Film FiLE

The Man in Grey

Lady Eleanor Smith

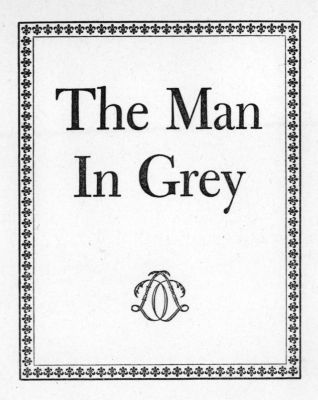

The Man In Grey

DOUBLEDAY, DORAN AND COMPANY, INC.
Garden City 1942 *New York*

PRINTED AT THE *Country Life Press*, GARDEN CITY, N. Y., U. S. A.

Contents

The Man in Grey

PART I

Narrative of Mary Rohan

I

I AM WRITING these words on a wild and stormy night in early spring.

I have never before been alone at Rohan, but David and I were married four months ago, and now he is with his regiment in France. I could have stayed in London with my parents, or I could have invited friends to stay with me, but I felt an odd inclination to be by myself for at least one week in David's home. He understood, as he understands most things. Rohan still seems strange to me, and that is wrong. It is *my* home now. I have said that to myself every morning, trying, I suppose, to make us more used to one another. I mean the house and myself.

If only it wouldn't rain so hard, I think everything would be easier. But since I arrived here three nights ago the rain has never ceased, and this morning the hollows in the park are flooded.

I went out with the spaniels, and wondered why one's dreams so seldom come true. Somehow, when I had visualised myself alone at Rohan, I always imagined wandering about in spring sunshine, watching newborn lambs, picking armfuls of pussy willows from the hedges, and finding birds' nests in the woods beyond the park. I never saw myself shivering in a wet mackintosh, battered by the wind, trying in vain to prevent my feet sticking in quagmires of mud.

This morning when I went out the day seemed lead-coloured. When I walked towards the lake and found that rain had broken one of the bridges to the woods beyond, the day darkened and assumed the tint of Indian ink. I began to realise how little I knew of country life. I had been to Rohan only once before, on our honeymoon. David, I remember, was apologetic.

"If it wasn't for this damned war," he said, "I'd have taken you to the South Sea Islands. Now all I can get is a week at Rohan!"

He was lucky, all the same, to get that week. He wouldn't have, later. But the war had scarcely started then.

During our honeymoon it was cold at Rohan, but cold with a fresh crispness, and with David there I was never, of course, lonely. The house only seemed strange to me then if, as seldom happened, I was left alone for half an hour by myself.

I remember one evening we were in the Long Drawing Room, and the short day was nearly over. David had been talking to me, for the first time since our marriage, of his family history. "One day," he said, "when there's more time, I'll tell you a lot about the past Rohans. Some of them are interesting. Others, of course, were just interbred bores—that happens, I suppose, in most families. Others, again, were wild enough. But——"

Just then Chaddesley, the butler, came in to say that the keeper wanted to see him, and he went away in the middle of his sentence. David is like that: his body is as quick as his mind, and he is the most impetuous person I have ever known.

Then, for the first time, when I was alone, I began to feel what I can only describe as "strange," although that sounds so foolish that I wouldn't dare say so to anyone. Perhaps the word I really mean is uncomfortable.

The sun was low, but one bar of crimson light struck through the windows upon some of the portraits in the room. Coming so soon after what David had said I wondered what they would have thought, these ancestors, if they could have seen me and talked me over among themselves. Would they have approved, or would they have been annoyed because I had no dowry, either of wealth or of brilliant connections, to bring with me to Rohan?

Some of the portraits—there was one, particularly disconcerting, of a sallow man in a ruff—some of them must have seen so many girls called Lady Rohan come home for the first time as brides, that the spectacle must long ago have lost any novelty, had those watching eyes been real instead of painted.

I looked, but in vain, for the Regency Lord Rohan. Everybody knows his wife, for the reason that she is the famous beauty whose portraits hang in so many galleries. I had not, I recollected, so far seen a portrait of this lovely lady in her own home. I reminded myself to ask David why her likeness was nowhere to be found.

I looked from the glossy, whiskered face of that Victorian politician who was David's great grandfather, and then to the pale mouth and haggard eyes of Sir Digby Rohan, the cavalier whose loyalty to his King had won him a peerage soon after the Restoration. There was, too, a Guy Rohan, who had been imprisoned for rebelling against Queen Elizabeth. I knew no more of David's family. But as I waited for him in the Long Drawing Room I realised, perhaps for the first time, that if I had a son he would be of their blood, the blood of all these long-dead people. He would not be made entirely by David and myself.

The feeling of discomfort grew on me. There was I, a girl of twenty-four, daughter of a fairly successful lawyer and of his blameless wife. I knew, of course, the names of my grandparents, but further back than that I had never bothered to enquire. But now, watching the portraits, I realised how many men and women had gone on living and dying, begetting and bearing children, to ensure the fact of my own obscure existence in the year 1940. For a moment I was fascinated by the thought.

I suppose that my own ancestors were respectable and worthy merchants. They would not be of any particular interest were I to trace them to or delve into their history. They were unlike the Rohans. I mused, then, on the violent lives of so many of those painted people on the damask walls. Hastings, Crécy, Agincourt, the Wars of the Roses, Blenheim, Waterloo, Arras, Mons. So many of them had fought and died in battle. Then I remembered that David at any moment would be fighting, too, and I shivered.

A log crashed in the grate, and the bar of sunlight fled from the windows. It was then that the house first seemed strange to me. I felt an intruder, not only in the Long Drawing Room, but everywhere—outside, in the great gloomy hall, with its chess-board floor; in the dining room; in the library; in the gun room, and on the polished steps of the immense coiling staircase; even upstairs, in our lovely rooms, where firelight flickered over the fantastic designs of the Chinese wallpaper.

I thought, then, that when David was sent away I would do what I am doing now—stay on alone and get used to Rohan. I didn't add then—being with him, and somewhat ashamed of my fancies—that I wanted Rohan to get used to *me*. But that thought, of course, was somewhere in the back of my mind. If

I had a baby, I would never want this sense of intrusion, of discomfort, to disturb my peace of mind. I could never bear to feel my child would be unwelcome in his father's house. It sounds an odd word to use, that one, but I use it deliberately. It is disconcerting to know just how unwelcome the pictures, halls, and corridors of an ancient house can make you feel when you are alone and still a stranger to ways and customs other than your own.

I suppose I had a feeling of panic then and wished that I had never married David. He could, God knows, have picked half-a-dozen more brilliant girls. I told him so once, before our wedding, and he laughed.

"I hate fashionable young ladies," he said.

"Why?"

"They bore me. I love you because you could never do that. I also love you because you can exist without quarts of gin; because you appreciate good music as well as enjoying jazz; because you read books for pleasure, not to show off; because you've got a lovely speaking voice, and because you're beautiful."

I thought of that, only one of many pretty speeches, as I waited for him in the Long Drawing Room and pretended to myself that I was not really a stranger in my own home.

David had no mother, only a very beautiful, rather disdainful-looking married sister named Bridget Greville, and I remember how I tried to console myself by thinking that things might have been even stranger had I acquired an alarming mother-in-law.

Then I heard footsteps, and started, because they were not David's, and, what with one thing and another, I had worked myself up into a low nervous state of mind. I think that knowing how soon we were to be parted had a certain influence upon my mind.

I know now that Rohan is a house and not a mausoleum. The mausoleum is somewhere out in the woods beyond the park. I have never seen it, or wanted to. I won't go there. I know just how depressing it is.

The footsteps, of course, were those of Chaddesley, the butler, coming to black-out the room.

It was nearly tea time. Suddenly my fancies left me and I was happy again. I longed for David; I wanted so much to ask him why there was no portrait of the lovely Marchioness of Rohan in the Long Drawing Room.

But when he came in he kissed me, and I forgot to ask him. When next I remembered, he was on his way to France.

II

TODAY it rained even harder. I went down to the fields where David's two remaining hunters were out at grass. They looked so drenched and dejected that I longed, when I had given them carrots, to take them back to their warm loose boxes. When I thought how David would have roared with laughter at this idea I felt more cheerful, but I wished, too, that I had been brought up with horses. Parading up and down the Row once a week in childhood is no preparation for peacetime life at Rohan, which is situated in Leicestershire.

I squelched my way back across the park, where the very deer looked as though they were drowning, and went into the flower room to dry the dogs. I seemed to spend a lot of time in this pursuit. But this time Chaddesley came in as I began to rub Rex.

"Oh, my lady," he said in a shocked voice, "this is a job for Thomas. I shall fetch him immediately!"

I like Chaddesley, who is one of the last remaining butlers I know who looks like an archbishop.

"I don't mind drying them," I said. "In fact, it gives me something to do in the mornings."

Then I thought Chaddesley looked sorry for me, and I added hastily:

"But perhaps you'd better get Thomas. I'm wet, too, and must change."

"I was looking for you, my lady," said Chaddesley, "to ask if it would be convenient if Mr. Langford cancelled his appointment for this week. Apparently he is in bed with a chill. His wife telephoned while you were out."

"Of course it will be all right."

Mr. Langford is the librarian, and I had not even known that he was expected. He is a little man, dry and dusty as the books he loves so much. I remembered then, as Chaddesley went to summon Thomas while I held on to both dogs, David once telling me nobody knew more about the Rohan family history than Mr. Langford. I felt sorry that he was ill. At least he would have been somebody to talk to.

I had lunch in the gun room, which is oak-panelled and comfortable, with a roaring crimson fire, silver cups and trophies, foxes' masks and sporting prints, and cases of old pearl-handled pistols.

Chaddesley brought in the coffee, and, as I sat drinking it, the wind rose, so that the rain was scattered like savage showers of gravel against the windowpanes. For a moment I faltered; thought of telephoning to my mother, or to a friend—nothing would be easier than for someone to come down to Rohan for a few days. Then I rebuked myself for my weak-mindedness.

Rohan was my *home;* I vowed to stay on there alone until the end of the week.

A Week Later.

I am still here, and still alone. But I am not solitary; I am no longer nervous. I have discovered something that enthralls me. I don't know, nowadays, whether it is raining or not; I don't care. I no longer mind sleeping alone in the vast bed with the damask canopy—best of all, my insomnia is cured. I am so tired, now, that I sleep at once until I am called in the morning, and then I can scarcely wait to get back to the library.

It happened, my discovery, the day after I heard the librarian, Mr. Langford, was unable to come to Rohan. I wandered then, for the first time since my honeymoon, into the library. I went there aimlessly enough, in search of something to do.

There was, of course, no fire, and everything looked dismal and forlorn. I saw a long, nobly proportioned room of white and gold, its walls lined with the morocco and calf and green of more than a thousand books. The ceiling is elaborately moulded, and there are two bay windows overlooking the Italian garden. So much I noticed before, turning, I saw a portrait I had hitherto overlooked. David, certainly, had never shown it to me.

The portrait was a small one, about two feet by one, in a frame of tarnished gilt, an oil painting, of a man in a grey coat. He had grey eyes, and although the face was that of a youngish man, the hair, too, was silver-grey. The complexion was olive-pale, the features prominent, the expression inscrutable. But the lips were curved and scornful.

I studied him, wondering what had been his history, for there was no name upon the frame, no date, no artist's signature. A strange face, I thought, and could not decide whether I found it more attractive or repellent.

"Whoever you were," I mused, "you were as hard as nails. And you look as though you were accustomed to having your own way. No, I don't think I really like you."

Yet the face interested me oddly, and I found myself looking at it again, when, dawdling round the room, I paused to examine a lovely rose-and-gold edition of Spenser's *Faerie Queene*.

It was a dull, dark day. Probably it was still raining, but I can't remember. In any case, I decided to take down the picture and look at it by the light. I climbed onto a footstool—the picture was hung between two bookcases, above a glass-topped treasure table—and unhooked it. As I lifted it down my hand brushed, and my bracelet caught, against the panel behind. To my astonishment a little door swung softly open, and I looked into what I supposed must be a concealed safe. I put the picture down on the floor, climbed up again, and found myself peering into a small aperture lined with shabby turquoise velvet and crammed with bundles of papers.

It was not a safe, since safes are modern, but it was to me something far more delightful—a secret panel. It did not look as though it had been opened for many years. The velvet was frayed and worn, the papers thick with dust, and a strange musty odour came from the hiding place. Mixed with it was a faint sweetness I recognised as the scent of sandalwood.

I was afraid of the panel closing, for never, never, I knew, would I again discover the secret of that hidden spring. Hastily, propping open the little door with my free arm, I began to bundle out the papers. Clouds of dust arose, and soon I was sneezing my head off, but I continued to pile them on to the glass top of the table below. The cabinet contained not only papers, as I discovered when my hand closed upon two hard objects, one larger than the other. They followed the papers, and only then, when there was nothing left inside, I let the little door swing to and once more looked at a smooth panel exactly like every other panel in the room.

I paused, almost panting with excitement. Then I glanced down at the portrait lying on the floor, and was made suddenly uncomfortable by the coolness with which the grey-eyed man stared at me. Impulsively I picked him up and hung him back where I had found him, guardian, perhaps, of a secret concerning only himself.

It was as well I did so, for at that moment Chaddesley came into the room to remonstrate:

"My lady, you'll catch your death of cold! If you're going to stay in here, may I ring for the fire to be lit?"

"Yes," I said; "yes, of course."

The fire was laid, but it was not one of Chaddesley's duties to light it, and he would never, not even in a war, have relinquished one jot or tittle of his hereditary privileges. So Chaddesley rang the bell, and soon a housemaid came bustling from about a mile away to put a match to the grate.

I said, rather defiantly,

"I'm going through some papers."

"Yes, my lady."

(I did not know until later that my face was smudged black with dust.) The housemaid scuttled away, and Chaddesley, on his way out, bent to cast a severe, expert eye on the smouldering wood. As he paused I asked impetuously:

"Chaddesley, who's the man in that picture there?"

Chaddesley straightened slowly, with his usual majesty, and directed a glance upon the portrait which seemed to indicate that he had never seen it before and didn't much care if he never saw it again.

"One of his lordship's ancestors, my lady."

"Yes, but which? Who was he? It doesn't say."

Was it my fancy, or did he hesitate for a moment before he answered:

"The Lord Rohan of Georgian days."

"Oh. Why, was *he* the husband of the lovely Lady Rohan? The one who was painted so often?"

"Yes, my lady."

"His lordship never showed me this picture. It's very good, isn't it?"

"I don't know much about it," Chaddesley said thoughtfully, "nothing but that they called it the 'Man in Grey' in an old catalogue I once saw. There's a reason for that, of course."

"Of course!" I cried. "I think that's why I like it. I love grey!"

Chaddesley hates being interrupted. I should have remembered that. He moved towards the door in his most episcopal manner. Before he went out, however, he relented.

"I was not alluding to the colouring of the coat or hair, my lady."

"Then——"

"That particular marquis went by a nickname, as many gentlemen did in those days. They called him the Ghost."

And he was gone before I could ask him any more. Perhaps it was as well. I was so excited by my discovery that I might have confided in him, and then I should have been sorry. It was my secret, and I wanted to keep it for David.

When I was alone I hurried to examine the two little packets that were part of my find.

III

I OPENED the larger one first. It seemed to be a paperweight, but it was such a paperweight as I have never seen before. It took the form of a hand modelled in alabaster. This hand rested upon a base of lapis-lazuli, or jade—I'm not sure which—but the clouded blue-green stone made the alabaster hand seem whiter, perhaps more delicate, than it could ever have been in life. Some hands express great character, and this was one. It was, of course, a woman's; the fingers were spatulate and strong, the nails long and shaped. They rested idly upon the clouded stone, and yet they gave an impression, not of idleness, but of force. The model might have been, not of a relaxed hand, but rather that of a clenched fist, for the modeller had been clever enough to suggest the bones of the fingers, so that an impression of nervous strength dominated the apparent frivolity of the whole charming design. On the third finger was placed a curious ring— a circle of gold adorned with a tiny skull of white enamel.

I examined it intently. This, I supposed, was a model of the great beauty's hand, Clarissa. I remembered that—her name was Clarissa. Yet I frowned, studying the model, for there was much that did not fit in. I recollected from so many picture galleries the face of the lovely Lady Rohan. That face and this hand did not quite go together. That is—I corrected myself—they did not go together in my own mind. And then I cursed myself for a fool. Just because, from one enchanting canvas, I treasured my own vivid memories of a long, tapering hand catching back some gauzy scarf it did not mean that contemporary artists, immortalising a celebrated beauty, had necessarily agreed.

And yet . . . No! I looked at those strong, powerful fingers which bore no relation whatsoever to what I remembered of David's most celebrated ancestress. And there was no clue. Like the picture, the alabaster model was anonymous. But it was beautiful. It might well have been some luxurious toy brought from Paris—either of the eighteenth century or of the First Empire. Probably it had never had any connection with a living woman.

I opened the smaller packet. This contained a small faded leather case which in its turn, being opened, revealed a man's gold signet ring. This ring bore the same device but this time it was of pearls—a tiny skull with ruby eye sockets. I knew, then, that the alabaster hand wasn't just a fantastic Parisian toy—it had been modelled for some particular reason, by some particular person.

By this time the fire was roaring like a lion, and the room, that had been so lost and dismal, now assumed a warm and crimson cheerfulness. Putting my two finds carefully upon the table, I picked up the nearest bundle of dusty papers.

Some years ago, when I underwent a fit of that inevitable but usually brief independence in which most young girls indulge, I worked as secretary for a long-suffering gentleman whose job at a museum it was to decipher letters belonging to the past. I worked with him for a year, and learned something of his own delicate methods. Therefore, glancing at the first bundle of papers, I knew, at least vaguely, how to decipher them, although to do so properly is more difficult than a crossword puzzle.

The paper was yellow and the ink faded brown, but as I held some sheets to the light certain phrases caught my eye. These were, of course, simple enough. They did not begin to get difficult until later.

I read, in a flowing, pointed hand:

"C will meet R all next week Grosvenor Square. I have it from her maid. I shall go to Rohan."

And:

"You must never reproach me about the past. Distasteful it must be for both—I had almost said *all*. Her stakes grow higher . . ."

Then in a man's finer handwriting:

"You can tell me of her play without that Subterfuge I disdain. I would be glad to make you comprehend I have no love of Informers . . ."

And once more, another, a feminine hand:

"G, I implore you, put this in the fire, but hear me. I have done wrong, yes, but shall you in your heart judge me? Oh, G, that would be heartless and cruel. . . . Blameless I am not, but——"

It was torn and I couldn't read any more. The papers, as I examined them, were a mixed collection. There were letters from at least three, if not four, different people, and there were some journals, too, bound in green velvet with silver clasps.

I wiped off dust with my handkerchief, which was soon black, and began to pick up any papers containing phrases easy to read at first glance. One sheet was headed simply, "Confession," but it was so illegible that I could only grasp a few words, such as "poverty," "the devil helped," "what did *she* care" (very clear this)—"we were alike" and I *think* without being sure, several times repeated, "have mercy, have mercy, have mercy." But the writing at this particular page trailed away into flies' tracks of illegibility.

I turned to the diary which, although obviously written by a woman, was inscribed by a more graceful yet a more careless hand than that of the "Confession."

"Spent the morning at my Mantua maker but am dissatisfied.

Return'd Home to Grosvenor Square where I was astonished to find S.R. who I had thought to leave at Rohan. I said, you are a pretty gentleman, to be sure! He seemed agitated, and said . . ."

Here half a page was torn away, but at the bottom I read:

"I did not play faro as I thought to, tonight, but stayed at Home . . ."

While I puzzled over this a slip of paper fell from the leaves of the journal. I opened it and read in faded printed letters:

"The Ghost Walks Tonight."

That was all. No signature. While I held this slip I noticed that the sweetness of the sandalwood I had noticed before came, not from my stacks of papers, but emanated from the velvet-bound diaries.

The clock struck, but I did not hear it.

For the first time since I have been alone at Rohan I was absorbed.

I knew, naturally, that Clarissa, Marchioness of Rohan, was the most beautiful woman of her epoch—who doesn't? I knew, for the first time, that her husband was nicknamed the Ghost. But of these other people I knew nothing. The woman who prayed for mercy was a stranger to me and somehow hostile, although I knew nothing of her nor of her life. Nor did the many significant initials dotted about the diary, and so common to the eighteenth and nineteenth centuries, mean more. In fact, since I was determined to decipher every word of my treasure-trove they only served to exasperate.

As for the alabaster hand, it was merely another link in a puzzle completely unsolved. The hand and the ring. Those jewelled skulls that must once have meant so much.

At that moment, I think, Chaddesley came in with sherry, to ask if I would like dinner at the same time in the gun room. I said I would.

Then as he was leaving I stopped him. I was really curious.

"Chaddesley," I said, "how long have you been here?"

Chaddesley enjoys this type of conversation. He paused, beaming. He looked like a bishop who has been sunbathing. He almost purred.

"How long have I been here, my lady? Well, before his lordship was born I was here with his late lordship. Thirty years ago I came here. As pantry boy."

"Then you know a lot about the family?"

But he wasn't listening.

"Well do I remember his present lordship's twenty-first birthday. An ox roasted whole in the park, with fireworks. A whole fair—merry-go-rounds, cocoanut-shies—everything! Beer and beef for every tenant. His lordship danced with every old lady in the neighbourhood. Very affable his lordship was, with the old people! And the peasants, if I may call them so, they much appreciated——"

I interrupted him again. Twice in one day. But I really couldn't help it.

"Then, Chaddesley, you must know a lot about the family?"

Oddly enough he didn't mind this particular interruption. He rubbed his chin and said:

"Your ladyship should have known Mrs. Perceval, the old housekeeper. She died, as his lordship may have informed you, in hospital. His lordship was very upset, and frequently visited her. She, of course, was with his grandfather. There was nothing about Rohan unknown to Mrs. Perceval."

"But she's dead," I said stupidly.

"Yes, my lady," Chaddesley agreed, as though intoning a psalm, "she is dead, subsequent to which"—he brightened up—"her late ladyship decided that there was no longer a place here for a housekeeper, his lordship coming here so seldom, what with London and what with abroad."

"Chaddesley," I said, "why is there no portrait here of the great Lady Rohan? You know—the Regency one? The one called Clarissa?"

This time there was no mistaking the pause. At length he said mildly:

"That's a long time ago, my lady."

"No, it isn't! For the portraits? What do you mean? They go back to before Queen Elizabeth, some of them!"

"Mrs. Perceval——"

For the third time that day I interrupted him, and this time I was shameless.

"Chaddesley, since I can't ask his lordship, please won't *you* tell me—*why* is there no portrait here of Clarissa Lady Rohan?"

"There should be."

He said that as though he hadn't meant to, and started to make a majestic departure. But this time again I stopped him.

"Her husband's here, although he's rather tucked away. You could never find him except by accident. But *she*—she's in every picture gallery! Why isn't she here?"

There was a pause, and then he said rather reluctantly:

"She *is* here, my lady. But I believe she's in the attics."

"The attics? Why? Is the picture so bad?"

"I couldn't say. I've never seen it."

He was no longer friendly; he was once more ecclesiastically remote.

I said helplessly:

"You know how little I know about Rohan, Chaddesley. That's why I wish you'd help me. Do tell me why Clarissa was banished to the attics."

He fidgeted for a moment with the glasses.

"Mrs. Perceval," he said, and cleared his throat.

"Yes?"

"Mrs. Perceval, my lady, once told me they were unlucky."

"They?"

"That whole lot, my lady, if you'll forgive the expression. What I call the Georgian lot."

"But the Grey Man's in the library!"

"A small picture, my lady, tucked away, as you just said. He's only there at all, I suppose, because he was once the head of the family. And that, at Rohan, still means something, in spite of Socialists. Socialists, indeed! The village don't like them, and never will!"

I evaded the Socialists.

"Chaddesley," I said, "don't you know *anything* about the Lord Rohan they called the Ghost?"

"No, my lady," said Chaddesley, now determined to leave; "no, I don't, and won't say I do. It's a pity you never knew Mrs. Perceval."

Once again he paused at the door. I now suppose he did it for effect—it is his favourite gesture.

"One thing I do know," he said deliberately, "and that is, they're supposed to be unlucky to the family. Always have been."

"*Who?*"

"That Regency lot," Chaddesley said again, and vanished.

IV

THE NEXT MORNING I directed the head housemaid to take me to the attics. There I found parrots' cages, hip baths, lacquer cabinets, Victorian wax fruits, samplers, china, sporting prints, and workboxes. But I found no portrait, either of Clarissa Lady Rohan or of anyone else.

At lunch I questioned Chaddesley. I almost, if I may be so irreverent, third-degreed him. But Chaddesley was of no help.

"I can only suppose," he said, "that his late lordship must have ordered the portrait to be destroyed."

"But why? Why should he do such a thing?"

"His late lordship might have supposed it to be unlucky."

"I never heard such nonsense!"

"Mrs. Perceval——"

"Can I have some more beans?"

It was no good. Chaddesley might so easily have been my confidant, but he chose not to be. If he is now against me, that's his own fault, not mine. He is really a very stupid person.

That same day, I remember, I had a letter from David.

BELOVED,

I'm delighted to know you're at Rohan, but I hope you aren't alone any more. Please, my darling, ask someone to stay. I want to hear you're happy—not lonely. I love you more and more. I'm writing in great haste, and of course can't say where we are. My darling Mary, I miss you so terribly, but at least we had a week. I'm glad now we spent that week at Rohan if it has made you love the place. Now I shall think of you both together! You and Rohan.

All my love,
DAVID.

I thought, as I read that letter, how delighted David would be to hear of my find. But of course I had no intention of telling him about it in a letter. Nor had I any intention of asking people to stay.

From now on I am going to spend all my time deciphering the papers I found in the secret door.

My mother rang up the other day, and so apparently did the librarian, Mr. Langford. But I managed to put them both off, although Mr. Langford might help me.

But I don't really want his help. I've found something for David, and I can't bear anyone else to interfere. I've found something about the Rohan family that's my own discovery. I want to type and tabulate this discovery before David comes back on leave. That's why I put off Mr. Langford. He might want to take charge, and I couldn't bear that. For better or for worse, this is my own affair.

I go through what I begin to think of as *my* papers every day now, and I find that what I thought of as some kind of romantic story about two people is nothing of the kind. More and more clearly *four* people emerge from the veil of the past. One of them is particularly dominating. Her name is Hesther. I would give much to know all about her, but I don't like to question Chaddesley any more, as he seems so reluctant to discuss family history. He's a strange, fishlike person.

Sometimes I wonder whether David warned him to keep off the subject. But on second thoughts that seems ridiculous, for of course David would love me to take an interest in his family. I wonder, though, whether all old families are as secretive as the Rohans seem to be. I have searched the library in vain for any records or personal documents.

And this Hesther—she seems to have played so important a rôle in the family that one would like to discover more about her, although of course I will probably be able to do so later, when I really get started. I don't know whether she was a relation or only a friend. In any case, somehow one would expect to have heard her name. Those great Whigs made their mark in history, and if Hesther was so mixed up with them it seems odd never to have heard of her.

But there is so much about Rohan that I never knew.

I knew that part of the house is Carolian, part of it is Queen Anne, part is early Georgian. Then in Victoria's reign more was added, so that, like many English houses, it is a jumble of beauty and ugliness. But knowing that isn't knowing very much. Most old houses make you feel strange and new. Rohan is no exception. That's why I am so determined to decipher those papers. I shall have done something then that no other member of the family has ever done before. I shall know about Hesther too. Perhaps even David doesn't know much about her. Perhaps he has never even heard her name. Sometimes I think he knows very little about Clarissa, or even about her husband— the Ghost. He has only mentioned Clarissa casually to me, and Clarissa, through her portraits, is almost national property. It's difficult, really, when you think of her age and epoch, not to mention her. But he has talked of her only as a stranger might— as so many people must have talked who filed, before this war, into picture galleries to warm their hearts with a glimpse of her lovely face.

As for Chaddesley saying that the Whig Rohans were "unlucky," that's the sort of servants' gossip that makes one understand how long ago ignorant people could have been stupid enough to burn witches.

I have decided, when I sort my papers out, to write a story of those Rohans concerned in all the muddle of diaries, and letters, and paperweights, and skulls. Clarissa has always appealed to me; to write about her will be a pleasure. About the Man in Grey I'm not so sure, although I don't think he will ever be dull. I may not like him, yet I long to know him better. But the mysterious Hesther intrigues me more than any of the others. I have an idea that the alabaster hand may have been modelled from hers. But why, and how? So far I have no proof. . . .

Later.

I have been much puzzled by the initials S.R. or R. occurring in so many of the documents. Of course I thought the person alluded to must have been Rohan himself, although I couldn't understand the S, as the Ghost was called Lucas William Roderick.

But this afternoon I came upon the name in full.

Swinton Rokeby. A name that means nothing—just another piece to be fitted into the jigsaw puzzle I have set myself. I decided, too, this afternoon, to read one of the velvet-bound diaries before I struggled any further with the papers. When I opened it, to my delight, after studying it for only a few minutes, I discovered that the diary was Clarissa Rohan's own private journal! I was so enchanted that I almost sat down to write to David. Then I remembered how much I wished to surprise him with my treasure-trove and stopped, only just in time, for if I'd ever begun the letter I know I should have finished it.

And Later.

I shan't write any more—of my own diary, I mean. I shall concentrate on Clarissa's and try to tell her story just as I learned it from herself and from her friends. How gay she must have been, and how simple, in spite of so much beauty and sophistication!

I can hardly wait to find out if she was happy with the Man in Grey. I hope she was! At the moment of writing, although I intend to read her diary late tonight, I still cannot discover any clue to the mysterious Hesther. But an odd thing happened when I tried to pump Chaddesley this evening.

I said innocently:

" 'Hesther' isn't a family name, is it, Chaddesley?"

This time I am certain that he looked at me oddly.

"I'm sure it's not," he said, and then he went straight out of the room.

I felt depressed for a moment afterwards. Perhaps David knows all about the secret panel. Perhaps my papers were all deciphered, and typed, and docketed, years ago. After all, dust accumulates so quickly . . .

But I shall still go on with my work. It gives me something to do.

The Next Day.

Since I wrote those last words the present, for me, has ceased to exist, and I think the past has taken me captive. The past and Clarissa Lady Rohan.

I can picture those old days. There were about twenty horses in the stable yard and the coach house was filled with chaises and curricles. If there was a party at Rohan there were dozens of candlesticks on the hall table and the silver sedan chair wasn't here at all. It was used, in London, to carry her ladyship back from routs to Grosvenor Square. No wonder Rohan seems quiet with only Chaddesley and one footman; in those dead days there was an army of powdered lackeys waiting to snuff the candles and to call the carriages. The ladies played Mozart in the Long Drawing Room and faro in the library. They laughed and were gay, they talked politics, and they toasted Charles James Fox. When Nelson died, they wept and wore mourning. They pledged the Prince and laughed at the King. They did nothing by half-measures. They were impetuous and subtle at the same time. They were as romantic as Byron the poet, as cynical as Byron the man. They were recklessly abandoned and at the same time exquisitely controlled. They were the privileged ones, rulers of the earth, and yet, through their passions, they suffered; nor did their extreme sophistication spare them from the anguish of their own untutored feelings.

They chattered away in French and Italian; they wrote Greek and they read philosophy; they were Whigs first and Christians afterwards; to win votes, they sold kisses; when they loved, they loved passionately, immoderately, and without restraint.

The gentlemen were orators and pugilists and whips. Born politicians, they, too, turned to poetry and philosophy. They, too, divided their recreation between Mozart and faro. Always they rode their horses hard and gamed their money, in idle moments, on fighting cocks. But if they ruled their world, this world, for them, was always ruled by politics.

By politics, and by love.

Never, surely, at any epoch can love have played a more dominant rôle than in the glittering story of these great Whigs, and here their Prince led them a hectic and a swaggering example. Nor were Nelson, Fox, Sheridan, or Byron, in any respect laggards. Nor were all contemporaries. But the story was always the same. The same, with variations.

And this is where Clarissa Lady Rohan——

But I am anticipating.

To begin her story we must disperse the mists of the past and post to Bath, when England was young and green and the King still sane, and the candles of the eighteenth century were burning low but not yet extinct, although they guttered, and were nearly done.

PART II

A School in Bath

V

THERE was once a certain white house, situated in a shady Bath
Crescent, from which it seemed that all day long music tinkled.
Sometimes girlish faces were to be glimpsed at the windows,
and it was to be observed not only that the young gentlemen
of Bath were much disposed to linger opposite the White
House, but that their business took them frequently enough
into this part of the neighbourhood.

Not that young gentlemen were ever encouraged by the lady
who presided over the establishment, for her name was Miss
Patchett, and for more than fifteen years she had ruled, with an
iron rod, her Academy for Young Ladies.

One has only to glance at her original prospectus, faded now
and torn almost to shreds, to realise at once that here was no

ordinary person, no ordinary school, or academy, as she herself preferred to call it.

Miss Patchett's Establishment

for

The Board and Education

of a Limited Number of

YOUNG LADIES,

The White House, Bath.

We read further and discover that board and education cost thirty-five pounds a year, while French, music, and drawing were extra, and the use of spinet cost the parents another five shillings a quarter. The prospectus concluded with the reminder that:

Each Young Lady must be provided with One Pair of Sheets, Pillow-Cases, Four Towels, a Dessert and Tea Spoon.

Perhaps it was the gentility of these last two items, perhaps it was the commanding personality of Miss Patchett—herself a governess honourably retired from a most noble family—or perhaps it was the charming situation of the house in Bath. Perhaps it was a combination of all these three advantages. In any case, Miss Patchett's Academy flourished, and it was a pretty sight to watch her young ladies troop to and from church on Sundays, for they wore white muslin with pink sashes in summer and white muslin in the winter, too, with blue sashes and blue pelisses, and the richer young ladies sported feathers in their hats.

It was a delightful sight, too, to see the pupils dispersing for their half-yearly holidays. The street, then, was crowded with chaises, lackeys, and fretting horses; parents, wigged, powdered, and plumed, stormed the very steps of the nunnery; once admitted, they listened to the young ladies performing on the spinet and were regaled with saffron cake and white wine.

Miss Patchett on such days was at her most majestic: sporting an elaborate auburn wig, clad imperially in purple, and beaming through her spectacles at the wealthier or more aristocratic parents. These, naturally, adored her; only a widow or two, scraping to educate an only daughter, found Miss Patchett unsympathetic and brusque.

There were always two young ladies who never went home for the holidays. Their situations, however, were very different. One of them, the pride and joy of Miss Patchett's heart, was a strange enough creature to find in any boarding school of that era, for she was a member of what the schoolmistress always alluded to as "a noble family," and in those days daughters of the aristocracy were usually educated at home, by governesses and tutors.

But Clarissa Richmond was an orphan. Daughter of the late Lord Carey, her mother had died when she was born, and her father violently—of a duel—when she was twelve. Lord Carey was succeeded by his brother, a taciturn naval officer, and it was to the casual guardianship of her uncle that the little girl was confided. Carey spent most of his time on active service and had no estates, not even a house. His brother had died heavily in debt, and on his own succession he was fortunate enough to sell the country seat in Shropshire. Nor did Clarissa's uncle possess a wife.

"There's time enough for that," he always said, and, in any case, there was a younger brother.

And so Clarissa, at the age of twelve, was sent to Miss Patchett's, in Bath. Now she was fifteen, while her guardian, still unmarried, had attained to the glories of being promoted admiral.

It may well be imagined that from the first moment of her arrival in Bath Miss Patchett denied her star pupil nothing. The daughter of a peer—soon the niece of an admiral! Clarissa was the parlour boarder, the spoiled darling, the pet, the poppêt, the princess of the school! The Hon. Miss Richmond could do no wrong! The Hon. Miss Richmond had fat on her plate—pray serve her another slice! The window was open—did not the Hon. Miss Richmond feel the draught?

After her first week at the White House Clarissa, suddenly fixing Miss Patchett with her great blue eyes, said:

"Ma'am, please to call me just Miss Richmond. Like the other young ladies."

It was observed by thirty other pairs of mischievous eyes that the schoolmistress swallowed, flushed dark red, and—obeyed!

So began Miss Richmond's reign.

Nor was the girl averse from being spoiled. She seemed happy enough to reign as queen of the White House. She kept her own pony, could hire a chaise whenever she desired, and on Sunday nights she wore her mama's pearls. She had fur-trimmed pelisses, her own mantua maker, and a hairdresser once a month to dress her hair, whereas the other young ladies depended on curling rags. Her guardian paid Miss Patchett a generous allowance, derived mainly from the past sale of valuable timber from the Shropshire estates of Clarissa's papa.

It is strange to reflect that the other young ladies adored her, for it would have been natural enough to suppose that they detested the very sight of her as a "toad"—the ultimate insult, this, at the White House. But they did not, and she was loved; the reason being that, despite the fawnings of Miss Patchett, she continued to possess a gay and candid nature, a simplicity, and, above all, a mischievous, merry sense of humour that has been, since times immemorial, the admiration of "young ladies" en masse, and possibly always will be.

For Clarissa was friendly with them all, even with poor Miss Jennings, a charity pupil, whose mama had once been at school with Miss Patchett, and who was, after some expostulation, accepted without fees, as an "apprentice," rather as a creditor accepts, no matter how resentfully, a bad debt. Miss Jennings was pinched and bullied by the teachers, ignored by Miss Patchett, and mocked by the pupils. That, until Clarissa—who didn't know who she was, and most certainly didn't care—gave her a comfit box and invited her to come out driving in a chaise.

"I am going to buy a poodle next week," Clarissa said to Miss Jennings; "you may share him with me if you like. He shall have a blue ribbon round his neck and we will call him Médor."

That evening nobody pinched Miss Jennings on her way to supper, and it was observed that Miss Patchett actually invited her to "partake" of a second helping!

Clarissa herself was the only person present to ignore the significance of this tremendous gesture. It was the same, then, with her, as it was always to be. She had been "nice" to Miss Jennings, not because she was sorry for her but because she liked her. She, whose name was to be associated with so much glittering sophistication, was never, and never could be, what is called "worldly." She was always completely natural. She was delightful to people, not from benevolence, but because, for some reason or another, they pleased her and attracted whatever mood was hers at the time.

Nowadays she would have been called the most unsnobbish woman in aristocratic society. Her own epoch, not yet having coined the word, described her as unconventional. But she had something else—she was always able to charm people, with the added charm of not even knowing that she did so.

She was, of course, helped in this by her great good looks.

It is sad to think that she was never painted until she was eighteen, or thereabouts, because it would have been interesting to compare the prettiness of childish immaturity with the poised beauty of so many famous pictures.

But she must always have been as lovely as a flower. One letter exists, written about this time to Admiral Lord Carey by a lady whose daughter was at school with his niece. It describes, gushingly—probably incorrectly—Clarissa's many accomplishments, and goes on to describe, with how much more sincerity, her personal appearance. We feel that the "accomplishments" were mainly invented (although she was intelligent enough when she chose) but that the description of her looks was written sincerely, by a simple and unenvious woman.

We read of her luxurious red-gold locks; of her large lustrous eyes, so dark blue that they resemble "the deepest sapphires"; of her tiny waist; her green-and-silver slippers, and her "rose-and-ivory" complexion. It is pleasant to know how gay she was, and that her laughter was "sweet and frequent." Pleasant, too, although the admiral may have been bored, to read of her many "silk gauzes," her long eyelashes, "that curl upwards," her sense of fun, her "lovely smile," and her passion for snowballs!

It must have been cold in Bath that winter. The picture of Clarissa, glowing like a rose in her fur-trimmed hood, encouraging the other young ladies to romp in the snow, will always remain agreeable, more particularly since the vision of Miss Patchett, blue with cold, shivering, yet determined not to thwart her "parlour boarder," remains as a possibility in our mind and as a not altogether unpleasing *vignette*.

Perhaps for the first time the admiral, trying his liver severely in the West Indies, may have realised that he was guardian not, it is true, of an heiress, but of a beauty. If so, he made no sign.

She was only fourteen when this letter was written. Nor is any reply from him recorded.

And so it went on.

Encouraged by Miss Patchett to do exactly as she pleased, she remained warmhearted and natural. Yet surely it was in Bath that she first grew accustomed to her own way. Most girls of her age and of her epoch spent their holidays with brothers and sisters and cousins. She, who had none, reigned in Bath winter and summer alike. When it was Christmas, it was she who wreathed the holly, who drew for kings and queens; at mid-summer, when the school picnicked, in white gowns and rose sashes, it was she who chose where they should go and who should sit beside her at the banquet.

The wonder is she was not spoiled and odious and over-bearing.

But she was none of these things, although she had never been crossed until she was past fourteen.

Then the first unfriendliness she ever met came from another "young lady," one who, like herself, stayed on at Bath for the holidays.

That is how Clarissa first met Hesther.

VI

Hesther, unlike Clarissa, was neither a pride nor a joy to Miss Patchett. Rather was she a thorn in the side.

Hesther Shaw was nearly fifteen when she first came to the White House.

She was the only daughter of what the schoolmistress referred to as a "Cornish gentleman," and her mother died many years before, when Hesther was a little child. But Mordaunt Shaw, her father, was a wastrel and a gambler. A yeoman farmer of respectable family and tradition, it did not take him long to squander first his land and then his house. He journeyed from Cornwall to Manchester, the child with him, where, ostensibly searching for some Shaw cousins, he encountered and married a well-to-do widow, a certain Mrs. Abbey. There, in her cold, bleak little house, Hesther lived for seven years. Her stepmother, passionately in love with Shaw, who was considerably her junior, took little notice of the child, who attended school daily and lived mainly in the kitchen, where as she warmed herself by the fire she listened precociously to the unceasing gossip of the two servants.

It did not take Mrs. Shaw long to discover that her handsome husband was a gambler and a rake. Quarrels, then, raged night and day.

"I don't think I shall ever marry," the child Hesther once said to the cook; "I might find a husband like my papa."

Then, listening for a moment to a furious altercation storming in the hall outside, she added:

"But if I did, I shouldn't allow my husband to behave as *he* does."

Hesther fed with the servants in the kitchen, studied her books there, and was described by her schoolteachers as a brilliant pupil. Mrs. Shaw, who did not pretend to understand children, avoided her, or, if she had to meet her, accorded the girl a sort of benevolent indifference which deceived neither, for Hesther despised Mrs. Shaw and made no secret of it. Nor was she attached to her good-looking and erratic papa. She was silent but observant, as the servants noticed. Pretending to study her schoolbooks, she would listen, quiet as a doll, to their gross and often ill-natured conversation.

One day when she was twelve the pie man called, to find her alone, and tried to kiss her. She tore at his face with her nails so that blood ran down his cheeks. She had not a friend in the world, and being fierce, lonely, and suspicious, she did not feel her loss.

When she was fourteen her father died. He was, in fact, run over by a coach when he was crossing the street, drunk. His widow had been inconsolable. How little had she appreciated this pearl among men! All was forgotten—his lies, his gaming, his drunkenness, his infidelities—all that was violent in his wild blood. For two months Mrs. Shaw tottered vaguely, black-veiled, about the house. Then it occurred to her to recollect Hesther, who was, after all, the beloved's child. She sent for Hesther to come to the parlour, where the girl stood facing her in a shabby black dress. Mrs. Shaw studied her for a moment, and tears coursed from her eyes. There was something about the girl, something uncompromising and haughty in her bearing, which reminded her so vividly of the deceased that for a few moments she wept in silence. Hesther watched her.

"Your . . . poor . . . papa . . ." the widow at length achieved, blubbering.

"Yes ma'am?"

"He wished—— Oh, Hesther—he wished——" The widow broke off in sobs.

"Yes ma'am?" Hesther said again.

She was bored, almost disgusted.

Mrs. Shaw gasped:

"You shall have the best—the best of everything! He would have wished it!" Once more she covered her face with a black-edged handkerchief and Hesther began to listen with more attention, for Mrs. Shaw was promising her an education. She was to go to a good school, the best Mrs. Shaw could find, and there she was to study until she was seventeen. Then, if her reports were satisfactory, Mrs. Shaw would invest some money so that Hesther might begin her career as a teacher.

A teacher! The girl did not allow her contempt to show. After all, an education was something, and it would be delightful to leave Manchester.

"Or a governess," Mrs. Shaw supplemented; "whichever may be preferable. I am determined, Hesther, to do my best for you."

"Thank you, ma'am," Hesther said.

"They say," her stepmother hazarded, "you are a clever pupil. Since you have no dowry, you must earn your own living. I would like to make your path as easy as I can."

Again Hesther thanked her.

Mrs. Shaw was meticulous in her search for the best school possible. It was finally decided that it was impossible to improve upon Miss Patchett's Academy in Bath, but just before Hesther's departure a shocking thing occurred. Mrs. Shaw was found in bed, dead of heart failure. For the first time in her life Hesther knew what terror was.

She lay sleepless at night, her hot cheeks pressed into the pillow.

"I shall be sent to the poorhouse! I shall be sent to the poorhouse!"

But she had no need for alarm. Mrs. Shaw, a businesswoman, had left exactly enough money to pay her stepdaughter's school fees until she was seventeen. There was a further provision. On condition that the girl's record was satisfactory another sum of money was set aside to be administered to Miss Patchett on her seventeenth birthday that she might be apprenticed to the school as teacher. Mrs. Shaw's solicitor was appointed her guardian; twenty pounds were to be spent on her wardrobe;

and a few weeks before her fifteenth birthday she departed, by coach, on the wearisome journey to Bath.

There, the young ladies beheld for the first time a tall, slender girl, pale-skinned, with dark heavy locks, grey-green eyes, and a full, sulky mouth. She came, on a winter evening, into the white-panelled hall, where candles blazed from silver sconces on the walls and where some very little girls were playing blindman's buff. There were older girls present, some reading or chattering, on the rug before the fire, some sketching, as best they could, by candlelight, and at least two laughing together as they tinkled the spinet, for this was the hour of recreation.

Miss Hatch, a junior teacher afflicted with chilblains, brought Hesther into the room and said briskly:

"Young ladies, this is Miss Shaw, who has had a long, inclement journey. Pray bid her draw near the fire and make herself at home."

So saying, Miss Hatch withdrew, leaving no doubts in the mind of even the most juvenile "young lady," aged eight, as to Hesther's social status, for had she been a pupil of importance Miss Patchett would herself have made the presentation. A little reluctantly waves of white dimity parted to reveal a fire burning bright as geraniums, and Hesther, tired, half-frozen, and shy, was glad to hold out her hands to the blaze.

"You have travelled far, Miss Shaw?"

This was Miss Seymour, senior pupil, and always a model of courtesy.

"From Manchester," Hesther said in a low voice.

"Manchester?" someone cried. "Do you wear clogs, then, Miss Shaw?"

The voice was mocking, and Hesther turned wearily, trying to distinguish her tormentor from amongst so many bright and laughing faces. But it was impossible.

"No," she said coldly, "I do not wear clogs. Nor yet a shawl over my head. It is not the custom."

She turned back to the fire, feeling so weary, so lonely, that tears stung her eyes. She might, she who so seldom wept, have shed tears then had there not come an interruption in the form of a new arrival.

A door banged; a wave of frosty air blew into the warm room; a gay voice was heard calling, and a girl came impetuously into the white-panelled hall. She was flushed like a rose from her cold drive; a strand of guinea-gold hair was blown across her cheek, and her blue hood was trimmed with white fur. She carried a white muff, and behind her Miss Patchett's small black page, grinning, bore an armful of little parcels.

At once the quiet groups broke up into wild disorder as the young ladies swarmed about the newcomer. Even the little girls stopped romping to hang about her skirts. Hesther was left alone by the fire with the sedate Miss Seymour. She stared in astonishment.

She had never imagined a schoolgirl so richly dressed. Nor had she beheld, in all her life, a more joyous, a more radiant being.

"I've sweetmeats for all!" Clarissa cried, as she flung off her pelisse and hood. "Siege the blackamoor—not me! They're his responsibility, aren't they, Toby?"

The little Negro grinned again, sidling close beside her, so that she began unwrapping the parcels, all untidy and disordered as she was.

"Rose leaves, Louisa, and a gingerbread man for Fanny, and sugar sticks, look, for Lavinia! Oh, and a pink cake for Charlotte, and comfits for Anne, and a marzipan bird for Sally! Wait—wait! I've not done!"

Hesther touched Miss Seymour's arm.

"Who is that?"

Miss Seymour answered, smiling indulgently, not at Hesther, but at the gay and noisy group at which, oblivious of manners, the newcomer pointed.

"Why, that's Miss Richmond, our parlour boarder! A sweet creature, is she not?"

Hesther said nothing, but a great bitterness filled her heart, and it was then, for the first time, that she envied Clarissa. She felt lonely and unwanted, standing apart in her mourning dress amid so much gaiety, laughter, and crisp white dimity. She thought moodily:

"No wonder that girl's happy in her rich gown, throwing her largess to the school! Were I her, I'd be happy, too, the pampered wretch! *She* will never have to work as a schoolteacher!"

It was as though Clarissa, in the midst of so much merriment, sensed this unspoken hostility, for she looked up then and saw Hesther for the first time, and if anyone had noticed they would have beheld her shiver. For, warm as it was there in the firelight, she had for one brief second the sensation once described to her by an old nurse as of "someone walking over her grave."

It has already been explained that when Clarissa was charming to people it was not usually from benevolence, but simply because, her life having been set in easy ways, most people pleased her. She did not think, then, that this pale girl in black was particularly pleasing, but she had, on the other hand, a warm heart, and the newcomer's mourning dress appealed to her sympathy.

So she went impulsively up to her and said:

"Please, won't you sample these sugared violets?"

But Hesther, her heart still filled with envy, looked at her steadily, and then said, turning her head away:

"Thank you, but I am not hungry."

It was Clarissa's first rebuff, and she did not like it. The pink of her cheeks deepened to scarlet, and she tossed her untidy golden head. Then she turned her back abruptly, and went on laughing with the other young ladies; then it was suppertime, and the gathering swiftly dispersed, and the candles were snuffed, so that the white-panelled hall was left in the quietness of the firelight.

VII

As the days passed Clarissa discovered that—unique among the young ladies of the academy—Hesther Shaw treated her with a contempt that was scarcely veiled. Nor was this the only trouble. Until the arrival of Hesther, Clarissa had been the only beautiful girl in the school. She would always, too, have been lovely, for such a flowerlike beauty as hers is not easily put in the shade—it will always appeal to the senses.

Nor was Hesther subtly her rival.

Where Clarissa was golden-haired, and bright-lipped, Hesther was pale, dark-braided, and ironically conscious of her charms. But there was a tilt to Hesther's eye, a curve to her vivid mouth, that made her certain slaves among the young ladies, and Clarissa had never known slaves other than her own.

To her, at first, Hesther was unsympathetic, and she wrote in her velvet-bound diary:

"I do not like Miss Shaw."

Those words should be noted, for they are possibly the only ill-natured ones Clarissa ever wrote or said in all her life.

But her situation, at the time, was not to be envied.

She had been, so simply, the queen of Miss Patchett's school. She had never thought herself grand, or smart, or condescending; it was Hesther who, for the first time, made her feel self-conscious.

It was Hesther who said, in effect, to her own followers:

"Of course Miss Richmond is sweet—but what does it cost her? She's pretty, and spoiled, and rich! Why shouldn't she seek to curry favour?"

And the pale Hesther had, even in those days, a power that made Clarissa's young favourites hesitate in this battle between the two rivals. Clarissa, like most sensitive people in a similar situation, became nervous, and nerves did not suit her. She was still such a child that coldness nearly killed her. Hesther's mocking eye became something that she would almost have died rather than meet, and it was then, for the first time, that she decided she would do something someday that would once and for all show the young ladies she was their leading spirit.

She wrote defiantly in her diary:

"I shall marry a Nabob, or a great Actor . . ."

She was, it may be observed, so unworldly that the idea of marrying into her own class did not even occur to her, and that despite Miss Patchett's teachings . . .

Then came the Christmas holidays, and there were only two girls left at the school. They were Clarissa and Hesther Shaw.

The White House was lonely on the first night of the holidays. The gaiety was gone, the fun, and the laughter and the music. All that foam of muslin skirts had vanished the day before, when coaches and chaises ploughed up the road, and Clarissa went down to the white-panelled hall subdued, a book under her arm.

There were few candles in the holidays and for a moment she

thought herself alone. But the fire was blazing, and she hummed a silly song as she crossed the room.

> *"The ladies of St. James's*
> *Go swinging to the play . . ."*

She stopped, and that song was never finished, for Hesther stood by the fire. Hesther was ivory-cheeked and dark-browed, in a dress of prune taffeta.

"I thought I was alone," Clarissa said.

"I'm sure," Hesther suggested, "you wished you were?"

"How foolish," Clarissa said, "since we have to spend some weeks here together."

"That," sneered Hesther, "must be most distasteful to your ladyship!"

Clarissa considered her.

"Why do you hate me?" she enquired with a simplicity Hesther could not begin to understand.

"Hate you, Miss Richmond? I am afraid, miss, I could never take the trouble!"

Clarissa answered serenely:

"Perhaps hate's a big word. But you do not like me. Why?"

"You're so lovable?"

"Until you came here," Clarissa observed, "they thought I was."

"Because you're rich and pampered?"

Clarissa considered this, her gold hair flame-tinted by the log fire.

"I'm not rich," she said at length, "for I have no portion. As for being pampered, well . . . Since you came here my friends have much forsaken me."

"You're good-natured," Hesther told her grudgingly.

"But you're better-looking than I am," Clarissa remarked, "although you sulk and scowl. Why do you so spoil your looks?"

"What have my looks to do with you?"

"You see," Clarissa produced, "you're like a hedgehog—cross and prickly! Aren't you pleased to be so pretty?"

Hesther was not used to compliments. But she had read Perault's tales, and to be flattered by this fairy princess touched something in her breast that might have been her heart. Watching the fruitlike curve of Clarissa's cheek she thought of pumpkins, of Prince Charming's court, ugly sisters, and of witchen godmothers.

She said roughly:

"I'm not pretty! But *you're* beautiful!"

Clarissa frowned, and then achieved, with a painful honesty,

"People might look at me for a moment in the mirror, but if you were behind my shoulder I think they would always look at you!"

Once again Hesther experienced a new and vivid pleasure. Would "they"? Was Clarissa right?

"'They'?" she said.

"The people," Clarissa explained, "we are supposed to marry."

This was all new to Hesther. She asked bluntly: "You are betrothed?"

Clarissa laughed and shook her head so that all the bright locks danced.

"Lud, no! But I will be!"

"To whom?" Hesther pressed.

"I don't know! My guardian will find a gentleman, we'll meet and like each other, and fall in love!"

"But if you don't?"

"Don't what?"

"Fall in love!"

"But we shall," Clarissa declared, "after we're married! Miss Patchett has told me so."

"Miss Patchett!" Hesther was shaken, dry-lipped. "Has *she* a husband or a lover? Don't trust, my dear, to Miss Patchett! What a comical idea!"

"I don't trust to anyone," Clarissa protested, "but I shall fall in love."

"No doubt. You're made for love!"

Clarissa at this point became very dignified.

"Pray, is that a sin?"

"Well," Hesther said, "if one looks like you it might easily become one!"

Clarissa paused, staring at the fire.

"But I'd like," she said at length, "to be made for love!" She thrust her toe into the grate, prodding a log. "What's wrong with that?"

"Don't you ever long," Hesther said, "to see outside these windows?" And she ran across from the fire to pull the curtains, so that they heard the galloping of a coach and saw a red light glowing, and then, in a flash, the coach was gone with all its clatter.

"You saw," Hesther said, and her voice was triumphant, "you saw that coach? It travels all the way to London!"

Clarissa, too, left the fire to press her face against the pane, but there were no more coaches, and they looked into darkness.

She said with confidence:

"I'll leave Bath one day, but not by coach! I'll travel by chaise!"

"And I," said Hesther, "will be lucky indeed if I can pay for my fare on a stage!"

"I'll pay for you!" Clarissa said eagerly.

But Hesther, watching her with greenish eyes, observed reflectively:

"I'm not a charity pupil yet . . . you know . . ."

Clarissa went back to the fire and held her hands out to the smouldering logs.

"I seem," she said, "to have offended you. Well, that again is Miss Patchett's fault. When I leave here I'm to have my own chaise, postillions, and horses. Why mayn't I share so much with you?"

"You're an angel," Hesther declared coldly.

But Clarissa was no fool.

"I've done wrong again it would seem," she said drily; "pray forgive me."

"Wrong? You're so spoiled you can scarcely do right!"

This was a bold move, and had an immediate effect.

"May I then not protect my friends?" Clarissa demanded haughtily.

"Ask Madam Patchett!"

"But," Clarissa persisted, "she does what I say!"

"And you have no shame, to know yourself so pampered?"

Clarissa no doubt would have answered, but at this moment Miss Patchett herself entered the room in her bottle green with a powdered wig and spectacles.

She was fulsome to Clarissa and forbidding to Hesther, whom she disliked.

"My dear child," she said to Clarissa, "we have an invitation to a New Year's party at Dr. Proudfoot's. Would it divert you to accompany me?"

"Yes," said Clarissa, "if Hesther comes too."

"Hesther? Miss Shaw?"

"You know her, madam," Clarissa reminded her, laughing: "she's sitting opposite you at this moment."

"Don't trouble yourself, Clarissa," said Miss Shaw coldly.

"Trouble!" Miss Patchett caught Clarissa's fixed eye. "Trouble! My dear Miss Shaw, we will be delighted. Will you accompany us?"

"I shan't go if she doesn't," Clarissa announced, for she had made a friend, and for Clarissa her friends could do no wrong, her enemies no right. So she was born—impetuous, hot-headed, and gallant—and she winked at Hesther over their glass of madeira.

And Hesther, realising exactly what she had to deal with, winked back.

Friendship!

It meant different things to both, and their lives were one day to be entangled.

But that night, behind Miss Patchett's majestic back they smiled secretly, and pledged each other, as the candles twinkled, and the fire roared merrily, and they were young.

They were schoolgirls, ignorant of the world.

But that night, for the first time, the curtain rang up on the drama both were to play. The fire, the candlelight were so pleasant; who could foretell that dark paths lay in wait for either one?

VIII

Hesther," Clarissa asked a few days later, "what will you do when you leave here?"

Hesther laughed.

"I am supposed to become a governess."

"But that would be monstrous! Governesses can't be so pretty. Why, Hesther, all the papas and the brothers will fall in love with you!"

"I shan't really become a schoolmarm," Hesther declared, not laughing any more, but in a dry tone of voice.

"Then what——"

"Oh, I shall run away," said Hesther recklessly.

Clarissa considered this.

"Run where?"

"Does that matter? Over the hills and far away."

"Could you not stay with me? I could ask my guardian——"

Then, poor child, she saw Hesther's dark brow and knew that once again she had done wrong.

"It would make me so happy," she finished lamely.

"You are kind," Hesther told her ironically, "but we shall never meet once we leave here."

"Why not, pray?"

"Our circumstances will be very different."

"Do you really think," Clarissa demanded, "that I would ever forget you, no matter if I married the Prince of Wales himself?"

Once again Hesther was touched; once again, not for the last time, she realised the generosity of Clarissa's nature, and she knew, then, definitely, that it was true: Clarissa *wouldn't* forget her if she married the Prince of Wales; she was one of those rare people who do not forget. She knew, too, that Clarissa loved her with the selfless worship only young ladies at school can achieve. She was Clarissa's first love.

So she pressed her hand and said truthfully:

"You are the only person, sweet, I care for in the world."

And then Polly, the housemaid, ran in, and whispered that there was a gypsy fortuneteller in the kitchen, if they liked, and please not to tell Miss Patchett.

"Oh yes!" Clarissa cried. "I've silver here in my purse! Quick, Hesther, before we're discovered!"

Hesther did not think she wished to know her future. But the charm of a gypsy fortuneteller, to young ladies at school in Bath, was difficult to resist, and so she followed Clarissa to the kitchen.

There, where copper glowed, and the fire roared, and a garland of Christmas holly hung above the warming pan, a woman sat by the kitchen table smoking a black pipe and drinking porter. Behind her hovered the cook, a stout body in a frilled cap; the kitchenmaid, an overexcited orphan child; and the small black page, all giggling.

"Be out, both of you!" cried the cook to the kitchenmaid and the page as the young ladies came in, their light dresses rustling, Clarissa with a candle in her hand.

For a moment they stood on the threshold, these two young virgins, their eyes brilliant, their cheeks flushed, for was not this an adventure? Still drawing at her pipe, the gypsy threw them a shrewd glance. Clarissa, golden headed, with her vivid, laughing face; Hesther, ivory-pale, with dark tresses and a coral mouth. They must have made, framed in the doorway of that old-fashioned kitchen, a delicious, youthful picture.

But the gypsy, a mercenary creature, was not concerned with their attractions.

"Come in, young misses," she growled, and put aside her pipe.

She was a wolfish, middle-aged woman in a red cloak and a black dress trimmed with tarnished sequins. Her jetty, grizzled hair was uncombed and stiff as a hedgehog's spines; her fierce eagle's face was seamed with the lines of forty years' sun and wind; her black eyes blazed, and she smelled of wild animals, wood fires, and toasted cheese. There were lumps of gold stuck in her ears.

"Who's first?" she demanded, finishing her porter in a gulp.

"You," Clarissa whispered, pushing Hesther.

But the gypsy would have none of this.

"No," she said roughly, "you." And she caught Clarissa's wrist, drawing her down at the kitchen table. She then demanded silver, and Clarissa, following an ageless tradition, crossed her hand. The gypsy looked hard at the girl's palm, breathing fumes of porter in her face.

She said in her rough, rather hoarse voice:

"I shall see you one day, my lady, at the races at Newmarket, but you may not remember the gypsy's face. You'll be on a splendid coach, in a pink dress, and you will be with a man in grey. Later you'll see me at Epsom. You and the man in grey will be near the King's son then, and one of them will give me a guinea. The man in grey will say it's for 'my lady of Egypt,' for that's what they call me."

She gave a ribald laugh, and, leaning closer, said,

"Women are unlucky to you, my pretty one—all women. Never forget that—make no friends of women . . . maybe you're too beautiful. If you're not careful a woman will harm you, and terrible will her harm be—perhaps there's no escape. Not for you. And there's a tall gentleman who'll call you over the seas. You go with him, my dear—he'll take you far away from danger."

"Shall I be loved?" Clarissa wanted to know, her eyes dancing.

"Not enough," the gypsy said positively.

"Not enough for what?"

"To make up for the danger." And the gypsy pushed away her hand, once again burying her face in a fresh tankard of porter.

"Your turn," Clarissa said to Hesther.

Hesther came reluctantly to the table, and Clarissa watched her with absorption. Behind them, furtively, gathered the cook, Polly, the kitchenmaid, the Negro, and Miss Patchett's coachman, a little the worse for drink, but suddenly very respectable on seeing the young ladies. Outside, in the street, link boys were shouting for a chair, and a curricle dashed past, spattering snow and mud, but nobody was listening as the gypsy looked at Hesther's hand, sitting under that wreath of holly hung beneath the warming pan.

There was silence for a moment, and then the gypsy looked up, her dark, fiery eyes fixed on Hesther's composed face.

"Well?" Hesther asked, smiling at Clarissa.

But the gypsy was silent.

"Well?" Clarissa demanded, exchanging a laughing glance with her friend.

The fortuneteller got up then, bundling herself hastily into her shabby red cloak.

"And my fortune?" Hesther asked.

The gypsy shook her head violently. The smell of her, that was rather the smell of menageries and of wild animals, seemed more pungent.

"I can't tell the young lady's fortune," she said. She picked up her basket and then, suddenly, she pushed across the kitchen table the fourpenny piece with which Hesther had crossed her hand.

"Why not?" Hesther asked curiously.

"I can't, my dear. I can't say it. Not *your* future. That I won't say."

And then she was gone, this wolfish, grizzled gypsy, just as though someone had chased her out of the firelight into the sleeting, hateful night.

"My lady of Egypt," Clarissa said, rather nervously. "I shall remember her!"

"So shall I," the cook said, "the nasty, artful creature! And they do say she stole the children's silver pheasant from across the road! Well, they'd steal anything—gypsies!"

"Even a character," said Hesther suddenly, getting up.

She went back to the white-panelled hall and there, a few minutes later, Clarissa found her.

Miss Patchett was writing letters to parents, and they were unlikely to be disturbed.

Hesther said, warming herself before the fire,

"I wish I'd reminded you to bring down your perfume of sandalwood."

"My sandalwood? Why?"

Hesther spread her skirts before the dying fire.

"That gypsy stank like a menagerie of wild beasts."

"She *is* a wild beast," Clarissa said to this.

"You liked her?"

"I like her race."

"Such beggars? Why?"

"I like the wild way they live. They care for no one. They love freedom and the road."

"I hated that woman," Hesther said.

"My lady of Egypt? Why? Because she wouldn't tell your fortune?"

"Perhaps."

Clarissa laughed.

"She may have been tired and tipsy with porter. She had a long way to walk, no doubt, and only a tent at the end, and perhaps a drunken husband and some hungry children. She was in a hurry to go back—can you blame her?"

"You have a magnificent imagination," Hesther retorted.

"I liked my lady of Egypt," Clarissa repeated, warming her hands at the fire.

"Because she saw you in a grand coach? Or because she smelled of wild animals?"

"Both," Clarissa laughed, and added: "I hope I shan't forget her. I hope I shall always know her face again."

"I'm going to bed," Hesther remarked. "Will you snuff the candles?"

"We'll both snuff them."

And they did, forgetting my lady of Egypt.

IX

It was a year later, when Hesther was seventeen and Clarissa a year younger, that Miss Patchett took them both to a garden party in Bath. The summer holidays had just begun; as usual they were the only young ladies left at school. By now Miss Patchett was resigned to taking Hesther with her to such mild outings as she devised for Clarissa; the younger girl insisted, and the star boarder's word was still law.

But the schoolmistress did not like Miss Shaw.

The girl showed affection for nobody in the school, with the one exception of Miss Richmond. She was reserved, haughty, ironical in her manner. A brilliant pupil, she showed no interest in her work, no ambition for the future. The other young ladies in the end came to dislike her, tolerating her only because of Clarissa, of whom they were all fond. Nor did the schoolmistress approve of this close intimacy between the two girls. It seemed unlikely to her that the friendship was, on Hesther's side, disinterested. Hesther, she considered, might later make claims upon Miss Richmond unsuited to their respective situations. Once, greatly daring, she had ventured to hint the same, and Clarissa had flushed crimson.

"Madam, the sight of Miss Shaw could never, no matter what the circumstances, be unwelcome!"

Miss Patchett contented herself with thinking grimly:

"Wait until you're my age, miss! Begging letters and bad debts—wait until you get to know them!"

But, sycophant that she was, she had long ago ceased to remonstrate. The star boarder must have her own way.

And so, in the chaise, Miss Patchett drove with her young charges to the garden party of a certain Lady Twemlow, widow of some obscure city magnate. It was a warm September day, and the sky was dappled with silvery clouds. The roads were soft with dust, muffling the beat of the horses' hooves; the coachman's face was red; and Miss Patchett, in purple taffetas and a monstrous wig, at which both girls were inclined to giggle, looked more than ever like one of his own equine charges.

The girls themselves were a bewitching foam of white frills and pink ribbons. Clarissa sat beside Miss Patchett, Hesther opposite. Miss Richmond, the schoolmistress reflected, had been inclined to protest about the arrangement, but her companions had soon overridden her wishes.

"Conceive," Miss Patchett said to herself, "of the Hon. Miss Richmond driving through Bath seated opposite a pupil-teacher like a maid! Yes, a very maid!"

Fortunately Miss Shaw herself had been the first to perceive the impropriety of such a suggestion. And so as the chaise rolled down the dusty streets of Bath Miss Patchett, inclining her head with dignity to various acquaintances, felt tolerably pleased with herself, with her equipage, with her star boarder, and even with her pupil-teacher, who seemed to be learning her place, and who even looked quite distinguished on this pleasant afternoon.

"That is, of course," thought Miss Patchett complacently, "so long as one does not compare the poor creature with Clarissa!"

And the schoolmistress, who knew little of men, would doubtless have been astonished to learn that any members of this mysterious sex could, and would, prefer Miss Shaw's pale, secret face to Clarissa's apple-blossom loveliness.

While she mused so inconsequently the chaise drew up before Lady Twemlow's door.

The garden party was a pretty sight. The lawn was not spacious, but it was charmingly framed with elm trees that cast dark velvety shadows on the green turf, and crowded as it was with ladies and gentlemen in gleaming silks and satins, it seemed, to the two young girls, a fête as sumptuous as any Versailles could have offered. Lady Twemlow, a birdlike old lady in grey brocade, pounced immediately upon Clarissa, who was drawn, reluctantly enough, into a circle of elderly Bath inhabitants while Miss Patchett paused to salute a minor canon.

For a second Hesther was left, uncertain, by herself, then the school doctor, a jovial, paunchy man, came up to her followed by another figure.

"My compliments, Miss Shaw! A delightful day, isn't it?"

As Hesther curtsied Dr. Ryan continued:

"May I present a gentleman who's dying for the honour?"

She saw, from the corner of her eye, a splendid uniform of red and white, and smiled consent.

"Ensign Barbary, ma'am, very much at your service!"

Again she curtsied.

The young man was extremely tall, with curly brown hair, a weak mouth, and a complexion like a girl's. His smile was charming. For a few moments they stood talking together, then, as a befeathered lady claimed the doctor's attention, the young man said quickly, in a low voice:

"Ma'am, may we not stroll for a few moments along one of these pleasant paths?"

"If you wish," Hesther answered quietly.

She was for the first time alone with a young man not, certainly, of her own age, since he was several years her senior, but a young man, all the same, and one, furthermore, clad in a magnificent uniform. Her heart beat faster, but no one would have known it from the composure of her face.

"I have seen you before," he told her suddenly.

"You have seen me? I don't remember."

"Last Sunday, in church. I watched you leave, and wondered whether I should ever be fortunate enough to be presented."

They sauntered along a shady path leading towards a little ornamental pool in which goldfish swam.

She seemed thoughtful, he observed, and wondered whether or not he had been too impetuous. But all she said was:

"I did not see you, sir."

Her skin, Ned Barbary thought, was like cream, and her mouth was red and silky. On so warm a day, when he was sweating in his fine uniform, she seemed cool and fresh as a sweet pea.

He stammered eagerly:

"May I, one day, wait upon you? It is the White House, is it not?"

Hesther was startled, and replied only to the first part of his question.

"Oh no! You could not—it's an academy, Mr. Barbary! A young ladies' school!"

"I know it is," he replied, smiling with great sweetness, "but such establishments are not nunneries, surely? And I have credentials. Dr. Ryan would vouch for me, and a dozen more."

But she shook her head, repeating in a low voice:

"It would never be permitted."

"Then where and how shall I see you again?"

"In church, Mr. Barbary." She lowered her eyes demurely.

"I shall contrive, if I may, a note."

"At your peril!" But she laughed. "I must return," she told him.

"One moment, I beg you! You know nothing of me, of my situation—barely my name!"

"Five minutes, then," she said, looking at the goldfish.

His tale took no longer; there was little enough to tell. He was twenty-one, the son of a Wiltshire squire. He was in Bath only for a fortnight more; he was with some brother officers, and they were soon to rejoin his regiment—the name of which was unknown to her—in York. Somehow, no matter what happened, he must see her again soon. Would she somehow contrive not to disappoint him? After all, the White House had a garden—he had passed it every day, in vain, since Sunday—and as for the wall, well, he was agile, and walls presented no difficulties.

"Mr. Barbary, sir," Hesther insisted, "I must return to my friends. We have been too long absent."

And so they turned and left the pool, retracing their steps towards the crowded lawn, where Miss Patchett was chatting with three or four other female dragons and Clarissa was talking to some school friends, now of course on holiday. Once, Hesther saw, she glanced about her, as though looking for her friend.

"On Sunday—a note——"

"You must leave me now," Hesther said quickly, and in a moment she vanished.

"Hesther," Clarissa said a moment later, "what do you think? Lavinia has had the drollest adventure——"

Ensign Barbary watched the charming group from a distance moodily, sheltering himself behind a cluster of ecclesiastics.

Driving home, Miss Patchett, still genial, amused herself by discussing the party.

The canon was so charming, Lady Twemlow the soul of affability, and Sir Weedon Dunstable so excessively courteous. Did not Clarissa agree?

"Oh yes," yawned Clarissa, who had found the party somewhat tedious. "What is Bath?" Clarissa thought. "I want to go to London."

"And you, Hesther," Miss Patchett condescended, "I saw little of you. Did you divert yourself?"

"Yes, madam," said Hesther in a low voice.

Clarissa, who knew her so well, thought:

"She's excited about something. About what? Surely not Dr. Ryan?"

She had not, herself, seen the young ensign in his splendid uniform. She looked curiously at her friend. But Hesther seemed tired, and her lashes were black fringes upon the pallor of her cheeks.

"Soon," Clarissa thought, once more restless, "soon I shall leave Bath and go to London. Soon, now, in less than a year . . ."

The chaise stopped at the front door of the White House.

"Tired?" Clarissa asked her friend, after they had most gallantly assisted Miss Patchett to alight.

"No," Hesther said, "I'm not tired."

The long day was nearly over; already candles blazed in the windows of the White House; the tobacco flowers in the garden smelled sweet, and Hesther laughed as they went indoors.

"Indeed," she said again, "I'm not tired."

The door closed behind them and the curtains were soon drawn.

X

THE DAYS PASSED, still lazy and golden, although September was nearly over, and soon the White House would echo once more with the sound of laughter and with the strumming of spinets.

But everything was quiet, still, although slashes of red and gold could be seen among the leaves of the green trees in the garden, where sometimes, early in the morning, before the maids were up, a flash of white skirt could be glimpsed in the distance among those shrubberies growing near the wall.

Clarissa found her friend moody, and complained.

"One would think you lovesick," she declared once.

"For whom? The coachman?"

Hesther could, she knew, have trusted Clarissa, but she never did. Her heart was already grown too secretive, her nature too reserved. She knew that Clarissa loved her, and sometimes she loved Clarissa, but then she reasoned, ungirlish:

"I don't need her help now. If I did, I would confide in her. And later . . . But we shall never meet again. I will be across the seas, in India, perhaps, when she is the toast of London and would not know me if we met across a room. But we never shall meet; our schooldays are nearly over, and we are no longer little girls."

Indeed the sands were fast running out.

Clarissa knew that the following May she was to stay with her godmother in Soho Square and make her curtsy at St.

James's. She supposed that Hesther would stay on in Bath, as a teacher, and pitied her with all her heart. But whenever she tried to arrange a future meeting, or an invitation, Hesther shook her head.

"It's better not."

"But why? Is this some sort of ridiculous pride?"

"No, sweetheart," Hesther answered lightly, "but you will have to learn to be more worldly. Your godmother would be the first to protest if you tried to adopt every waif and stray you meet!"

"I shall choose my own friends," was Clarissa's only retort.

Sometimes, during those September nights of long ago, Hesther was wakeful, and lay for hours staring out of her windows as though waiting for the dawn to break. It was then that she asked herself whether or not she loved Ned Barbary, and it was then that she decided she did not love him. She knew him little enough but already felt herself the stronger of the two. He was completely dominated by her imperious will, and the careless affection she felt for him was as far removed from his own passionate worship as frost from fire.

"Later," she thought, "perhaps I shall learn to love him. After all, why not? It's a charming creature."

Soon there were only three more days until the beginning of term, and Clarissa wondered why, for the first time since Hesther had come to the White House, she would be glad for the holidays to end. It was Hesther's fault, she decided: her friend had been unusually silent during that last week. Absent-minded too; sometimes she started, when addressed, and remarks had to be repeated twice before she heard them. She was also twice rebuked by Miss Patchett herself for "daydreaming."

"A fault you must learn to conquer," the dragon told her, "before the commencement of this new half-year. You will be a teacher in the future, my dear Hesther, pray recollect, and no longer a pupil."

Hesther bit her lip but said nothing, and it was as well the dragon could not read her rebellious and contemptuous thoughts.

The next evening, as the two girls sat embroidering in the white-panelled hall, Hesther yawned, explaining she had a headache.

"I think," she said, "I shall go to bed."

Clarissa was astonished.

"Already? On the last day of the holidays?"

"You forget," Hesther told her, "I am no longer a schoolgirl."

"And *you* forget," Clarissa retorted crossly, "that I have told you it will make no difference. You're a provoking creature, Hesther, and look! I've tangled my skein, and you know I can't unravel it."

"Give it to me," Hesther said, and deftly put it right. "There!"

She got up and crossed to her friend's chair.

"Good night, Clarissa. Don't disturb me tonight, there's an angel! I have a migraine."

She was usually undemonstrative, and the girl was surprised to find that pale, cool cheek brushing hers.

"I'm so sorry," she cried impulsively. "Do you really feel ill, Hesther?"

"I shall be quite recovered tomorrow," Hesther returned, and again kissing her lightly, left the room.

Clarissa sat by herself, sewing glass beads supposed to represent drops of dew onto the floss silk of her roses, and thought how dull life had become, and that she was too big a girl to stay on at school for another half-year, and she wished poor Hesther needn't teach but could come with her to London. She yawned, kicked her slipper off, pricked her finger, and thought that life could be hateful.

"I shall marry the first man to ask me," she decided, "so long as he's handsome and rich, I suppose, since I'm not, and of course I must adore him, and he must be in love with me, and we will have a lot of beautiful children, and Hesther shall come and teach them if she wants to, and is so proud, and she shall keep me company when they've gone to bed. And I'm sure," she reflected, yawning again, "I wish it was now and I hadn't to wait."

She put away her embroidery with a sigh, and went to the drawing room to serve tea.

"And where," Miss Patchett demanded, "is Hesther Shaw?"

"She begged me to excuse her, madam," Clarissa explained glibly—for the friends had a mutual understanding regarding the dragon—"she's off to bed with the migraine."

"Indeed?" And Miss Patchett raised her eyebrows. "She seems *distraite* these last weeks, does she not, my love? It is to be hoped she's not sulking."

"Sulking?" Clarissa asked haughtily.

"She is on the threshold of a new career. Let us only hope she appreciates her prospects."

Miss Patchett's tone betrayed no very sanguine expectations, and Clarissa shot her a mutinous glance. What a hateful, hateful evening!

The dragon, changing the subject, then began a long dissertation during the course of which she urged Miss Richmond, during her last half-year, to concentrate upon Italian and the harp.

"Your French, love, is excellent, your voice true, and your Greek passable. With the spinet, I am satisfied. Your mathematics are scarcely a strong point, but one cannot excel in all fields."

"No, madam."

"Your handwriting has improved, you express yourself vividly, and your general deportment is most pleasing. I can only urge a greater application to Italian, an ambition to excel at that most lovely instrument, the harp. You see, Clarissa, one day you will doubtless adorn an exalted station!"

"Yes, madam."

"It will be through no fault of mine that you do not shine in any sphere."

"No, madam."

She thought of the gypsy fortuneteller who had refused to look at Hesther's hand, my lady of Egypt. That was a name she would never forget. And the woman had seen her on a grand coach, in a pink dress, with a man dressed in grey!

"I wish——" she said suddenly.

"There is something you want?" The dragon beamed.

"Nothing," Clarissa sighed. It would only hurt Miss Patchett's feelings to say how much she longed to leave school.

"Yet you seem restless," Miss Patchett noted, sipping her tea.

"It's only . . . I'm no longer a little girl!"

"Indeed, no, my dear. You are quite the young lady—a very accomplished, charming young lady too!"

"Then——" the girl began, and broke off.

"Then what, dear?"

"Nothing, madam. Only I wish I had not to wait until May for this visit. Couldn't my godmother receive me at Easter?"

Miss Patchett was displeased, and did not trouble to conceal it.

"You had better write, my dear, if you wish to make fresh plans. But your Italian and the harp——"

Clarissa looked at her then, this woman who had ordained her life for many years, and saw, beneath the spectacles and the overdressed wig, a commonplace and vulgar snob, not even over-clean. Wasn't it true special insect powders were sold to ladies whose "heads" were so elaborately dressed as Miss Patchett's? And this was the famous female pedagogue of Bath!

She thought resentfully:

"When I am married I shall wear my own hair! And I shall bathe every day, and put on a clean shift whenever I please!"

It has been said, in the course of this tale, that the candles of the eighteenth century were guttering low. They burned so feebly when Clarissa Richmond was sixteen that their light was already waning. Miss Patchett's day was done, although she did not know it, but when the new century was born it would blow away more than her own monstrous wig.

Hooped skirts would soon be finished and done with, so would satin coats for gentlemen, and powdered hair, and swords, and women would no longer be burned alive for petty thefts, nor would there be public whippings in the tranquil streets of Bath. Negro pages, carrying their mistresses' prayer books to church on Sundays, would become less familiar, as would scolds' bridles, and witch-duckings, and pillories, and the stocks.

Prince Florizel, courting Perdita, little knew how much, be-fore he ruled, his times would change; haunting the lowest tav-erns with his friends, he was often shocked, but soon forgot, the fearful things he saw. But, unlike his stupid father, he loved beauty—music, and painting, and architecture, as well as women. Already in London the Whigs, despising their King, rallied around their Prince, although the young ladies of Bath knew nothing of these grand doings.

Yet one, brooding, her lip stuck out as she poured a third cup of tea for Miss Patchett, was to play a glittering part in the fairy tale that was her own near future.

And yet another . . . But Clarissa, fearful of waking her friend, took off her shoes before she ran upstairs, gliding like a shadow past Hesther's door.

She went to bed, and thought again what a hateful day it had been, and then she slept, and when she heard horses galloping down the road supposed herself to be dreaming, for it was late, the watchman had called the hour long ago, and the White House was silent beneath a sky peppered thick with stars.

XI

WHAT can one say about the elopement of a young lady from Bath that was not said, so many years ago, by many people who are now dust in the churchyard?

The scene in the kitchen, after Hesther's bed was found tenanted by a bolster in a nightgown, would have been worthy of Hogarth; there was the cook, and there were other female servants, flushed with sleep, bristling with curling papers; there was the coachman, unshaven, florid, bundled in shawls; the small black page, oyster green with fear, the orphan girl, sniffling, and some leering faces from across the way, from where the fortuneteller had stolen the silver pheasant. There was mulled ale for all, that early morning in the kitchen of the White House, and there were plenty to say that they had always thought Miss Hesther queer. And they had known of Ensign Barbary.

September was nearly done; the sun shone, but for the first time there was frost in the air, and how they chattered and argued as they pushed near the blaze of the kitchen fire! Their ruddy faces were reflected in the copper pots and in the warming pans; the cat stole cream without being observed, and still the argument was the same.

Who would break the news to Miss Patchett?

There were many who pressed for the black page, but so ghastly was his appearance, so palsied his limbs, that it was reluctantly decided "the heathen" could be of no use. Not that he benefited; on the contrary, he was elbowed from the fire, his feet were stamped on, his arms pinched, and his ears boxed, so that soon he was glad enough to leave the glow of the kitchen for the chill of the scullery where at least he might blubber unseen and cosset his bruises with only the cat to bear him company; but, unlike the boy, the cat was not hungry.

Finally, among those in the kitchen the cook was elected, by a popular majority, to break the news, and so the cook tramped upstairs with chocolate, her red face creased by lines of anxiety, the frills of her goffered cap trembling with agitation.

Into Miss Patchett's majestic maiden bedroom it is almost indecent to pry. So, no doubt, thought the cook, but, knowing her duty, cried in a quavering voice as she put down the tray near the bed:

"Madam, Miss Shaw's eloped with a soldier, and will we have chops for luncheon?"

Clarissa was perplexed not to find Hesther at breakfast, and the servants' confused and secretive faces puzzled her even more. Yet she was scarcely prepared for a summons to the drawing room, and, once there, eyed the dragon with bewilderment.

Miss Patchett's famous wig was crooked and the paint was daubed unskilfully upon her cheeks. She stood upright, holding a chair, and the girl noticed that her hand trembled.

"Clarissa, pray sit down."

"Something's the matter. What is it?"

Miss Patchett tried to speak, cleared her throat, tried again, and at length achieved hoarsely:

"Your friend . . . Miss Shaw . . . eloped last night . . . an officer here on leave. You knew?"

There are some blows that strike with a cruel kindness, numbing before they maim, and this was one.

"You knew?" Miss Patchett repeated, as the girl only stared at her.

"Knew . . . ?"

"You were her friend. You were in her confidence. She has ruined my school. You *must* have known!"

The parlour boarder had never before heard these harsh tones, but they fell on deaf ears. She looked dazed, and sat down suddenly.

"Hesther has—run away?"

"I've just told you, miss! She eloped with a penniless ensign! Do you realise what she's done to me?"

"Eloped?" Clarissa repeated stupidly. "But she could not without telling me. There's some mistake. Do you think I wouldn't have known?"

"You did *not* know?"

There was a pause, and then Clarissa came back to life. She was only sixteen, but she faced Miss Patchett with a dignity the schoolmistress was never to forget.

"Madam, if Hesther has really run away I know no more than you. Only this: a message must have miscarried, or a note been lost, for she is more than my friend—she is my very dear sister. Do you suppose she would have left me without a word?"

"I know not what to suppose!"

"Why, she would rather have died," Clarissa declared passionately, "than leave me in such anxiety! She's thoughtful, full of sensibility—can you really suppose her to be so selfish? Surely you know the love and trust between us? She said, herself, a hundred times, we were not only as sisters, but as twins! Oh no, madam, she must have been abducted——"

Miss Patchett without ceremony interrupted her star boarder. "This Ensign Barbary? You don't know his name?"

"I never heard it! She knew no officers! Why——" And she paused, as a strange, insignificant incident forced itself into her mind.

"Why what? Come, Clarissa, if you know something, your duty is to speak!"

"I know nothing! Only last Sunday, in church, a young officer jostled Hesther as we came out, and she said how rough these gentlemen are who spend their leave in Bath! But she did not know him. She was angry, and they never even looked at each other!"

There was a pause.

Then Miss Patchett said drily:

"I believe you, child. I believe you know nothing of this scandal. You may go."

Clarissa got up then and, flushing, said impulsively:

"If she's gone of her own free will I shall get a letter. That I know! You can't break friendship in a moment. How can you? It happens so seldom, and can never be replaced!"

The dragon, more cynical, contented herself with retorting:

"You really think this girl will take the trouble to communicate with you?"

"How can she not? She was my friend!"

The scandal spread over Bath, and soon it was learned that Miss Shaw had married Ensign Barbary up in Scotland, at Gretna Green. It was as swiftly learned that his family were furious, since he had been, from the age of sixteen, betrothed to some neighbouring heiress. The Barbary family would not, it seemed, recognise the marriage, regarding Hesther as a penniless adventuress. Such money as the young man might have hoped for was willed away from him, so that the couple had only his army pay on which to live.

In Bath winter fell and Clarissa Richmond still waited for her letter. But no letter came, and it would seem that Hesther Barbary had forgotten her.

Since her nature was both proud and loving, she endured a double loss. Her love, that had been so generously given to Hesther, suffered, but there was also her pride, that was as gravely wounded.

For weeks, months, she awaited the post bag, and could not still believe that one who had been as her sister could treat her with such cruel indifference. For more than a year she and Hesther had been as Shakespeare's twin cherries: they had loved each other, and been young, and laughed, and worked, and played together. They had made girlish pledges, they had roasted chestnuts in the winter, they had peeled apples, fearfully, before the mirror, on Halloween, they had drawn for kings and queens at Christmas, told ghost stories in their bedrooms, laughed together at Miss Patchett, and stolen down together to the kitchen to consult a fortuneteller. How many times, before the fire, or in the garden, had they sworn eternal pledges, and that despite Hesther's pride and resignation to their parting?

So now, when no word came, at first Clarissa was incredulous, then anxious; then—and it took many months—contemptuous.

"She never loved me," Clarissa thought, when spring came and the garden was sweet with lilac, "but she liked what she could get from me. Now all that is finished, and I am only a name, if she even remembers that. . . ."

Like many good-natured, warmhearted people, when at last she glimpsed the truth she was coldly angry. It was forbidden at the White House to mention Hesther's name, and she was glad; she had no wish to speak ungraciously, as she might, of one who was once her friend.

But she could scarcely wait to leave Bath, for it was there that she was first disillusioned, and although such women as Clarissa can never learn better, it was in Bath that she first suffered bitterness.

She, who had been spoiled from childhood without her head being turned, now learned that even favoured beings, such as herself, can be left friendless and forsaken. She remembered the fortuneteller's words, and knew that she would rather die than make another woman friend. But she was lonely, and longed to leave Bath.

She prayed for London, and for Soho Square, and for the Court of St. James, although people said the King was a sick man and his court dowdy.

She wrote passionate entreaties to her godmother, Lady Rune.

Finally she was permitted by her guardian, the admiral, to leave school six months earlier than had been arranged. Miss Patchett's fury was controlled, as was Clarissa's pleasure. Their last words before the chaise arrived were typical.

"With your French, Italian, and Greek, my love," Miss Patchett said, "I am delighted. But the harp——"

Clarissa interrupted. She was so happy that she could not help it.

"If Hesther should ever write, madam, will you let me know?"

The dragon, realising that this was a safe promise, nodded and beamed, as, behind her, without hearing a word of the conversation, the cook beamed, and the coachman, the maids, the orphan, and the little page.

Pointing to the latter, Clarissa said, just before the chaise drove off (and her new French maid thought her unconventional), "One day, madam, if I may, I'd like Toby for my own!"

For she had never liked the dog collar about the page's neck, giving his name and address, nor had she enjoyed the manner in which he so meekly followed them to church on Sundays, carrying Miss Patchett's prayer book on a blue velvet cushion.

The chaise had started, and, closing her eyes, she remembered Hesther's scornful rejoinders to her protests:

"Well, he's black, isn't he?"

Closing her eyes, she thought for one painful moment of Hesther, and then her pride dispelled this vivid ghost. Was she not grown-up, and travelling to London with her own French maid in a private chaise?

Hesther, who had behaved so monstrously, could go to the devil!

"Anyway," Clarissa thought, "I shall never see her again!"

The chaise rolled on, away from Bath, and she could not help wondering if highwaymen were as evil as the legends said.

She remarked as much, in French, to the maid, who gave a faint scream. She knew, then, that she could not talk to the maid. But she was already resigned—she was not yet seventeen—to loneliness, and so she said no more.

PART III

Mariage à la Mode

XII

CLARISSA RICHMOND made her debut in the year 1800, when bread cost 1/5*d* the loaf and London had become long ago accustomed to the many French *émigrés* who had escaped, by flying to England, the worst horrors of the revolution.

An attempt was made that summer to assassinate the King as he sat in his box at Drury Lane, and it was rumoured the Prince was "damned sorry" it had failed. The Prince himself had been for some years secretly married to Mrs. Fitzherbert although none but his most intimate friends was aware that the ceremony had taken place. In June Napoleon achieved the triumph of Marengo, and the war with France had lasted seven years.

London was a rambling red-brick town with cobbled streets and green meadows winding to the villages of Chelsea and Kensington. All day and most of the night coaches rumbled, chaises clattered, and lavender-singers were up at dawn. Watchmen, known as "Charlies," called the hours and the weather, while great ladies still rode out in sedan chairs. Out at Tothill Fields there were fierce and bloody spectacles to be seen: bearbaiting, bullbaiting, and cockfights. In Newgate hundreds of half-starved wretches waited to be hanged or transported for petty thefts. Down near the slime of the river wharves men, women, and children lived like swine in the fever-laden atmosphere of their swarming, filthy huts, but swine are more fortunate, for they eat, and these were famished.

In fashionable London the street criers were ceaselessly noisy. Apart from the lavender-sellers there was the chimney sweep, the milk girl, the pie man, the chair mender, and the little humped man who sold gingerbread. On May Day the sweeps celebrated, got drunk, and danced round London begging, with one of their number dressed all in leaves as Jack in the Green.

Ranelagh and Vauxhall were still the great pleasure gardens of the city, and there every night were to be found fireworks, fairy lights, concerts, acrobats, dancing, masquerades, and hot punch. All over London there were coffeehouses, oyster saloons, gin shops, and taverns; there was a street market on the Fleet Bridge, beggars and vagrants at every corner, and a pillory at Seven Dials.

The neighbourhood of Drury Lane was a rookery of bawdy houses, one of which was kept by a female rejoicing in the name of Old Mother Damnable. The fashionable districts of London boasted innumerable gaming houses, and Tom Cribb's Saloon in Panton Street was the haunt of the more modish bucks of the time. Here, chatting with the ex-pugilist as they sipped hot gin-and-water, sat splendid gentlemen whom two perspiring valets had shaken into their breeches, whose handkerchiefs were drenched in scent, who were better whips than

any coachmen on the road, and who were not ashamed of
knowing how to use their fists.

The lives of these great ones were set in spacious ways. They
were usually Whigs, and great land owners—they possessed, the
majority, a handsome house apiece in London, and certainly one,
if not two, country estates. The younger sons were frequently
army officers, or attached to foreign embassies; their elder
brother was invariably a politician, engaged either in the Lords
or in the Commons, as his circumstances disposed. In the
country they were magistrates, landlords, sometimes lord lieu-
tenants.

They were, in fact, a governing class that knew how to gov-
ern. Why not? They were born, bred, drilled, and trained, with
this one object in view. Despite their surface wildness, their
racing curricles, their fighting cocks, their mistresses, their
"mills," and their gambling, they remained essentially sensible
of their great responsibilities. Not for them the selfish, airy
frivolity that had led, some years before, to the downfall of the
French aristocracy.

These men read deeply, knew Cicero as well as they knew
Pope. In an age of golden oratory they soon learned the necessity of speaking vividly. They wrote verse in Greek and Latin
and French, as well as in English. Some of their sonnets were
admirable. They studied agriculture and learned to farm their
land. They were, of course, out of office, and, since they despised
their foolish King, the weak, brilliant Prince was the sun of
their ambitions. Warily they waited their chance. Intellectual
and sensual at the same time, they collected pictures, hunted,
spoke in Parliament, talked politics day and night, amused
themselves with courtesans, and frequently gossiped with Tom
Cribb.

A full and pleasant life, but not too full for these men, whose animal energy was boundless. They played as hard as they worked, slept little, drank heavily, and cultivated everything, anything, that charmed their vital minds. They were capricious and often arrogant, but they were generous, too, just as they were cultivated and sophisticated.

Outside, in the teeming streets, they had their shoddy imitators, who kicked the watchmen down, and pulled knockers off the doors, and who thought themselves rakehells; but most gentlemen were contemptuous of such vulgar tricks, and it was related of one of them, the Marquis of Rohan, that one night he had set upon such a fellow, thrashing him with the flat of his sword until he squealed for mercy.

Now gentlemen no longer wore swords and no longer powdered their hair save for formal occasions at Carlton House. Nor did they wear silk stockings in the daytime, but Hessian boots, or close-fitting pantaloons. Times were changing, although outside in the street there was the usual din, the clatter of chaises, shouting link boys, a coach galloping by, and the watchmen bawling the hour. It was 1800, it was summer, and that evening there was to be a grand ball.

Some of the gentlemen at Tom Cribb's were dressed, and some were not. Some called their carriages and went straight to Melbourne House, where the ball was to be given, others went home to change, and some could not be troubled to go at all. But among those who went, already dressed, despite his boredom, was this same Lord Rohan who once had thrashed a youth for knocking down a watchman.

That same night Clarissa Richmond made her debut. We learn that she looked ravishing in white gauze, and that her bright hair was worn simply dressed. Of her success there is no question, for she was the most beautiful girl in the room; she was new, she was fresh, and she was unaffected. They called her the radiant child from Bath, the Belle of Bath, the lovely Richmond. Afterwards, as dawn was breaking, she scribbled in her new diary:

"Enjoy'd myself vastly, for never have I seen such brilliant Company, such splendid rooms, with hosts of dazzling Tapers. I stood up for every Dance, and the Gentlemen to whom I was presented were charming and cordial. Lady M. very pleasant in her manner, as were the sons, but some quite old Gentlemen were nothing but a Pest. I drank champagne for the first time, but was not tipsey, and I think my shoes must be worn through with so much Dancing. . . . My godmother vr. affable and said I was a pretty love. Tomorrow we go to Almack's, so I must now to bed. . . ."

Lord Rohan was not presented to her that night, nor did he stay late, having an appointment to gamble, but when asked his opinion of the new sensation he answered briefly:

"She will be a beauty in a few years."

"You're impossible, Rohan," answered his friend Craven; "do you not even want to meet the lady?"

"No," Rohan said, "I detest young girls. Good night!"

"There's a queer fellow," Craven declared petulantly to his friend "Apollo" Raikes.

"The Ghost? Let him be. His tastes perhaps are more sophisticated than yours."

"His tastes? Who knows anything about 'em? He's damned secretive, and always has been."

Rohan went off in his carriage to gamble. He played late and high, winning a considerable sum of money, but he did not look happy when he returned at four in the morning to his great house in Grosvenor Square.

He went straight to the library, where a fire was burning, for, like the Prince, who was his friend, he felt the cold intensely and there were few nights warm enough for his taste.

He stood motionless for a moment, his hands spread out to the blaze. He was thirty, but he looked ten years older. That afternoon his mother had called upon him, beseeching him to marry. She had talked of his duty to the family, of his position, his career.

"So be it," he had said. "I'll marry."

" 'Tis not a death sentence!"

"To me it is."

And to a man so solitary it was. His mistresses were never permitted to interfere with a life in many respects austere. He was not, for his age and life, sensual. He loved politics, and Charles James Fox, high play, his horses, and his country house. Long ago he had been in love with a woman who had treated him ill, and who had, by her desertion, frozen much in him that might have been warmer and less cynical.

The idea of spending his life with any woman bored him to extinction; already, at the mere prospect, he sighed and was desolate. But that, he supposed, was his fate, for his sense of pride and family was strong.

"God damn it!" he said aloud, and then, after a pause, "God help her, whoever she may be!"

He supposed that he must now look about for some young woman, and he hated young women. This reflection reminded him of the girl he had seen that night at Melbourne House.

"She might do," he thought moodily as he went to put out the candles.

XIII

A few nights later Rohan was presented to Clarissa at Almack's Club.

Patronised by Lady Jersey, she was happy enough in the vast ornate room with its crimson curtains, its glittering crystal chandeliers in which candles burned, its hosts of waxen tapers, all its gaiety and glamour and its springtime music. To Clarissa, it was fairyland.

It was Lady Jersey who introduced them.

"Miss Richmond, may I present Lord Rohan?"

She looked at him frankly, expecting someone young, cheerful, and charming. Instead she saw a man who seemed to have no age—a man of middle height, slim and wiry, in a dove-coloured coat. She saw that his hair was frosted grey, and so were his eyes that looked, to her, like silver coins. His skin was olive-pale, and she observed, with distaste, his high-bridged, arrogant nose.

He said:

"May I escort you into supper?"

"I would be delighted."

"My God," Rohan thought. "How does one begin to court these misses?"

He watched her closely. Her brilliant colouring did not appeal to him, but he noted, as a connoisseur, the lovely modelling of her face. Those exquisite high cheekbones; the dark swallow slant of her eyebrows; her deep vivid eyes, and the curves of her mouth. Watching her, he thought that she would grow old gracefully. Her bright hair, guinea-gold, had no charm for him, who favoured dark women, but he stared at her, handing her a jelly, and said:

"You've conquered the town, Miss Richmond."

"You say that as though you were displeased. As though you were angry. Why?"

"You mistake me. My social conversation is not my strongest point. Yet I would like to congratulate you upon your success in London."

"They call you the Ghost, don't they?"

"I believe some people do."

"I see why," Clarissa told him.

"You do?"

"Yes. You're all grey."

"You find that displeasing, Miss Richmond?"

"Not at all."

"How the devil," he thought, "can I carry on this conversation?"

He pressed a handkerchief to his lips, and begged her to accept another jelly.

"No," she said, "and I don't want to be tedious and press you with questions, but they call you the Ghost, I suppose, as I said before, because you're all grey?"

"Perhaps," said Rohan, and made up his mind. He added harshly:

"You stay with Lady Rune, don't you? At Soho Square?"

"Yes."

"I shall call."

"I hope you won't call looking so cross!"

"I beg your pardon?"

"Well," Clarissa protested, "you seem a very angry gentleman!"

He did not think this funny.

"I beg your pardon"—with a cold bow—"I shall hope to improve!"

And then a young man came to ask her to dance.

Rohan watched them, his handkerchief still pressed to his mouth. He thanked heaven, then, that he was rich and had no reason to wed an heiress. "This girl," he thought, "is beautiful and healthy and will give me sons. What more can I ask?"

But he left Almack's tempestuously, and sat gambling late. He won, and was still bored. The idea of marrying Clarissa seemed to him horrible. He found her loveliness tedious; the thought of making love to her embarrassed him.

All the same, he called three days later at Soho Square where, to Lady Rune's delight, he made a formal offer for Clarissa's hand.

"You'll remember, won't you, sir," she reminded him, "that my goddaughter's an orphan and a lonely creature?"

"Then we shall have something in common," he replied, and asked to see Clarissa.

Left alone with her in the library, he was once more conscious of embarrassment.

"Grey again!" she remarked, pointing to his silvery coat.

"Miss Richmond," he said abruptly, "I have a request to make."

She looked at him in surprise, thinking that this could scarcely be a declaration, as she had at first supposed from his manner.

"Yes?" she said, waiting for him to propose that she should exercise a horse for him, or some such favour.

"I'm thirty," he said, "and you, I believe, are seventeen?"

"Yes, I am seventeen," Clarissa agreed, thinking that thirty was old enough in all conscience, but that he looked many years older.

Rohan hesitated, wishing himself dead, and then said:

"Miss Richmond, I have come here to ask your hand in marriage."

Saying which, he looked at her for a moment with those strange eyes that were like silver coins, plunged his hands into his pockets, and went across to the window, where he stood staring at the trees of Soho Square.

She did not know that he was praying with all his soul for a refusal, but she did know that this, her first proposal, was singularly disappointing.

"Well?" he said, after a moment, his back still turned.

Clarissa, astonished, asked impetuously:

"But why do you want to marry me?"

Why, why, why! How tedious young misses are, he thought, hating the interview. But he turned round and told her suavely:

"You're very beautiful. And we could be happy together, don't you think?"

"I don't know," she said, and this was the truth.

"Oh!" he rejoined impatiently, "I realise I'm a stranger. But soon we'll grow to know each other better and be friends."

Friends!

Surely, she thought, staring at him, one marries because one's in love!

"You doubt my regard?" he demanded, not understanding her look of perplexity.

"Regard," she answered, awkwardly, "seems such a formal word."

"Why, yes," he said, "of course it is! I see I should have conducted this matter properly—on my knees, kissing your hand! I've played my part ill and I don't blame you for your hesitation!"

"Now she'll refuse me," he thought, "and I can go on my way, my duty done."

"I wasn't hesitating," Clarissa said to this, "I only wanted to know why you offer for me when you do not seem to—to——"

"To what?"

"Well, to love me!"

"I see," he said again. "I should have written notes and sent you flowers and sweetmeats. I should have courted you instead of coming here to put a duelling pistol to your head. I stand rebuked, Miss Richmond! At my age I should know better!"

She retorted with the childish dignity of seventeen:

"I don't want flowers and sweetmeats, Lord Rohan! In any case, I'm too old for sweetmeats! But you don't really want to marry me, do you? I mean, you don't sound as though you did."

"Hell!" he thought, "I'm making a mess of this—and she's a lovely child."

He walked towards her, put his hands on her shoulders and said lightly:

"I think we might become very fond of each other. Don't you agree, ma'am?"

"Perhaps we might," Clarissa agreed dubiously, wishing with all her heart that he were younger and handsome.

"Very well! Isn't that a pleasant start?"

"I don't want to decide anything——"

"But of course not," Rohan agreed coolly, "we'll leave everything in abeyance while we learn to know each other better. Meanwhile, I'll call for you at three tomorrow, with my curricle, and take you driving in the Park. Agreed?"

"Oh yes! I'd love that."

She was too ignorant to know that such an outing would immediately proclaim their betrothal. But Rohan knew as he kissed her hands. The game was his, but his heart sank.

He went off to White's scowling, pitying her almost as much as he pitied himself.

He thought:

"Poor little devil!" and his temper was sullen for the rest of the evening.

"But what's the objection, child?" Clarissa's godmother demanded the next morning.

"It's not exactly an objection, because I like him. But he's older than I, and so stiff, and his hair's grey!"

"Do you know," the godmother enquired solemnly, "why Lord Rohan's hair turned grey at the age of twenty-five?"

"No ma'am."

"Well," the godmother continued, her eyes on her charge, "it was a wild, reckless proceeding."

"What happened?"

"His lordship, with some other gentlemen, made a wager to ride some devil-may-care steeplechase one night at midnight if there was a moon. Well, there was no moon, but his lordship still insisted upon the chase. They rode across country in the darkness, their finish being the house of a beautiful lady in Leicestershire who waited to provide them with food and drink. Lord Rohan was thrown, child, and his horse killed. He was not found until morning, and then he was unconscious. For weeks he lay like a dead man, and while he was so ill his hair turned grey."

"He's a good horseman, then?"

"A splendid horseman, and a better whip."

"Oh"—she digested this, and then produced—"he's never said he loved me, so I can't suppose he does. I'm afraid he only wants to marry because he knows he should settle down."

"Do you not think instead that he's an honourable man, one

who would disdain to make love to a young girl unless he were betrothed to her?"

"No," Clarissa said, and laughed, "I don't think such scruples would trouble Lord Rohan."

"Really, my dear——"

"But I don't!" Clarissa repeated, shaking her head and still laughing.

"I'm afraid, Clarissa, you don't appreciate this wonderful offer. Do you realise Lord Rohan's position? His wealth?"

"Oh yes. But he doesn't love me and never will!"

"I suppose"—and here the godmother became lugubrious—"I suppose that, like most young ladies, you are waiting to swoon in love with some impossibly handsome and romantic young man?"

Clarissa blushed, thinking this picture attractive.

"Can you not realise," the older woman insisted, "that Lord Rohan is considered more fascinating than any youth? Are you really surprised to hear that?"

"Not surprised," Clarissa said, "but you see, ma'am, I'm only seventeen, and so he seems old to me, especially as his hair is grey, but I *will* try to like him, and I only wish he liked me more than I think he does!"

"So long as you promise you will try!" And the godmother brightened.

"I *will* try," Clarissa assured her.

But she could not help thinking that Hesther must have had more fun when she ran away with Ensign Barbary, who was at least young and romantic, and who must have been fond of laughter.

Lord Rohan looked as though he never laughed.

XIV

A FEW MONTHS LATER they were married, and they went to Brighton for the brief honeymoon that was customary in their day.

What are called the facts of life disturbed Clarissa; having lived so long beneath Miss Patchett's maiden sway she knew nothing of such matters and was terrified. Rohan, perplexed and bored, was of little help, for he had never before wooed a young girl. Between them they immediately made a pretty mess of their marriage. She was alarmed, disgusted, and shy; he was by turn embarrassed, bored, shy too—and impatient.

They found it difficult to talk when they dined together in the honeymoon villa that had been lent to him by Colonel Hanger.

"When we return to Grosvenor Square," he said, "we will have our own rooms and our own customs. You will do what you please, and with your permission so will I."

"You mean," she asked, "that we will have separate bed-rooms?"

"Why, yes, if that is what you want."

"Well, I should prefer it. You see——" She stopped and bit her lip.

"See what? Won't you please continue?"

"I just prefer it," Clarissa repeated, staring down at the table-cloth.

"I understand."

"You're not angry?"

"Why, no," he said; "I think it suits us both."

She asked:

"Are all husbands and wives like us?"

"Like us? Like what?"

"I mean—do they make the same arrangements we have made after their honeymoon? Is that the custom?"

"Not invariably."

"Well," she declared, "I can't understand it!"

"What can't you understand, Clarissa?"

"I don't want to be discourteous," she said, "but I can't understand why people like being married!"

"I know what you mean."

And he sipped his port, thinking what a failure he had been. Already this lovely child loathed him physically, and he was bored with her, always had been.

He said:

"We must have a son, and then . . ."

"But," Clarissa protested, "I don't know that I want to have a baby! It's very painful, isn't it? And I don't much like newborn babies."

"Those matters," he said, "are arranged for us. We can't direct them."

"Perhaps not," Clarissa agreed; "but I'm the person who has to have the baby, aren't I?"

"But of course!" he agreed.

"How soon will I have one?"

"Why, who can tell?"

"Cannot you tell? You're much older than I, and much wiser!"

"I can't tell," Rohan declared, thinking moodily of his own illegitimate child by an opera dancer. "How should I? These are women's matters! Ask your godmother!"

"Well," Clarissa said positively, "I don't like being married, and I think someone might have told me about it before. Don't you?"

"No. Had they done so, you'd not have taken me!"

"I shouldn't," she declared frankly, shaking her head.

"Am I so distasteful, then?"

She hesitated, trying to spare his feelings, and then she murmured, blushing,

"It's not exactly that . . . I just don't like being married."

"Poor Clarissa!"

"You don't, either, do you?"

"Oh yes," he drawled; "I'm perfectly content."

"But surely you were happier before?"

"I was not," Rohan declared, with a sort of grim courtesy, "and I was fortunate to marry someone so beautiful as yourself. I appreciate you, my dear. I've settled down to domesticity and I'm happy."

She wished, with a sigh, that in that case he would not look so gloomy, but she said no more.

Meanwhile, thinking with distaste of the long evening that lay before them, he asked her if she played picquet or backgammon.

"No," she said, "but I would gladly learn if you would be so kind as to teach me."

"Good!" He rang for a servant.

He was surprised to find her quick and clever. For the first time since their marriage she looked alert and gay; her eyes were bright and her cheeks flushed.

"I find you a born gambler," her husband announced in a tone of amusement.

He was not to be so much amused by this discovery before their story was finished, but since he was not gifted with super-

natural powers he continued to smile at her quickness, and the
evening passed more tolerably than any the ill-assorted pair
had spent together.

She asked him later:

"Rohan, will you let me have something on which my heart
is set?"

"Let us hear first what it is you want."

"A little black page!"

"I shan't grudge you one. By all means. You'll make a di-
verting contrast, Titania!"

"You, at least," she smiled, "are more reasonable than Ob-
eron!"

And so within a few weeks Toby arrived in Grosvenor Square
from Bath, to become Lady Rohan's most faithful and devoted
servitor.

They stayed only a few days in London and then went down
to Rohan, to celebrate their marriage with a tenants' ball, fireworks, and an ox roasted whole.

Clarissa enjoyed the celebrations and was impressed by the
stately beauty of the house, but she did not like "Old Lady
Rohan," as she privately referred to her mother-in-law. This lady
was a handsome, faded woman of about fifty who still powdered
her hair and whose rather peevish prettiness had lost its bloom
early in her married life. She had borne six children, of whom
only two were living, her son and her daughter, who was married to a secretary at the St. Petersburg Embassy. Her delighted
relief at Rohan's marriage was swiftly succeeded by doubts
concerning the wisdom of his choice. The girl was bred right,
she admitted, and her son rich enough to dispense with the
usual heiress, but she found Clarissa both giddy and wilful.

"Most of us were at seventeen," Rohan returned to this.

"What sort of companionship can she give you?"

"I need none."

Well, she reflected irritably, that was his way, and no one, most certainly not an inexperienced miss, could hope to change him. Not for the first time she thought him inhuman.

"If you let that girl run wild in London she will assuredly get herself into trouble of some kind!"

"Madam, I must ask your leave to conduct my affairs in my own way."

"So be it," she grumbled; "but there's no sign of her breeding, is there, yet?"

"Let it be!" he said impatiently, "there's plenty of time!"

"If she rode a little less——"

She broke off as Clarissa came impetuously into the room. She was flushed, for she had been riding for two hours, and now announced frankly that it was a pity ladies did not hunt.

"It seems to me," she declared, pulling off her plumed hat, "as though everything pleasant in the world were reserved for gentlemen!"

"Really, Clarissa!" her mother-in-law remonstrated, while Rohan laughed as he went out.

He walked slowly down an avenue of arching beech trees towards the gilded iron gates that bore his coat of arms. Above his head the rooks produced that harsh yet subdued cawing he had known all his life and found a soothing music.

Sometimes he thought himself happier at Rohan than anywhere else; he was an able and intelligent landlord who enjoyed supervising his estate; he liked shooting, and hunting, and talking to his keepers. He had a good memory for village faces, and knew the family histories of his tenants. He loved the dignity and beauty of the house that had always seemed a part of him, as though their roots were somehow intertwined.

When he thought thus he was ready enough to live in the country for the rest of his days.

But after a few months, sometimes after a few weeks, the old restlessness would grip him, so that he must be off to London without delay. For there waited so many attractions: the glamour of the Whig cause, the clash and battle of politics, and men with whom he loved to exchange ideas. There, too, waited the gambling rooms thick with smoke, bright with candles, and behind them, as a background, all the dirt and glitter of the teeming London streets.

"I'm never satisfied," he thought. "At Rohan I hunger for London and when I'm in London I think of Rohan as paradise."

The trouble with this man of thirty was that he was lonely and cynical beyond his years. His mother had denied him nothing, as an only son whose father died when he was at Eton; he had no sooner come down from Oxford than he attracted the attention of one of London's greatest ladies. He enjoyed twelve months' mingled bliss and misery before he was cast aside for another man. On an aloof and sensitive nature such as his this reverse could only have a disastrous effect. Never, since then, had he loved a woman, although he would have been considered singular in that age and in his situation had he not diverted himself with various mistresses, the majority of whom he had found more tedious than amusing. His love of politics, his faith in the Whig cause and in Charles James Fox sometimes seemed to him, as it seemed to many others, an interminable period of waiting. The King would live forever.

Younger than many of his political companions, he was less sanguine than they as to the future greatness of the Prince, who often seemed to him no more than a weak-minded libertine. Young William, he often thought, was the pick of *that* bunch.

But he kept these reflections to himself, for he had no love of being laughed at.

Rohan had always dreaded the thought of his marriage. Now that it had happened, it seemed to him worse even than he had imagined. For the rest of his life he was tied to a high-spirited, impetuous girl with whom he had not one single idea in common. He did not understand young girls. This one he had chosen for her beauty. She was, too, less affected and more intelligent than her contemporaries. But the calamity was as great. Already, he knew, they bored each other, and his mother's comments nearly drove him mad.

He thought:

"When we return to London I must see that that pretty creature is painted. . . ."

Then he caught sight of his head keeper and instantly forgot all about her.

XV

SHE WAS KNOWN before she was eighteen as the lovely Lady Rohan.

She had thought, in her ignorance, that she would be lonely in Grosvenor Square, since her husband was engaged so often in the House of Lords.

She need not have feared.

From the first she was courted and flattered. She grew up, then, swiftly. For the first time she tasted real power. Her sheltered life as a favourite parlour boarder seemed a long way away. Now in this rich house she reigned as queen; she had only to clap her hands for fairyland itself to dazzle her. Banquets, theatres, dinners, and balls, all were hers for the asking. She seemed to move perpetually beneath the bright blaze of a hundred waxen candles; she danced, laughed, and went to bed at four o'clock in the morning.

The Prince tried to make love to her and was repulsed, almost with mockery. At the same time she accepted her husband's political standards and became an ardent Whig. Her interest pleased him and was to become, for many years, their only taste in common, for they never gambled together, and indeed she hid her play from him.

They met seldom save in public, when they were friendly, and she thought sometimes that she would have liked him had he been her elder brother. He had returned soon enough to the habits of his bachelor days. Not that he would have neglected her, or seen her lonely; but to his relief she was gay enough.

They had been married two years before she found herself pregnant. She had, as she herself wrote in her diary, "grown up so fast" that she was no longer terrified, but content. At last she thought she would give an heir to the two Rohans who were sometimes so much akin—the man and the house.

But she gave birth to a daughter, Lucinda, and nearly wept herself into her grave. Rohan, too, was bitterly disappointed.

She soon recovered, and appeared even more beautiful that same winter, when she entertained more splendidly than before. It is easy, even now, looking at her pictures, to recapture for one nostalgic moment the charm of Clarissa Lady Rohan. The obvious loveliness of bright hair, an apple-blossom skin, and deeply fringed eyes, darker than sapphires, are as nothing compared to the vivid gaiety, the sparkling fun, and mischief, the radiance of that incomparable face. She has been painted many times, and every portrait is a fresh delight, for somehow, no matter if the painter is incompetent, there is always a charm, a tenderness, a subtlety, in every curve of lip and cheek; a gleam of sunlight caught, captured for a moment even by some artist who has no other claim to immortality. As for the great painters, they have made her live and move forever. She seems to step, from at least three immortal canvases, living and breathing, her arms filled with flowers whose scent is really that of spring. Of all the women of her epoch she is the only one who seems timeless. Her hands stretch forth as though to bridge the vast gulf of a century; men today still want to kiss her mouth, and so it will always be, unless her pictures are destroyed, for like Mary, Queen of Scots she was born a honeypot, and the memory of such women does not die.

Rohan's indifference was soon so known that many men tried to court his wife. But she would have none of them, and, since she had never lost her heart, she was not even tempted. But often, looking at her friends, she thought that she was missing something other women had. She had friends who lived feverishly for love, and love, to them, compensated for many things: for angry husbands, and debts, and for innumerable children—those "children of the mist," so notorious in Clarissa's time.

She soon found out her husband had an illegitimate daughter of nine.

"Where is she?"

"She is being educated by a decent woman in Chelsea."

"I would like her here."

"Indeed? Well, you can't have her, and you mustn't interfere with the arrangements I have made!"

"But I want her," Clarissa persisted; "she would amuse me."

"You have your own daughter."

"My own daughter's a baby."

"I'm sorry, Clarissa—it's out of the question!"

Oh yes, she thought, when spring came to Rohan and the lilac was sweet, she had missed something other women knew and took for granted. She thought that it would be heaven to fall in love, and even tried to fall in love with her own husband. She was not successful, but soon she found to her joy that she was once more pregnant.

They had been married five years.

"Of course," she thought, her mood changing whenever she felt ill, "it will be another girl. . . ."

But she was mistaken: the child which came gasping into life on a breathless summer day of long ago was a boy.

A son and heir. Exhausted, she lay back on her pillows, her eyes closed, wave after wave of happiness breaking across her weary mind, so that she smiled even while her face was still damp with sweat, and put her hand in Rohan's when he came to congratulate her.

"So . . . pleased . . ." she whispered, as he pressed her hand and went out to buy a great diamond for her finger, as though she had not enough jewels to weigh her slender body down. That night her husband entertained at White's Club in honour of the infant who was soon to be christened Roderick Hilary Charles, Earl of St. Ives, and who was heir to his father's titles, estates, riches, and to all his worldly goods.

The little sister of three soon found herself neglected in the nursery, and was sharp enough to understand why. Lucinda was a pale little girl with her father's grey eyes and her mother's red-gold hair. Clarissa was fond of her without at all understanding children.

"Mama," the child asked her, "everyone won't love Baby more than me, will they?"

Clarissa, still in bed, her gold locks combed loose upon her shoulders, her shoulders white in the rosy foam of her nightgown, laughed, touching the child's cheek, although her heart smote her.

"I love you both alike," she said.

"Does Papa?"

"Of course he does."

"Then *I* shall love Baby too."

"To be sure you must!"

When she was quite recovered, she gave a ball to celebrate the birth of her son, and once more there were fireworks at Rohan, although she was not there to see them.

A change came, then, into her relationship with her husband. They had a son and heir; there was no longer any reason for an intimacy in which neither one had ever pretended to be interested. The matter was never discussed between them, but tacitly they understood one another, and he no longer came near her rooms. The relief to both was heart-felt, and sometimes, on the rare occasions when they dined alone together, they found that they had plenty to say to each other.

Except when they dined abroad together their interests were usually different. He remained a frequenter of clubs, attaching himself more closely even than before to the Whig cause, more vigilant than ever in his attendance at the House of Lords. When he wanted relaxation, he found it in Panton Street, with Tom Cribb and his friends. He raced at Newmarket, attended "mills," and continued to gamble. He supped often at Holland House.

Clarissa was intimate with all the young Lambs, and amused herself at Almack's, of which club she was soon made a patroness. She was friendly with Lady Jersey, but detested Lady Holland's sharp tongue, and seldom directed her coachman towards Kensington. But she, too, loved to gamble, and on one occasion, at least, met her husband on the doorstep of a famous gaming house in St. James Street.

A contemporary diarist notes that "he looked cold, and she confus'd." Nor, apparently, did she play that night, but went home in her sedan chair, a vehicle she continued to use long after the majority of her contemporaries.

"I like a chair," she said, "save for long distances. You can think in a chair, while a carriage whirls you too fast."

And her chair, silver-panelled, lined with oyster satin, still faintly sweet with the essence of some long-forgotten perfume, stands today in the great hall at Rohan.

It must have been a pretty sight to watch that silver chair process homewards towards Grosvenor Square, borne by two men in the peach-coloured Rohan livery, and preceded, proudly, by black Toby, dressed in satin, waving the brightness of his torch. Always behind the chair marched a huge footman carrying another torch, with a stout stick in his other hand; the streets were so dark and footpads so numerous that he was a necessity as watchdog, and it was rumoured he was some pugilist found for Rohan by Tom Cribb. In any case, he carried a pistol in his belt and there was never an attack upon her ladyship's chair.

Soon they had been married six years, and little Roderick had his first birthday, with a sugared cake and one candle.

Sometimes, with the children, they went to live for two or three months at Rohan, where they would entertain for the shooting. Clarissa liked these visits better since Charlotte, Lady Rohan, had been banished to the Dower House across the park. Not that this formidable lady could be prevented from frequent and, to Clarissa, interminable visits.

XVI

No more children?" the Dowager one day demanded of her son, leaning on his arm as they walked slowly round the rose garden.

"Does not Roderick suffice you?"

"He's a fine boy, but I'd like to see another four of such. Did I not bear six children?"

"Times have changed, Mama."

"H'm. In my day your father would never have permitted me to gad about as is Clarissa's custom! Is she unfaithful?"

"I don't think so," he answered, "although her suitors swarm around her. But I have nothing with which to reproach her."

"And you? They still call you the Ghost?"

"They do, madam. It's more familiar to me than my own baptismal name!"

"I see you still wear grey. What whim is that?"

"Just a whim," he answered. "My hair is grey, my eyes, and sometimes, I think, my face! That's another nickname; I believe the lackeys christened me the Man in Grey!"

"When I think of your father! When I think of his silks, his satins, and brocades——"

"Times have changed," he said again, not without melancholy, "and my grey coats do me well enough."

Clarissa said to him in the library:

"I wish your mother would not criticise me as she does!"

"She is unsympathetic; you're impatient! You are not together many months of the year; can't you really contrive some truce?"

"I find it difficult." She sighed. She was dressed for riding in a close-fitting purple habit and a hat with a curled violet plume beneath which her hair sparkled.

"Will you ride with me, Ghost?" she asked. "We could send a message now to the stables."

"Alas! that's impossible. I'm driving fifteen miles across the country!" He rang the bell.

"Business or pleasure?"

"Both, I've money on a boy who is fighting in a mill."

A servant came in with a many-caped driving coat of dove-grey and a tall beaver hat.

"You miss our guests, Clarissa?" he observed, adjusting the coat.

"I think I must. Have you any objections to my returning to London at the end of the month?"

"Why, no"—and he picked up a handful of new whip points—"you must please yourself—you usually do. You will leave the children?"

"Yes. They shall stay over Easter."

"Then do as you please."

She went over to the window and watched him leave.

The delicate-looking curricle, spider-wheeled, waited on the gravel sweep outside the door. Two grooms stood, one at each horse's head. The horses were young, nervous thoroughbreds, grey like everything else in the Ghost's stables.

"Grey, grey!" she thought impatiently, her face pressed to the pane. "How I long for something bright!"

Rohan sprang into the curricle as the grooms jumped away from the horses' heads. Away he went, skimming round a sharp corner, flying down the long avenue at breakneck speed, his mastery of the hot young pair so quietly skilful that even his wife was ravished.

"Indeed," she reflected, "I married a great whip—whatever good that may ever do me!"

She ordered her own horse, then, a bay mare—for she took no part in her husband's whim—and rode away across the park followed at a suitable distance by her groom riding one of Rohan's grey hunters.

She rode far, and in silence. The groom was disappointed, for her ladyship was usually the most delightful companion, and she would talk to him for hours, not only of horses, and bits, and steeplechases, and training, but also of his wife and family, showing in these a deep interest, and never forgetting either their names or their complicated stories.

But she flung only one remark at him that morning.

"Wright," she said, "I'm thinking of buying my own phaeton and pair, and driving myself in London!"

Well, Wright wondered, scratching his head, what would the Ghost have to say about that? Not, he was bound to say, that her ladyship couldn't do it, because she could. But it sounded daring, and of course the old lady would have a fit if she ever heard of it, and doubtless she would, for she couldn't keep her prying nose out of anything.

He would have liked immensely to continue the discussion of this project, but her ladyship seemed in no way ready to oblige him.

She rode on ahead, across green pasture land, down an ancient Roman lane, over a ford, and through a spinney of tangled beech and elms. The path was thick with moss; she was walking her mare, and the animal's hooves made no sound. Thus it was that she saw, framed in a thicket of brambles, a pair who did not see her.

They were ordinary enough, no doubt.

The man was little more than a youth, long-limbed, in his

loose ploughboy's smock, sunburned, and red-headed. The girl
was brown-haired, rosy, in her print dress, and comely in a peasant way; they lay close together in their glade that was sheltered
from the wind, and he held her in his arms.

For one moment, before she disturbed them, Lady Rohan
saw their faces so clearly that she thought the sun had burst
out to make them bright, but there was no sun; she was mistaken.

For that brief moment, before they heard the jingle of her
horse's bit, their look of ecstasy, of shared joyousness, trans-
figured them with such a glow that it made her heart beat
faster. Then, hearing her approach, they sprang apart, bashful,
eyes downcast. They were no longer young gods or young
animals; the magic had gone, quenched as fast as though a
light had been blown out in both their faces, and they were
left gaping, an awkward pair of rustic lovers, as she touched
her horse's side and rode on through the wood.

Her own face looked white as she rode towards the gate
Wright had pressed forward to open for her. Noticing this,
he supposed that the sight of the courting couple had shocked
her, although she had never been what he thought of as a
squeamish lady. But she said nothing, and rode away down
the hill in the direction of Rohan.

Why, she was wondering, has that never happened to me?
Why, why, why? It was not that she was ugly—she was beautiful and young and brimming with health. Many men had
courted her, but never a one yet had touched her heart or moved
her senses. Rohan once had told her she was cold, and she believed him bitterly, hating herself for what she thought of as
a frigid abnormality that must set her apart, all the rest of her
days, from women more fortunate than herself. The simple,
shared ecstasy of that rustic courtship was not for her and

she thought it never would be although she had so many things other women could never possess—her great houses, her silks and jewels, her son and heir, her horses and her gilded carriages, her servants, all her luxury, and a life that was set in pleasant and spacious ways.

Well, she thought angrily, she would rather have what she had than a few snatched kisses beneath a bramble hedge! Then:

"Damnation!" she muttered angrily, "why can't I have a taste of both? I'm only twenty-three!"

She forgot, indefinitely, her wish for a phaeton and pair of her own, but a year later, during another, similar visit to Rohan, she thought of it again. She was, as before, to return to London some weeks, perhaps some months, before her husband; she decided she would take Wright with her and buy both the pair and phaeton before there was time to consult the Ghost. Not that she thought him likely to object, even to a whim likely to cause gossip; she realised he grew daily more remote, and they met seldom in private.

A few days before she was due to leave for London she was seated, on a bitter February afternoon, before the fire in the Long Drawing Room with her mother-in-law opposite to her, and Rohan, over at the writing table, preparing some speech, when he, who was facing the windows, uttered a sharp exclamation.

"What is it?" Clarissa wanted to know, laying down her embroidery.

"That child!"

"What child?"

She sprang up as he went across to the window, knocking angrily upon the pane.

Outside, on the frosty terrace, the five-year-old Lucinda danced with glee, having escaped her nurse, and seemed oblivious of her bare arms and muslin dress. She turned her head mischievously as she heard Rohan call:

"Lucinda! Come in at once! And come here!"

The child, who had seldom heard her father speak so harshly, gave him a scared look and vanished immediately.

"What's that damned nurse doing?" Rohan demanded of his wife.

"Lucinda must have run away. I shall speak to Nurse, although it's the maid's fault. Nurse is busy with Roderick."

Charlotte, Lady Rohan, looked up and said sharply:

"Lucinda needs a governess!"

The child came peeping into the room, paused, and ran across to her mama.

Rohan asked sternly:

"How dare you run out in the cold without a shawl?"

"I did not think," said she, and sucked her thumb.

"Surely, madam," Clarissa said to her mother-in-law, "at five she's too little for a governess?"

"A what?" the child asked, looking up at her mother.

"Run away to the nursery, Lucinda, and stay there!" her father said. And when she had obeyed:

"It's an idea of which I approve. She is too wild to be all the time with nurses. When you are in London, Clarissa, you can look about for someone suitable."

"I am not sure that *I* approve," Clarissa retorted, glancing at her mother-in-law.

"Oh, settle it amongst you—it's women's work!" Rohan answered, returning to his desk, a scowl upon his face.

"Of course," the senior Lady Rohan hinted, "were the child more often with her mama . . ."

"Is she not?"

"Here, perhaps, you see much of the children. But in London——"

Clarissa interrupted:

"I consider my daughter too young for a governess, madam. There is nothing more to say."

She was glad to drive away from Rohan, glad to know her carriage rolled upon the London road. Wright was driving, and she had with her, not the French maid, whom she disliked, but a little mouse-haired spinster named Molly, to whom she was devoted.

She felt as gay as a schoolgirl setting forth upon a holiday.

XVII

London that March seemed grey and bleak. Not many months before the Duchess of Devonshire had died, soon to be followed to the grave by Charles James Fox. Rohan's grief at this latter death was something she had not known how to comfort; how should she, when they were strangers? Yet she herself, so much his junior, had shuddered to hear that the great Fox had gone forever from their lives and times; with the passing of this mighty rebel the last memories of the brilliant eighteenth century seemed already to be growing a little dim.

Napoleon continued to triumph, and there were those who believed that these wars with the French would never end—not in their lives, they said, shaking their heads, perhaps not even in their children's lives.

Melbourne House was shut up that early spring, for the family was out of town; Clarissa missed her friends, but was so content to be away from Charlotte, Lady Rohan, that even the comparative emptiness of London charmed her.

Driven by Wright, chaperoned by the faithful Molly, she visited tea gardens, horse fairs, puppet shows, and the street market on Fleet Bridge. She saw a crowded, colourful, squalid London of which she had never dreamed; she saw for the first time the dirt behind the glitter, and being of a frank, enquiring mind, she took an immense interest in what she saw.

It was amusing when she and Molly, drinking ratafia in a tea garden, were pestered by a pair of city clerks from whom they had the greatest difficulty in escaping to the carriage. Not that Molly found it amusing; on the contrary, she was terrified.

"Only think, my lady, what his lordship would say to this adventure!"

"He shall never know of it," Clarissa laughed, "so don't fear!"

Meanwhile, although Wright had found her exactly the light phaeton that she wanted, it seemed impossible to discover a well-matched pair anywhere in London. The only two horses remotely answering to a description of what she wanted were a pair of greys, and she would not even see them. Grey! That was the Ghost's colour, if you could call it a colour, not hers!

So she shook her head, and said lightly to her coachman:

"I've no wish for my lord to steal horses from me when I've had such trouble finding them!"

Then a few days later Wright came in to see her with the information that at Oxford there was a pair of bays for sale— thoroughbreds, well-matched, well-broken.

"Then I'll have them sent here for me to try," Clarissa declared.

That, Wright regretted, was impossible. The bays were to be sold at auction in three days' time.

"But if your ladyship were to give me the responsibility——"
She interrupted him.

"I'll go myself, with the chaise! I'll take Molly, and Toby
too! What time tomorrow can you be ready?"

And so, lightheartedly, she set off on what was to be the most
momentous journey of her life.

She left Grosvenor Square early in the morning, travelling
in her claret-coloured barouche, its doors gilded with the Rohan
crest and coronet. Wright was driving a pair of iron-greys, their
harness aglitter, and was swaddled in his peach-coloured top-
coat, its cape trimmed with gold braid, for the morning was
cold. Beside him the black boy Toby, wrapped in a yellow cape,
hugging a white poodle, grinned so hugely that he threatened to
split his face in two.

Clarissa came out in a cloak of leaf-green, sable-lined, wearing a high bonnet with a huge green ostrich feather, brown-
clad Molly hovering at her heels. Molly carried her lady's jewel
case, and, since the heavy luggage had long ago been stowed
away, there was nothing to delay them.

Clarissa stood for a moment, smiling up at Toby, and called:
"Be sure you take good care of Médor II!"

"Oh yes, missie! Never fear!"

Then she got into the carriage, watched by a pie man, two
urchins, a chimney sweep, and a very old Irish beggar to whom
she gave a silver coin.

Wright flicked his whip, and the grey horses sprang forward
on the first stage of their long journey.

"Now, Molly," Clarissa said, "you shall see what a pleasant
time we're going to spend!"

"I only wish your ladyship had brought a footman," Molly
observed doubtfully.

"We want no more weight. I like to travel fast."

"Footpads . . ." Molly began, but Clarissa laughed.

"In this year of grace 1807! Really, Molly, I declare you're languishing for the sight of some gallant gentleman in a black mask!"

"Indeed I'm not," Molly said firmly, "but I don't think his lordship would like you to travel without one of the footmen!"

"Well, his lordship will never know!"

They drove away from the fashionable squares and palaces of Tyburnia, through mean and muddy streets so badly paved that even the barouche jolted, streets where ragged children fished in the gutter, lean pigs snuffled, and the air stank of rotten vegetables.

"I wish we'd soon reach the country," Clarissa remarked, pulling up the window.

"It won't be long now, my lady."

It was not, and soon she let down the window with delight, for they were bowling down a long road bordered by hedges that glittered with diadems of frost, and it might, as she said, be Christmas instead of spring. The sky was a pale, milky blue, and soon the sun came out to dazzle the countryside as though the fields were sprinkled thick with diamonds. The air smelled fresh and sweet after London, and soon her spirits rose.

"We'll dine, Molly, at the first pretty inn, and change horses at the posthouse tonight. I only hope there won't be fleas in the beds."

The roads were empty in those spacious times that were Clarissa's. Sometimes they passed farmers' wagons and carriers' carts; there were occasional chaises, and gentry riding gingerly, because of the frost, on the grass beside the road. Once or twice Wright swore to himself as the rumble and clatter of the public coaches forced him to swerve aside, which he considered greatly beneath his dignity, but the stagecoachmen were usually low and violent fellows who drove ruthlessly before them, and cared nothing for the accidents they caused upon the King's highway. The mailcoachmen, Wright conceded, drove with more care if with less skill; but oh! how much he prayed, with all his heart, he might just once fight to the finish, in some tavern brawl, one of those drunken, ham-handed fellows they called stagecoachmen!

Not that he confided these desires to the blackamoor who was, in Wright's opinion, a "heathen," although her ladyship seemed so fond of him. But, he consoled himself, she was very fond, too, of the poodle, for which he had had already to stop once or twice, so that Toby might let it run on the grass.

There wasn't, Wright reflected, watching them dispassionately, as they ran together beside the road, much difference between them, save that the poodle was pretty.

"Not 'uman," he thought, shifting his whip, "neither one. Not like 'orses." " 'Orses" were nearly " 'uman," to Wright, and already he dreaded the strange ones he must drive before the end of her ladyship's madcap adventure. There was the worry, too, of wondering whether the greys would be properly tended at the posthouse before being collected for the homeward journey. Young Pollux was one for catching a cough, and Castor was nervous with strange grooms. . . . " 'Eathen names, those," he ruminated, "but his lordship had queer ideas when it came to naming 'orses. . . ."

They lunched at Clarissa's "pretty inn" and soon resumed their journey.

She was delighted, once, to pass a gaily-painted caravan of gypsy carts plodding along slowly, hung about with baskets, drawn by mules and asses and spavined old horses. She woke

Molly, who was dozing, and together they gazed back at the trudging, alien figures in their gaudy rags.

"Molly, once when I was a girl an Egyptian told my fortune and said I should marry a man in grey! That's strange, isn't it? I never thought of it since!"

"Witchcraft?" Molly hazarded.

But Clarissa was frowning, for that memory recalled others, less agreeable, and for a long time she was silent.

"Remind me," she said abstractedly, after a pause, "to write to my old schoolmistress when I return. I have been remiss."

An ice-blue dusk enfolded the countryside as they drove on towards the posthouse where they were to lie that night. Rooks cawed, swooping above the ploughed fields, silhouetted against the glacial sky like clusters of black fruit. Wright stopped for Toby to light the carriage lamps, and then, when the greys stepped out once more, tired now, and no longer fresh, their imperious hooves smashed the ice, formed, film-like, on puddles, with a brittle, tinkling sound.

It was pleasant to find the glowing marigold windows of the posthouse. It proved itself, by daylight, just another dingy coaching inn, but it seemed cheerful enough, that night of early spring, and they were all glad to stretch themselves.

There was a huge red fire, supper in a private room, a cot placed for Molly beside Clarissa's bed, and quarters found for Toby and the poodle, while Wright went straight to the stables, there to superintend the grooming of the Rohan greys.

XVIII

"WHAT sort of horses have we, Wright?" Clarissa asked at nine o'clock the next morning.

He made no audible reply, but pointed gloomily towards the yard. She looked outside, to behold a sorry pair being led towards her splendid carriage. A brown horse and a dun, one ewe-necked and ancient, the other with a suspiciously big leg.

"Lud!" Clarissa exclaimed, "we'll be fortunate to reach Oxford tonight!"

He nodded lugubriously.

She went, then, to give a guinea piece to the ostler who was to be responsible for the greys.

Once more they set forth, but soberly, now, and Clarissa realised, not for the first time, that the Ghost was an excellent judge of horseflesh.

She thought:

"He does so many things well. He speaks beautifully, and his brain works fast. He's read everything and can talk of what he's read. He rides well, he's an incomparable whip, and they tell me in a brawl he knows how to use his fists. Why, then—*why* is it we bore one another so much?"

But this familiar riddle was one impossible to solve. She shrugged her shoulders and forgot it.

They lunched at a posthouse, eating beefsteak and apple dumpling, and there she insisted on the extravagance of another change.

"These horses," the ostler protested, "will carry your ladyship to Oxford and back again!"

"Perhaps," Clarissa shrugged; "but I happen to dislike over-working horses. Get me your best pair!"

They changed—for the worse, she thought—and went plodding on towards Oxford. It was pleasantly warm inside the softly swaying barouche. She leaned her head against the peach silk upholstery and once again watched the cold blue twilight steal down like a shadow upon the blanched and frosty countryside. She was sleepy, and her head nodded. Soon, she thought, very soon they would be in Oxford at the Crown where she had bespoken beds. She dozed.

She started, thrown violently upright, for the carriage had stopped abruptly and she could hear Wright swearing. It was no longer twilight; a deeper shadow fell across the land—that premature darkness of early spring that is like the soft duskiness of black grapes.

"My lady! My lady!" Molly was twittering.

"What is it? Why do we stop?"

"It's what I said, and Wright has no pistol!"

"What you said?"

"It's High Toby! Listen to the fellow!"

She woke up then completely, to hear a deep, resonant voice addressing her coachman.

Clarissa was wilful and obstinate but she had many qualities. She had, to a high degree, courage. So now she put her head out of the window and called:

"Sir! Whoever you are, to hold up my carriage, your business is with me, not with my coachman! What do you want?"

There was a pause. She repeated:

"Pray come here and address yourself to me!"

A man then came towards her, while Toby, acting on Wright's hissed instructions, jumped off the box and followed him to her window, swinging one of the carriage lights. But the glass of this lantern was cracked, and the flame flickered uncertainly, so that she saw only dimly a very tall man in a dark green riding coat and muddy boots. His face she could not see at all.

"You wait, just wait," Clarissa cried in a fury, "until the thief takers catch you! Do you know, sir, you shall hang for this?"

"Madam——"

"I'll never rest till I've set the Runners on your track. You——"

"Madam," said the stranger firmly, "you mistake my purpose. I'm no cut purse."

"Why, then——"

"You must be travelling to Oxford."

"What is that to do with you?"

"Just this," he said easily, but leaning deliberately against the door. "I was riding to Oxford tonight, but there's a cursed frost, madam, as you may not know, in this sweet, perfumed carriage of yours! Well, my horse fell and threw me on the road. He was lame, and I was forced to leave him in a ditch tavern two miles back, so mean a place they had not even a mule to mount me."

"This does not excuse——"

"Wait, madam, wait! Were you never told not to interrupt? Now for business reasons I must be in Oxford tonight within an hour. I waited for a coach, but the coach passed by, disdaining my need. Can you really blame me, madam, for halting your splendid carriage?"

Clarissa said, her mind working fast,

"You are so desirous of reaching Oxford?"

"Desirous? My state's graver than that, madam! I *insist* on reaching Oxford!"

So saying, he clambered into the barouche without another word, flinging himself down beside her on the peach silk cushions.

"May we now proceed?" he asked, heaving a sigh of relief.

"Oh, my lady!" Molly breathed in anguish.

"A ladyship?" the stranger remarked cordially. "Well, I am in luck it seems!" And again, "May we not proceed?"

Clarissa darted him a look of fury.

"I have, it seems, no choice," she said.

"None whatever," he agreed serenely.

She called out of the window to Toby.

"Tell Wright to drive on. The faster the better!"

There was a short pause, and then the barouche plunged violently forward into the night.

Molly, on the seat opposite, was rigid with terror. Automatically, her hands clasped, like a vise, upon her lady's jewel case, and she prayed fervently, beads of sweat bubbling on her face.

"Do you still regret the footman, Molly?" her ladyship asked coolly from the darkness.

"I—— I—— Yes . . . Yes . . . I do!"

"*I* don't," the stranger said to this; "a footman might have shot me."

"I think he might," Clarissa agreed.

"You'd have enjoyed the spectacle?"

"It would not have displeased me."

"I never met a lady of quality before," he remarked, "but I've always heard they're bloodthirsty."

"Bloodthirsty?"

"Yes," he said. "And why does the female I suppose to be your maid tremble so much? Pray assure her I shan't cut her throat!"

"Molly," Clarissa said, her voice sounding amused, "you're not at all afraid of this person, are you?"

"No, my lady," Molly replied in a quavering tone of voice.

"Capital," he said genially, and then to Clarissa, "It's odd, isn't it, travelling together in the darkness, as strangers? I wonder so much what you look like."

"I would not in your place," Clarissa answered, "for darkness is kind to me."

"Indeed, ma'am?"

"Yes. You see"—her voice trembled—"I—I have the misfortune to be pock-marked."

"Badly?"

"Yes sir. Very badly."

"And you're young," he commented, "for your voice sounds young. It sounds like singing birds."

"I *am* young. Does that make ugliness any easier to endure?"

"Why, no," he said, and shifted, as though uncomfortable, upon the silken cushions. "I pity you, ma'am, from the bottom of my heart."

"Thank you."

There was a pause.

"Do you wonder at all," he asked, "what *I* look like?"

"It had not crossed my mind," Clarissa retorted.

"Well," he continued, ignoring her, "my mother would have thought me bonny had she lived to see me. But she didn't, and now no one else ever will."

Clarissa stifled a yawn.

"I'm black," he said with a sigh.

She started then.

"Black?"

"Yes ma'am. Quite black."

"Great heavens! You're a Negro, like my Toby?"

"Your blackamoor on the box? Yes. If anything, I'm darker."
Molly groaned.

"I'm black as a hearse horse," he insisted, sighing again.

She flew then into a fine temper.

"How *dare* you ride inside with me? You could have gone on the box with Toby and my coachman! Oh, this is too much. I'll put you out!"

"That would be difficult," he objected.

"How *dare* you so much as speak to me?"

He stretched his long legs.

"Well, ma'am, I'm as black as you're pock-marked!"

"What do you mean?"

"The light," he reminded her, "shone for a moment on *your* face. *Not* on mine. Form your own conclusions."

She was glad then of the darkness, for she knew that she was crimson, and she could think of nothing to say. There was a moment's pause. Then he leaned back and began to sing softly:

> *"Cupid and our Campaspe play'd*
> *At cards for kisses ... Cupid paid ..."*

Clarissa observed icily:

"I see lights, and suppose we are approaching Oxford."

He stopped singing and agreed:

"Correct, ma'am. Soon, very soon, now, I'll be leaving you. What perfume do you use? It's sweet as the tropical flower we call the tuberose. You have none here. They would die of your frost."

"You're a sailor?" she asked, unable to control her curiosity.

He laughed.

"Hardly that. But I am familiar with ships, and with the sea. Oh, I'm a man of uncommon parts. Madam, you may now direct your coachman to stop the horses!"

"I'll be glad to," she answered curtly. "Molly, tap on the window!"

They stopped, and there was another pause while he seemed to study her in the darkness.

"Come, sir!" Clarissa urged.

He got up then and opened the carriage door. The street was lighted, but so badly that still she could not see his face.

"You are keeping my horses waiting," she reminded him with asperity.

"True," he said, and then with a sudden formal courtesy: "Your servant, ma'am!"

Mechanically she put out her hand, and for a moment he took it in his. Then to her astonishment and disgust he seized her face, cupping it in his hand, and kissed her full upon the mouth. It seemed to her that she was still struggling as he jumped off the step to disappear into the night. Then she heard him call back a remark so senseless she knew him for a madman.

"Sometimes," he shouted, "I really *am* black, you know!"

And she heard him laughing in the distance.

"My lady . . ." Molly began in a faint voice.

Clarissa was furiously wiping her mouth with a lace handkerchief.

"That—that fiend! That—madman! Oh, I'd like him whipped!—I'd like him in the stocks! To dare—to dare—— Why are you waiting, girl? Do you want him back? Tap on the window!"

And so they drove into Oxford.

XIX

For some time after their arrival at the Crown Inn she continued to rage. She was by no means soothed by her oak-panelled parlour with its glowing fire, nor by the excellent supper of roast venison, cheese cakes, and syllabub with which she was regaled. She was, indeed, so angry that she felt her limbs trembling as though with an ague.

To think that a common man—a pirate for aught she knew to the contrary—a low fellow tramping the roads—should dare to kiss her brutally, as he had done, and laugh at her, and call himself a blackamoor! Great heavens! Clarissa gasped, he may have been, for aught I saw of his face! And once again she shuddered.

Wright expressed his deep contrition regarding what he called "the incident."

"It was not your fault," she answered a little stiffly.

"My lady, I thought our last moment had come! High Toby, I thought, and what his lordship would say——"

"Well, there was no harm done," she answered, almost with indifference, for at least Wright had not witnessed that shameful kiss, and then suddenly:

"Wright, did you see the person's face at all when first he held us up?"

"Only dimly, my lady."

"What—was—did you see what sort of person he appeared?"

"He was a young gentleman," Wright produced after a pause.

(Gentleman, indeed!)

"Did you notice—was he dark or fair?"

"I couldn't say, my lady. But he seemed handsome."

At least, she thought with a deep sigh of relief, at least he is not a blackamoor!

Later that night, as Molly helped her to undress, she said casually, rather as though she were jesting:

"Such monstrous impertinence as that—one doesn't often find it nowadays on the road! Such manners belong more to the eighteenth century!"

Molly whispered, awe-struck by the sacrilege:

"To dare to—to kiss your ladyship!"

"The person was drunk," Clarissa said disdainfully, "or mad, or both!"

"But, my lady, he talked like a gentleman!"

"Some tipsy squire holding up chaises for a bet! My comb, Molly!"

"I thought it was a footpad. I thought I would have died! And your ladyship's jewel case! There was I holding it, and——"

"Well, the adventure's ended now. Did they put the warming pan in my bed?"

"I did so myself."

Long after she had snuffed her candle she lay wakeful, still raging. That common man! Before her maid! The insolence, the bravado. And then, as though a tiny voice spoke in her brain, she heard the words: "But his voice was not that of a common man . . ." So much the worse, she decided. He hadn't even the excuse of tramping the roads. He must have been what she had so scornfully described to Molly as a drunken squireen, holding up carriages for some bet made in his cups. Again that tiny voice: "But he wasn't drunk . . ."

Then, of course, he was mad. But that, to Clarissa, wasn't

the worst part. Always honest, she forced herself to realise the appalling fact that the stranger's familiar kiss had not disgusted her so much as she would have liked to pretend. She had, naturally, been kissed a number of times, and always such snatched or furtive embraces had bored her intolerably. But this unknown man, pressing his mouth to hers in darkness, had, despite her anger and repulsion, most certainly not bored her. Perhaps, she thought, she had been too furious to be bored.

"Ah, no," she confessed to herself a moment later, "he made me feel like a slut! That's the worse part. For a moment I didn't mind. For a moment I was sorry, when he went."

And she felt her cheeks hot as she tossed so restlessly upon her pillows.

The next morning she was up early to try the bays. She liked them so much that she determined to buy them, and directed Wright to bid for her at the auction held that same afternoon. This, of course, entailed another night spent in Oxford, and the thought was tedious as she returned that morning to the inn. But as she walked through the hall, pulling off her gloves, her attention was caught by a printed notice pinned to the wall.

"Why, Molly," she said, "look, do you see? They're giving *Othello* tonight at the theatre here. We will go; tell Toby to bespeak me a box."

Molly privately thought they had had adventure enough to last them a lifetime and was furthermore convinced that she wouldn't understand a word of *Othello*. But she sighed, and gave the command to Toby, hoping very much that the "heathen" would misunderstand his orders. But Toby, who loved his mistress, had no intention of failing her, no matter if she asked for the moon, and he soon came back to tell her he had bespoken the stage box.

"You shall come with me too," Clarissa told him, "and see a fine play about a jealous blackamoor!"

Once again his dazzling grin threatened to split his face in two, and Molly thought sulkily that sometimes her ladyship had no sense. The idea of taking that heathen to a box at the theatre!

"Will your ladyship be dressing?"

Clarissa, having obtained her bay pair for £150, was in radiant spirits. She seemed, the maid thought, entirely to have forgotten their unpleasant adventure on the road.

"I shan't be making a *grande toilette,* if that's what you mean, but I shall bathe and change. I'll wear the white gauze and my blue cloak lined in ermine. Oh, and my pearls!"

She arrived in good time.

As she walked into her box a minute before they rang up the curtain she noticed with pleasure a graceful, old-fashioned theatre upholstered in wine-red plush, its boxes draped with gilt fringes. The familiar smell of hot candle wax and orange peel rose to her nostrils, and she relaxed in her chair with a sigh of pleasure.

"The playbill, my lady," Molly said, handing her a sheet of paper.

"Thank you," Clarissa smiled, as the fiddlers struck up, but she did not glance at the playbill. She was sure the actors would be unknown to her. Her hands clasped on the front of the box, she waited like an eager child for the magic to begin, serenely unconscious of the many eyes turned inquisitively upon her. So beautiful a lady, and a stranger, too, especially one accompanied by a Negro page in a spangled turban, caused considerably more excitement among the spectators than the prospect of the play itself. Soon an orange seller told the callboy, who told the stage manager, and then, in a few moments, all the actors knew that some great lady had taken the stage box, and all were curious, for their season had not so far been successful.

Clarissa, oblivious of the fact that she was not only to see one drama played that evening behind the footlights, but was herself to participate in another, continued to watch the shabby red curtain while she waited for the fiddlers to subside. At last the listless scraping finished, and the curtain rose.

It was not until the second scene, however, that Clarissa, giving a violent start, clutched wildly at Molly's arm, for, as the Moor walked onto the stage, tall, swarthy, and black-bearded, to say:

> "Let him do his spite:
> My services, which I have done the signiory,
> Shall out-tongue his complaints. . . ."

she recognized him immediately. There was no mistaking that rich, vibrant voice. Even the tall figure, seen before so dimly, could only have belonged to the stranger of the carriage.

"A player!" Molly gasped, conveying, by the horror of her tone, that even a footpad was socially preferable.

Clarissa stared straight before her.

His face was quite concealed by the black beard that had most certainly, as she had every reason to know, not been there a few hours ago when . . .

She felt her face grow hot, and was thankful that she had brought her fan. She held it up to her eyes until she reassured herself that there was small possibility of her being recognised in the darkness of the box. She was behaving, she told herself, like some foolish little gaby of sixteen. She laid down the fan and continued to stare haughtily at the stage until the entrance

of Desdemona all but caused her to fall out of the box in
her astonishment.

For a second she thought herself dreaming; she thought that
everything which had occurred since her departure from London must be unreal and that soon she would wake up in her
bedroom at Grosvenor Square. Surely everything since was a
dream. First, the stranger, pushing his way so rudely into her
carriage, talking to her with such familiarity, kissing her—final
outrage—with such monstrous impertinence. Then, a few hours
later, the stranger again, black-bearded now, striding upon a
stage as the Moor of Venice. And then, strangest hallucination
of all, even more fantastic than what had gone before, the sudden
apparition of a Desdemona who was not Desdemona at all,
but Hesther.

Hesther Shaw.

If this was a dream, she wanted to wake up, for so much con-
fusion was making her head ache. For a moment she closed her
eyes, only to hear Hesther's voice, clear and unmistakable:

> ". . . I do perceive here a divided duty;
> To you I am bound for life and education;
> My life and education both do learn me
> How to respect you . . ."

Yes, Clarissa thought, opening her eyes, aware now that she
was not dreaming; you *were* bound; you were bound to Miss
Patchett but you escaped. You ran away with someone called
Ensign Barbary. It seems a hundred years ago, and what you
are doing here, on this stage, God only knows, but I intend to
find out!

She watched Hesther, sitting motionless. Mrs. Barbary had
scarcely changed. She was slighter, perhaps, in her white, clinging robe; her face, too, seemed thinner than Clarissa remem-

bered, but there was no mistaking her eyes, her gestures, her black, satin-smooth head . . . While she watched, as though in a trance, she felt a light touch on her shoulder, and turned to discover Toby, the page, at her elbow.

"Miss Clarissa, dat lady—you remember? Miss Shaw, in Bath . . ."

"I remember," she whispered back.

Strange. Toby, whom many people thought slightly deficient, had never been known to forget a face.

She settled down to watch the play.

XX

Soon it dawned on her that Hesther was a poor actress. Despite her subtle good looks her voice soon became monotonous and her gestures were those of a marionette. Clarissa, accustomed to the mighty ones of Drury Lane, decided that she was both inexperienced and untalented. And he? His appearance was splendid, his voice rich, but he was little more successful in his rôle than Hesther. More competent, perhaps, and more assured, but inclined to rant, undisciplined of speech and gesture. Iago played him off the stage, and Iago, Clarissa knew, was just an ordinary provincial actor.

Then an idea came to her that made her feel strangely uncomfortable. Perhaps the stranger was Hesther's husband? He was obviously a wild man, such a one as might well have been cashiered from the army. She remembered, vaguely, that Ned Barbary's family had cut him off after his runaway match with Hesther. Perhaps that was it: they had been left penniless, somehow to grope their way into the fustiness of the provincial theatre there to perform ill enough, and to live, she was sure, precariously.

She did not think she wanted to discover that the stranger was Ned Barbary.

At the end of the first act the candles were lit once more in her box, and she looked eagerly at the playbill.

Desdemona, Mrs. Barbary. She had not even tried to disguise her name! Othello, Mr. Rokeby. Mr. Rokeby? Surely, if she played under her own name he would scarcely—— Why, he *could* not be Hesther's husband!

"Toby," she said, "I want paper and a quill or pencil. Please will you find them for me? Ask the candle-snuffer."

When they were alone Molly ventured:

"To think, my lady, he was naught but a strolling player!"

To which her ladyship made the singular reply:

"He is not the only ghost I have seen tonight."

"That's what he meant, I suppose," Molly discovered, "when he shouted back he really *was* black sometimes."

"I suppose so."

"And he is, I declare! Nearly as black as Toby. And that false beard!"

"The beard," Clarissa stated, not without irony, "is most certainly false."

"A strolling player!" Molly said again, and shuddered.

"You forget," Clarissa reminded her in the same tone, "you forget Mrs. Siddons, Mr. Garrick, and Mr. Kean."

"They would never have behaved so on the road," Molly insisted; "not even Mr. Sheridan!"

"Well," Clarissa admitted, "it's indeed difficult to imagine Mrs. Siddons as a footpad!"

"That's just what I mean, my lady."

Toby came back with some paper and a pencil, but she only began to write in the interval before the last act. Seeing Molly's horrified glance, she said:

"I am not writing to the footpad, Molly. Only to a lady I once knew."

She wrote:

DEAR HESTHER,

If you care to have supper with me at the Crown Inn, I will await you. It would please me much to see you after so many years. I will send my carriage back to call for you. I am alone. Pray do not dress. If your husband should accompany you, I invite him also to wait on me.

CLARISSA ROHAN.

She folded this note, addressed it to Mrs. Barbary, and instructed the page,

"Toby, you must go to the back of the stage and make somebody give this letter to Miss Hesther."

"Yes," he said solemnly.

She came to a sudden decision.

"Molly and I are leaving now. I shall send the carriage back. If Miss Hesther comes, you must escort her. If she cannot, you will return with Wright."

"Yes," he said again, and disappeared.

"Come, Molly," Clarissa said. "I have had enough."

For she knew definitely she had no wish to watch Mr. Rokeby smother Mrs. Barbary in the last scene of *Othello*.

"Of course," she thought, on the way home, "Hesther will not come. She has hidden herself away for many years. Why, now, should she disclose her circumstances when they must be so miserable?"

Yet when they arrived back in her dark-panelled private par-

lour she ordered the fire to be built up, and bespoke supper
for three. She ordered roast ducklings, cold meat, and apple pie,
and gave directions as to wine.

"That is," she said, "if my guest—if my guests—arrive. Otherwise, you need not bother."

She went to the bedroom, combed her hair, powdered her
face, and brushed the hare's-foot across her cheeks.

"You may go to bed, Molly."

"But are you sure——?"

"Quite sure. Toby shall help the waiter serve me. Be off!
Good night to you."

She went back into the parlour and stood by the fire, stretch-
ing her hands towards the blaze. It seemed to her that she
waited for a long time. Hesther could not be coming now.
But Toby——

Suddenly, outside, she heard footsteps, and turned.

The door was thrown open as Toby's high-pitched voice
announced:

"Mrs. Barbary!"

Hesther came into the room alone.

"Am I glad," Clarissa thought, "or sorry that she's alone?"

For a moment the two women looked at one another, uncertain, and the gulf of eight years seemed to both impossible
to span.

Hesther, hesitating for a moment on the threshold, saw, as
though temporarily dazed, the tall figure in its white, flowing
gown and scarf of azure gauze. Clarissa, but changed, grown,
of course, less girlish; almost imperious in the composure of
her gaze and gestures. But the loveliness itself was undimmed;
was more brilliant, indeed, than in her girlhood. She had assumed, if anything, a more vivid beauty than was hers in Bath;
she was very much a woman, but she was also, equally, a great

lady, such as Hesther had never seen before. She had, too, the dignity of complete naturalness; the little Clarissa had always been unaffected, but Lady Rohan wore the same simplicity as a crown brighter even than her own hair.

"Toby," she said in the warm voice that Mrs. Barbary remembered, "order supper at once. Come in, Hesther, to the fire, and take off your shawl."

Hesther wore a gown of green velvet that might have been rich once but was shabby now. The shawl was too thin for so cold a night. There were dark shadows beneath her eyes, but her skin was as creamy-pale as ever and her mouth as red. Her glance, too, was more ironical than Clarissa remembered.

They smiled but did not kiss.

"So you recognised me?" Hesther said, coming close to the fire. "I had no idea 'twas you until your Negro brought me that note."

"Recognised you? You are not very different!"

"I had thought——" She broke off.

"It is only eight years, Hesther."

"I know. But they have been hard to me, those years, while to you . . . Were you not ashamed, Clarissa, to see me posturing thus on a public stage?"

"That is not the sort of thing," Clarissa said, looking straight at her, "of which I should ever be ashamed!"

"True. I must be forgetting. How long have you been married, Clarissa?"

"Nearly seven years. I have two children. And you, Hesther?"

"It was thoughtful of you," Hesther answered, "to ask my husband tonight, but scarcely practical as invitations go. I'm a widow. He died three years ago."

"Oh, I'm very sorry!" Clarissa cried, but her heart beat faster. Mr. Rokeby was not Hesther's husband!

Toby came in, and she said:

"Serve supper quickly, and we'll help ourselves. Tell the waiter I'll ring when I want him." And then to Hesther, "Don't you remember my blackamoor?"

"Why, no. How should I?"

"The small page at Bath?"

"Is it the same?"

"Yes. He remembered you."

They sat down to supper alone in the oak-panelled parlour.

"Tell me," Clarissa said, "how you became a play actress."

"It's a long story," Hesther answered, shrugging her shoulders, "and too tedious for words. Ned, my husband, left the army. He had to. Affairs went badly then. We tried many things. At last we were offered our keep by a miserable touring company. We had no option. And after his death I had to earn my bread. So I stayed on."

"You always said you would never become a schoolmistress. Do you remember?"

"I remember," Hesther said, adding, in a bitter voice, "but if second chances were offered in this world I wouldn't be so high and mighty now! Not again! Never!"

"But at least this engagement——" Clarissa suggested delicately. "I hope matters are—will be—better?"

Hesther raised her large dark eyes.

"The 'engagement' you saw finished tonight. We are disbanded. We were not successful. By the way," as Clarissa digested this, "I have a letter for you. Here it is."

"Indeed? Who from?"

"Why," Hesther answered, watching her, "it's from our Othello. A Mr. Rokeby. It appears you were made the victim of an ill-mannered prank."

Clarissa laughed.

"Why, yes, indeed, on the road. I was annoyed and my servants frightened. But pray how was I recognised?"

"It seems he saw you through the curtain, in your box."

"Well," Clarissa said indifferently, "the letter will keep . . . Some more duck, Hesther? And who is this Mr. Rokeby who plays Othello on the stage and holds up chaises on the road?"

Hesther laughed, helping herself to pie.

"No more an actor than I'm an actress. You must have seen that for yourself."

"I—— But who——"

"Rokeby's a rolling stone. Born in the West Indies, he's Jack-of-all-trades—always has been. He's been in turn tutor, actor, sailor, pirate, too, they say. He's a scholar and a blacksmith. He writes poetry, breaks horses, and has sailed before the mast!"

"I'm indulgent towards such highwaymen," Clarissa remarked lightly, "you should have brought him with you, Hesther, and he could then have made his apologies in person."

"Indeed I could not. He took the midnight coach. He left, I think, for Southampton."

"What to do there?"

"Lud, Clarissa, how should I know? To look perhaps for a ship, or for a theatre, or for a poet's garret! Swinton Rokeby's a law unto himself."

Her voice sounded cold, as though she disliked talking of the young man. Clarissa, too, felt cold, although the room was so warm. But it was fortunate, indeed, that he had gone away from Oxford. An unsuitable person in every way—the sort of person, she decided, who inevitably turns out to be a blackmailer. And she had never seen his face, so——

"Tell me about your husband," Hesther was saying.

"The Ghost? Where shall I begin?"

Hesther laughed.

"Is that what you call him?"

"Not I. Everyone. Or they call him the Man in Grey."

XXI

It was an hour later, and the supper table had been cleared away.

"That still does not excuse your silence," Clarissa said after a pause.

"How could I write? It was so soon a miserable failure. I was ashamed."

"I thought you trusted me?"

"I did," Hesther replied, "when I ran away. That was why I did not want to involve you in my troubles. It was better for you to know nothing. And afterwards—afterwards I grew up so fast. You could not have kept pace."

"I married when I was seventeen," Clarissa reminded her. "Hesther, did you—Ned Barbary—did you love him?"

"Why, yes," Hesther answered smoothly, "of course I did. He was a delightful boy. But we were both so young. And we never had a penny."

Clarissa was silent.

She had found Hesther again, and Hesther was the same— almost the same. Yet there was something Clarissa could not quite understand. Something a shade evasive in Hesther's answers, some glibness of tongue, or elusiveness of glance, that made her seem strange despite her quiet manner, another being from the affectionate school friend of the White House.

"Why," Clarissa thought impatiently, "we were children,

then, and it's long ago. Why should either of us be the same? People don't stand still."

"You see," Hesther said, as though reading her thoughts, "you've never been pressed, Clarissa, have you?"

"No——" But Clarissa hesitated, and looked away.

"You married a rich man when you were seventeen. You've never had to think of money. You've always had everything— houses, and servants, and jewels, and coaches, and horses. You've never known what it is to have bailiffs in your lodgings, and your own possessions, your dresses and trinkets, taken in distraint! You've never——"

"Hesther! But your husband——"

"Died of fever," Hesther said quietly, "in the Fleet Prison." *"Hesther!"*

"That's true. It's where they send debtors, you know."

Clarissa was so much appalled that she could not for a moment speak.

"I've shocked you," Hesther murmured in her soft voice.

"Shocked me! You *knew* I'd married Rohan! You could have written!"

"Oh no," Hesther said, not without weariness, "we'd grown too far apart."

She got up then, as though to reclaim her shawl, to leave the warm and pleasant room.

"Where are you going tomorrow?" Clarissa now demanded.

"Oh, tomorrow. There's a tour being arranged for Liverpool. If I'm lucky I may get an offer."

"You are coming with me to London," Clarissa announced.

"Ah no! I've never yet lived on charity!"

Clarissa's cheeks flamed.

"I was not suggesting that you should!"

"I've scarcely the talent for Drury Lane, you know," Mrs. Barbary observed, not without bitterness.

"Hesther, will you please to listen?"

"I thought you changed," Hesther declared, leaning her elbows on a chair and scrutinising her hostess, "I had thought you changed at first, since you are taller, and grander, more sure of yourself. Now I see you're the same impetuous child who once terrorised Miss Patchett. Come, Clarissa, our schooldays are over and you can no longer enforce your word as law. We're grown women now, and we live in different worlds. This is no longer Bath, but Oxford; we are no longer even living in the same century!"

Clarissa, wilful always, tried desperately to control her impatience.

"Hesther . . . please . . . you said just now, speaking of second chances, that you wished you had not run away from the school in Bath. You did, didn't you?"

"I may have. What difference does that make?"

"You said you'd have been more content teaching school."

"As I *was,* I meant," Mrs. Barbary corrected her coolly, "not as I *am.* I could never be a schoolmarm now."

"Oh, Hesther, you can go to the devil if you will continue to interrupt me!"

"I beg your pardon!"

"You see," Clarissa continued, "I've a daughter of six, Lucinda, and my lord thinks she should no longer be with Nurse, but with a lady—that is for a few hours every day—to learn her letters—and he asked me to find someone! Now do you understand?"

"Did he ask you to find this same person barnstorming in a theatre?"

"Ah, Hesther!" And she began to talk, less impetuously now,

and with simplicity. She described her home and circumstances; the remoteness of her life with Rohan; and the "old lady," who *would* interfere with the children, and her own loneliness.

"Hesther, you *must* come! You've *got* to come!"

"To keep you company, or to teach the child her letters?"

"Both! Rohan's generous; he'll pay you a handsome salary!"

Hesther was silent for a moment. Once again, despite that curious hostility towards Clarissa, she experienced a surge of the old affection. What an offer! What good fortune! And yet . . . She knew, glancing sideways at Lady Rohan, that she had not been entirely frank regarding her past life. What right had she to go into Clarissa's home and teach her children? Then her eyes narrowed. Those great Whig ladies were no better than anyone else. Why, their morals were common gossip! And the temptation of the luxurious Rohan houses would no doubt in any case have proved too great.

She thought with a frigid horror of her own squalid life. Smelly, flea-infested lodginghouses. Dark, draughty theatres, and little frowsy dressing rooms that smelled of mice. Winter nights, with rain pouring, and outside seats on the coach; an empty belly, and everyone taking turns to swig at the bottle of gin. Tawdry costumes, stale with other peoples' sweat, the smell of orange peel, and the last rushlight dwindling before she had had time to comb her hair. Beggars, she thought, can't be choosers, and she shivered.

"What do you say?" Clarissa was asking.

"I say yes," answered Hesther Barbary, with defiance.

"I'm so pleased," was all Clarissa said, but her eyes glowed.

"Clarissa! You won't tell Lord Rohan where—and how—you met me?"

"Well, now," Clarissa admitted candidly, "it would be better not."

"Then what shall you say?"

"The truth—almost. That you're an old school friend from Bath, a widow whom I met walking down the street here in Oxford!"

"What am I doing in Oxford?"

"Why, staying with an aunt!"

"To be sure! An aunt! Do you always deceive Lord Rohan thus?"

"Why, no, only sometimes. About gambling."

"Indeed? Have you become a gambler since last we met?"

Clarissa frowned.

"Only sometimes," she said again, and changed the subject, "Can you stay here tonight?"

"Indeed I can't. I must pack at my own tavern."

Clarissa pulled the bell.

"The carriage shall take you."

"Clarissa, are you crazed? It's round the corner!"

"Then Toby will escort you. Here he is!"

Hesther looked at the Negro youth and said:

"You have grown, Toby. I did not recognise you."

"No ma'am. No, Miss Hesther."

For once he was not grinning, and he showed the whites of his eyes.

"But you remembered me?"

"Yes ma'am. I nebber forgets."

The ladies said good-bye then, and this time they embraced with something of their old affection.

"Ten o'clock tomorrow then," Clarissa said.

XXII

LEFT ALONE, Clarissa poked the fire. Mr. Rokeby's letter still lay unopened upon the mantelpiece, but for a moment she had forgotten it.

She was wondering just how angry the Ghost would be were he ever to discover that Hesther was a play actress whose husband had died in the Fleet Prison. He had, she knew, a marked streak of conventionality where his home and family were concerned; his pride, too, was strong. And yet, she mused, he seldom interfered with her private arrangements, and there was no reason to suppose that he would ever discover Hesther's secret.

She thought, looking into the fire, that it would be pleasant once again to enjoy Hesther's companionship—to share a friendship with someone who had no connection whatsoever with what Miss Patchett was wont to refer to as the "beau monde." Clarissa thought that it would be restful sometimes to dine alone with Hesther, to forget politics, Brighton gossip, chatter from Almack's, and Lady Holland's latest outrageous remark. She sighed, then, and wondered whether the old intimacy had become too remote, with the passing of the years, ever again to recapture the warmth of their youthful days.

Hesther had said truly that they were no longer schoolgirls, but women grown; possibly Clarissa appeared as strange to Hesther as Hesther seemed to her.

"Perhaps," Clarissa thought, "she finds me grand, or even pompous. Why, no, I am scarcely that, but self-willed, eager to have my way."

Yet again the little qualm returned to her; surely Hesther had become almost peculiarly reserved? Her story and her husband's story—surely she had omitted more than she told? A few casual references and so many silences. The outlines of a picture that had no background. So many years unaccounted for. So much unsaid, that for a moment the room itself had seemed to stir, as though in protest at those silences of Hesther's; for a moment the clock ticked; a log dropped in the grate; mice scampered in the wainscot; Clarissa shut her fan and sat still, isolated in the pool of her own slience. She had always, Clarissa recollected, possessed this quality of stillness, but surely, never in the past, had she seemed so withdrawn, so apart, as she had been that night?

"She had not suffered then," Clarissa reflected; "she shall be happy, now, for a change."

And then, unable any longer to resist the temptation of Rokeby's letter, she snatched it from the mantelpiece and tore it open.

She read:

HONOURED MADAM,

When I perceived, through the Curtain tonight, that you were supporting our ill-omen'd Venture I felt I must ask pardon for my beggarly manners on the Road today.

And yet, Madam, what other choice had I, poor devil of a rogue and vagabond that I am? To leave the company sans their Othello would have been well-nigh as impossible as my own performance. Do you not agree?

Yet while I ask your pardon for my Turpin manners, I still cannot crave forgiveness for the manner in which I said Farewell.

Your sweetness was so close it craz'd my mind, and although

*I should be penitent, how can I regret a Moment that is per-
haps all I shall ever know of Paradise?*

*Honoured Madam, when you read this, I shall be far away,
but one day I shall most assuredly return to ask your forgiveness in Person.*

Your most faithful and obedient Servant
SWINTON ROKEBY.

The fire sank into a glowing ruin as Lady Rohan sat staring at
this letter. Over and over again she read it, until she knew it by
heart, and even then she still stared at the plain, beautiful hand
which reminded her of Greek characters.

The fire sighed, expiring, leaving the room cold. She got
up then and went into the bedroom, where she put Rokeby's
letter away in her jewel case. The folded paper slid softly
amongst diamonds and rubies, and the secret clasp snapped.

Mrs. Barbary opened the door of a bedroom in a meaner inn
not far away. Here, in a damp attic room where plaster walls
dropped beads of moisture and the floor was bare, she found
a woman seated before a spotty mirror at a table illuminated by
one rushlight. The room contained two truckle beds and little
else. There was a bottle of gin on the dressing table together
with a messy heap of paints and powder. The window was shut,
and the room smelled of a sweet frowsiness that was partly gin,
partly cheap scent, and partly lack of air.

The woman, who had played Emilia in *Othello,* was a flabby-
looking creature with tow-coloured hair, a loose mouth, and
drooping breasts scarcely concealed by the loose wrapper she
wore. She was rubbing salve into her face.

"You're late, Hesther."

"Yes."

The woman pointed to the half-empty gin bottle.

"This is yours—this Blue Ruin. Want some?"

"Yes," Hesther said again, and then suddenly shook her head.

"You don't?"

"No. That's got to come to an end."

"What has?"

"Gin drinking."

"Not so easy!" the other woman tittered.

"To me it will be. I'm off to London tomorrow."

"With your aristocratic lady friend?"

Hesther nodded.

"Some broken-down players are more fortunate than others," the woman said, not without spite.

"They are. Did Rokeby get his place on the coach?"

"How should I know? Is that something to be given up, like Blue Ruin, now you're turning respectable?"

"That," Hesther said very distinctly, "was given up long ago. Even before I knew you."

She went to throw open the window.

"This room," she said, "stinks like a badger's earth!"

"You were always overnice!"

Hesther smiled.

"Tomorrow I travel to London in a gilded carriage upholstered in peach-coloured silk! Can you wonder I feel gay?"

"The same Rokeby held up on the road?"

"The same."

"And you've finished with the theatre?"

"Yes, Dora," Hesther said, "pray God I have. Forever."

The flabby woman suddenly achieved a half-tipsy dignity.

"You! You were always an amateur! What do you know about the profession? Nothing! You do not even know how to walk across a stage!"

"Now, Dora——"

"And don't you 'now, Dora' me because you think you're too grand for people who are proud of being rogues and vagabonds! Proud! Were I born again tomorrow I'd ask to be born as I was —in a dressing room—of a family who were busking the roads when Elizabeth was Queen of England!"

Her tipsiness passed then, so that the dignity was real and for a moment transformed her.

"Your Mrs. Siddons doesn't make the profession," she said, "nor did your Keans and your Garricks. They're the bright lights, the lions of Drury Lane. It's people like *me* who carry the torch—people who don't come alive until the curtain rings up; people who drink gin the moment it rings down! People who shiver on night coaches, who sweat in stuffy dressing rooms, who leave unpaid bills in doss houses such as this! We're a rough lot, God help us, but at least we do *something*— we give the people a taste of beauty they'd never know without us; we give 'em a taste of fun, too, and send 'em home all soft and sweet and happy! That's a lot, isn't it, in Bony's days, when the Frenchies might come here at any minute?"

"But, Dora——"

"Did you say you weren't drinking this gin?"

"I'm not drinking it."

"Then I shall!" And she tilted the bottle to her painted mouth. "Good luck, say I, to the buskers of this world!" She gurgled happily for a moment, then resumed: "Good luck to the rogues and vagabonds! They need it, don't they? You and your gilded coaches! Give me a dirty theatre—*any* dirty theatre—at rehearsal! That's all I ask of life!"

"That *is* your life——"

"That is my life, and I'm toasting it!"

Hesther got into bed.

"The candle's nearly out," she said.

"It always is when I put on a scene!"

"Good night, Dora."

There was some grumbling, and then the creaking of a mattress.

Then:

"Don't you think, either, that Will Shakespeare was any better than I am! All this talk, talk, talk, about Will! He was as much a strolling player as anyone else in the profession!"

Silence from Hesther. Then, from the other bed, more creaking, and finally:

"He knew how to write plays! Knew how to write parts! But if you ask me whether he ever thought he was great, I'll gamble he didn't! Great! He wasn't troubling about that! He was trying to write good parts, that's all, and, listen, Hesther . . ."

But Hesther did not listen, for she was fast asleep.

PART IV

Conversation Piece

XXIII

WHEN Rohan arrived in London a few weeks later he went to White's, and it was not until twilight that he walked home to Grosvenor Square. He went to the library, ordered some sherry, and began writing a letter to Lord Holland.

When he heard a footstep he paid no attention, thinking it must be the wine he had ordered; on discovering his wife, he sighed, and wished she would not pester him when he was busy.

Clarissa seemed in glowing health and spirits. She wore a gauzy dress of grey-blue with a ribbon of the same colour to bind her shining hair.

Rohan rose courteously and kissed her hand.

"Ghost, I want to speak to you," Clarissa declared. "Are you busy?"

"I am," he said. "Can it not keep until later?"

"Later I'm dining out. Surely you got my letter?"

"Which one? Oh, about the phaeton and pair, to be sure. Why, Clarissa, it will look singular enough, and my mother will fume, but if you want it so much——"

"Why, no," she interrupted, laughing, "not the phaeton and pair—not *that* letter! I wrote to you about Mrs. Barbary!"

"The lady you decided might teach Lucinda her hornbook? Why, engage her, by all means!"

"Oh! he's impossible," Clarissa thought. Aloud, she said, as though addressing a deaf person:

"Mrs. Barbary has been here with me for the past five weeks! I wrote and told you all about her!"

"To be sure. A school friend of yours. It sounds a capital arrangement. And now, Clarissa——"

"Please let me finish! She has come to be more my companion and friend than Lucinda's governess. You never think, do you, that I am often lonely?"

"I think you are very seldom lonely," he answered with dryness.

"Because I give dinners and go to balls? It's dull eating alone, Ghost. That's why I am so pleased to have Hesther here."

He said again:

"It sounds a capital arrangement. Now, Clarissa, I must continue my letter!"

"How much salary," Clarissa persisted, "am I to pay her?"

"How should I know?" he answered, firmly opening the door. "Do what you think is right!"

And he shut her out.

Clarissa went upstairs to her sitting room, sent for Hesther, and protested:

"Rohan hasn't seen me for six weeks, yet he turns me out of the library!"

Hesther smiled. She was finishing a piece of embroidery

started by Clarissa. Already, after a few weeks of rest and good food, she had lost much of her peakiness. She looked sleeker, and was not so thin.

"He approves," Clarissa went on, "of your being more my companion than Lucinda's governess. He says I may do exactly as I please."

"I don't know," Hesther said, "why you complain so much of Lord Rohan. It seems to me he always yields to you and lets you have your way."

"Oh, he dislikes being bothered," Clarissa retorted, and enquired: "Hesther, may I ask you—you said you were in love with *your* husband, didn't you?"

Hesther hesitated for a moment.

"I was devoted to Ned," she answered slowly, "but I always knew myself the stronger of the two. Now, looking back, I am sure I was not in love with him."

"Well, I was certainly never in love with Rohan," Clarissa declared, now in a rare fit of ill temper.

"Why did you marry him?"

"I knew no better. I did not know I should hate——" She broke off.

"Hate what?"

"We have not lived together since Roderick was born."

"Really?" Hesther looked up with a sudden interest.

"We were both glad, I am sure, when my son was born. I know I was. It was no longer necessary to pretend."

"I suppose you have many lovers?" Hesther asked casually.

It was almost with violence that Clarissa answered:

"No, not one! I have never been in love in all my life!"

And she thought with shame of the letter from Swinton Rokeby still carefully treasured in her jewel case. She was too proud to ask Hesther very much about him; she had once made some trifling enquiry or other, to which her friend replied only that Rokeby was a wild fellow, one who had never been born to die in his bed.

"And I have never even seen his face," Clarissa thought, unconscious of the fact that Hesther had long ago guessed her secret.

It was during this conversation that an idea crept for the first time into Hesther's mind. It was, in those early days, simply a plan to divert Clarissa, and was not, as yet, in any way calculating. All that would come later. At that moment all she thought was that it would be amusing to present Rokeby to Clarissa, to see what they made of one another.

"But he's vanished," she thought, "and perhaps I shall never see him again."

There were many things she might have said of Rokeby, but did not. She had been his mistress for a season, and they had fought like cat and dog. She was still in some ways conventional, despite her wild life, and it had been the young man's delight to tease her. But soon he had despaired. She still remembered their last conversation as lovers.

"You see, Hesther," he had said, "a man gets tired of playing Petrucchio all the time. He needs a taste of something called tenderness, and of that, dear heart, you know nothing, for you hold a pistol to my head whenever I want to rest that same head on your lap!"

She had made some protest or other, to which, she remembered, he replied:

"It's got nothing to do with going to bed. If a man really wants a woman, he wants her for other things—not only for making love. Are you really too self-centred to know that, or are you still playing cat and mouse with me?"

She had asked him, icily, what he meant.

"Why, just that all your damned feminine tricks have grown tedious!"

They had never, since that conversation, been lovers again, and although neither regretted it greatly, she possibly regretted it more than he.

She thought, too, of that night at the theatre in Oxford when, peering through the curtain, he had said:

"That woman in the stage box is the loveliest creature I've ever seen. And *she* has tenderness—don't ask me how I know, but I do!"

Hesther, explaining how long she had known Clarissa, was swiftly interrupted, for he turned on her impetuously.

"And of all women in the world that's the one I chose to hold up on the road tonight!"

"Well," Hesther had retorted, "she probably enjoyed it!"

He grinned then.

"I don't think she minded. And, you know, I kissed her before I left the carriage!"

Clarissa, Hesther reflected, had never told her of this kiss. Nor had she ever mentioned Rokeby's letter.

Once again, watching Lady Rohan, Hesther reflected that it would be amusing to introduce Swinton Rokeby into her life.

"But," she thought, "I must be careful. I'm still a stranger in this house and have not yet met the master of it. I suppose my future will depend entirely on some whim either of his or hers. They agree ill—that's obvious—but if he took against me I believe he'd make her send me away."

"You're very silent," Clarissa said; "you're in a brown study. You've even forgotten the embroidery!"

"I'm sorry," Hesther said.

"I was proposing something nice," Clarissa continued, her good humour restored.

"What?"

"You're coming to the play tonight, in my box. Some gentlemen are meeting us, and we shall have supper here afterwards."

"That sounds delightful, but scarcely part of my duties."

"Oh yes," Clarissa exclaimed, "and if you have not a dress my maid will help you. But, Hesther, my husband left me to make any arrangements I might think fit—about—about your salary, and you must have plenty for your dresses, for we shall go out together very often, I hope."

Hesther had earned her living for so long that she was able, with complete composure, to discuss a suitable salary with Clarissa, to whom the whole matter was an embarrassment.

But Hesther knew before they parted that she was to earn almost double what she had expected, and once again her affection for Clarissa was tinged with contempt for someone so unworldly as her friend.

XXIV

It was not until a fortnight later that she met her host. She had been shopping in the afternoon, and as she came into the dark hall of Grosvenor Square she saw him emerge from the library towards her.

He was easy to recognise, although she had formed, from Clarissa, the impression of a tired and prematurely aged man.

But Lord Rohan looked slim and wiry in his dove-coloured coat; despite the grey hair, and the strange eyes like silver coins, despite his olive skin, his cold and rather arrogant expression, he seemed to her not only young, but exceptionally attractive and filled with vitality.

He bowed, and said in his somewhat harsh voice:

"You are Mrs. Barbary, of course? I should ask your pardon for not having been presented to you before. Will you come into the library? I should so much like to speak to you."

She followed him into a long room, book-lined, where a great fire burned. He asked her to sit down, and then for a moment there was a pause.

She said at length:

"Your daughter's coming to London next week, I believe? You know I'm supposed to teach her her letters?"

"Let her be," he said.

"Let——?"

"She's a baby, my daughter. She has no need for letters yet. No, I welcome you, Mrs. Barbary, for other reasons."

"May I know those reasons, Lord Rohan?"

"Why, to be sure," he said; "that's a reasonable request. It's not my daughter, but my wife. You're good for her. Look after her, and we shall all be pleased!"

"I could scarcely interfere," Hesther murmured.

He sat down opposite to her and took some snuff.

"Interfere? Let us be frank! My wife is devoted to you, isn't she?"

"We're old friends."

"Exactly! She's sometimes bored, as possibly you've noticed, Mrs. Barbary. When she's bored, she gambles, and I don't like her gambling. Do you understand?"

Hesther opened her eyes and looked him straight in the face.

"Not quite, Lord Rohan."

"Well," he said, "she's no excuse for boredom now you are in the house. You see? Make her go out when she has nothing to do. She has a box at the opera and a box at the theatre. She doesn't use them for weeks at a time—make her use them!"

"I will try to," Hesther said.

"Good!"

He looked at her, and wondered why Clarissa had never told him Mrs. Barbary was beautiful.

He said:

"You must forgive this unceremonious interview—I have an appointment. Perhaps this week we might dine, the three of us? Will you suggest that to my wife?"

"Yes, Lord Rohan," Hesther said, rising.

"Ask her not to invite anyone else."

He smiled then.

"I would so much like to make your acquaintance," he continued; "you see, I think we're going to pull well together!"

When he had gone Hesther walked upstairs to her room, taking her time, for she was absorbed in deep reflection.

So that, she reflected, was the eccentric—the Man in Grey about whom Clarissa so often grumbled! Not for the first time she thought Clarissa a fool.

"For he," Hesther decided, "is the most attractive man I've ever met, and, furthermore, I mean to conquer him!"

The dinner took place about a week later. During this time Mrs. Barbary had spent her first advance of salary in buying some pretty frocks, and she looked charming in a dress of soft yellow gauze. She sat before the drawing-room fire and waited some minutes for her host and hostess, neither of whom was remarkable for his sense of punctuality.

But she was happy enough, waiting in the warm, scented, luxurious room, so rich, with its brocades and tapestries; so bright with its wax candles glittering in the crystal fall of candelabras; so sweet, with the flowers that bloomed exotically in every corner. She was content, remembering her past, to sit and dream, knowing that soon she would eat an excellent meal and later sleep that night in a soft bed. For a moment the animal comforts of her new life absorbed her senses completely; then she remembered, with a feeling of deep excitement, that soon she would see Lord Rohan once again.

Then as the clock struck the door opened, and she turned eagerly. But it was only Toby, bringing in a decanter of madeira. As usual, the proximity of the Negro filled her with a sense of distaste. She thought Clarissa ridiculous to dress the boy in silks and satins and to spoil him as she did, but there was something else, something she did not herself understand. She only felt that the black boy did not like her.

"Good evening, Toby," she said.

"Good evening, ma'am."

But he did not grin, and it seemed to her that he deliberately made a *détour* as he crossed the room to set down his tray. It was as though he did not want to come too near her; that he avoided her as some people will try instinctively to avoid a cat.

"He's jealous, of course," she thought, and then forgot all about him, for Rohan came in to kiss her hand, and once more she felt that tremor of excitement she had felt, or thought she had felt, for Swinton Rokeby once, and for no one else.

"I, at least," Rohan was saying, "have an excellent excuse for my unpunctuality. I've been at the stables with my groom and a sick horse and got back late to dress."

"I hope your horse is better?"

"Indeed, yes. Not only the mare, but her foal as well!" He went to get her a glass of madeira remarking, as he did so, "my wife, as you doubtless realise, has never learned to tell time!"

Hesther laughed.

"She was always the same."

He frowned.

"It's an abominable habit."

He sat down beside her on the sofa and glanced at her quickly beneath his lids, reflecting that Clarissa had stimulated him for the first time by bringing Mrs. Barbary to his house. No woman, indeed, had interested him for years and of this one he was not yet sure. But he knew that he wanted to see more of her, and that was as good a start as any.

"Are you happy here, Mrs. Barbary?"

She looked at him then, and met his cool gaze that told her nothing.

"Indeed I'm happy. Compared to my life before—I mean—in Oxford——"

"You lived very quietly?"

"Yes, Lord Rohan."

"I see."

He got up then abruptly.

"I hear my wife," and he went over to the door.

She was discomposed; it seemed to her that his voice had changed since she mentioned Oxford, and for a moment she was filled with terror, wondering whether he was mocking her, having discovered something of her past.

Clarissa came in with a vague apology, and soon afterwards they went down to dinner. Here, at a candlelit table set at one end of the enormous dining room, she was able once more to savour the change in her fortunes. For a moment, watching Clarissa's delicate face and Rohan's bitter one, glancing at the deft footmen in their peach-coloured livery, she had the odd sensation of once more acting on the stage, of appearing in some play of contemporary manners, or in some brilliant comedy of Sheridan's London.

"But," she thought, "we never did it exactly right."

And she knew that the theatre could never quite capture the careless ease in which these people lived: their unstudied elegance, and the simplicity of their assurance.

There was Clarissa, laughing at some political joke and calling Toby from behind her chair to peel a peach. And Rohan, lounging with his legs crossed, taking snuff, while he told them, with a dry humour, of Lord Alvanley's latest bet. She noticed something else.

She saw that Clarissa and Rohan were profoundly bored with one another. At first, listening to Clarissa, she had imagined them to be the usual quarrelsome pair of what, in those days, were described as "fashionables." Now she knew, watching them, that they were nothing of the sort. Their mutual indifference was too great to allow of much bickering; the gulf between them too vast; their lives too sharply separated. These two were strangers; their charming and graceful manners did not conceal from Mrs. Barbary's quick eyes their ignorance, their lack of curiosity concerning each other, nor did their courtesy entirely mask the discontent each one so clearly felt in the other's company.

Once or twice she was conscious of Rohan's glance, and wondered again if Clarissa lied when she insisted that she had never taken a lover.

"Not," she thought sardonically, "that his lordship would care."

But she could not imagine anyone of Clarissa's vital beauty either unloved or unloving, and the situation continued to puzzle her throughout the evening.

She was, however, by no means displeased when she went upstairs to bed, for she could have sworn that the Ghost was determined to see more of her and, since her opinion of him

was even more favourable than it had been before, she waited
his next move with an almost feverish impatience.

XXV

She would have been gratified, that night, to overhear a conversation between her host and hostess.

Rohan, in his wife's sitting room, suddenly enquired:

"Clarissa, what are you going to do about Mrs. Barbary?"

"Do about her?" Clarissa demanded in astonishment. "What
do you mean—do what about her?"

"Only this," he said. "Mrs. Barbary's a young woman like
yourself. Because she is supposed to shop for you, or write your
letters, or some such thing, you cannot condemn her to be shut
up like a prisoner in the house!"

Clarissa noticed an unusual enthusiasm in his voice.

"I still don't understand what you mean."

"It's very simple," he replied. "Introduce her to people, give
a dinner for her, see that she has a little pleasure in her life. I suspect that she could do with some."

"She's charming, isn't she?" his wife asked carelessly.

"Most charming," he replied as casually. "And this house,
you know, when we are not entertaining, might as well be the
mausoleum at Rohan! Your friend must often be infernally
lonely!"

"You are quite right," she answered, "and most thoughtful!"

"Then I shall say good night!"

He kissed her hand and disappeared, leaving Clarissa quite
as thoughtful as she had just declared him to be.

She perceived clearly enough that, apparently for the first

time since their marriage, he was interested in another woman, and she could feel only relief. But Hesther . . . She really could not think that Hesther would be made any happier by so peculiar a developement in their already strange situation.

And yet there were women, she knew, who found the Ghost attractive. Quite a number of women, she recollected, on due reflection, although he had never seemed to return their interest, or indeed to take much notice of them.

But for all she knew Hesther might be attracted by her husband.

"I shall say nothing to her," Clarissa decided. "I shall know nothing about it, and they must work matters out for themselves."

But after a fortnight, when she had given two dinner parties for Hesther, from both of which he had absented himself, she began to think that she had imagined his interest in her friend.

Hesther herself, while apparently delighted by her own social triumphs, was inwardly sunk in despair. To meet Clarissa's splendid friends on equal terms was, to this waif, like some brilliant dream come true, and Rohan spoiled it all. It has been said that she attended two dinners; at each one, amid a cloud of gauzy dresses, amid groups of blue and green and buff coats, amid clusters of scarlet uniforms, she looked always for one grey figure, and when she knew that she looked in vain her rage and disappointment turned her cheeks white and her heart sick. Her triumphs, then, were like the taste of ashes on her tongue.

What did it mean, to be admired by all these young Lambs and Cavendishes and Ponsonbys, since *he* was not there to witness their admiration? Where was the joy of meeting such celebrities as Lord Petersham and Lord Alvanley and Lord

Hertford when Lord Rohan continued to avoid his own house?

It was charming of Lady Morpeth to invite her to a dish of tea; astounding—if terrifying—to be presented to Lady Melbourne; gratifying, to see as he glanced at her, the appraising look in Lord Hertford's cynical eye; dazing, to be approached—three times—during the course of the evening by Lady Caroline Lamb with the soft but persistent request:

"Dear Mrs. Barbary, please won't you persuade Clarissa to part with black Toby? All my pages are white, and I'd so much love a blackamoor!"

All this friendliness would, a few weeks back, have meant much to the Hesther whose life had known more bitterness than gaiety. Now the Ghost had spoiled her happiness, and because she was reluctant to blame him and determined at all costs to blame somebody, she decided that Clarissa must have forced a quarrel upon him. Of course. That was it. That was why he kept away.

She looked, beneath her lashes, at Lady Rohan, who sat on a big sofa chatting with Lord Hartington, and with Mr. William Lamb, and with Mr. George Lamb, and his wife. Clarissa wore a dress, a slip, rather, of snow-white satin that clung, as was the fashion, to every line of her body and that was scarcely veiled by a drapery of silver net. She wore a great diamond on her finger and the Rohan pearls were twined milkily about her neck. Her golden-red hair was dressed in loose and careless curls which had taken her maid exactly forty-five minutes to achieve, and, as was usual when she was in the company of friends, her face danced and sparkled with fun and animation.

Compared with her, Hesther decided, sighing, the other women did not count. Lady Caroline was too thin, Mrs. George Lamb too luscious, the Cavendish sisters merely plain, and Lady Elizabeth Foster faded.

Once again, watching Clarissa, the old dislike returned, but more vividly, this time, since it was flicked with hatred. Clarissa had everything—even her husband, who bored her, and whom she had no doubt driven from the house. Hesther, apparently attentive to Lord Petersham, remembered once again the first time she had ever seen Clarissa Richmond. She saw, as clearly as though it were actually before her eyes, the white-panelled hall of the school in Bath and Clarissa coming in, cheeks pink with the cold, to offer her largess of sweetmeats to the young ladies who were her devoted subjects.

Hesther had hated her then. Now .... She listened to Lord Petersham's somewhat tedious description of his snuffboxes and continued to snatch occasional glances at the sofa.

Something Clarissa said made them all laugh uproariously, and then Lord Hartington took both her hands and pulled her up to dance some silly dance with him while the George Lambs ran to the spinet to accompany them, and everybody laughed again, even Lady Melbourne.

"No wonder," Hesther thought, "he hates all this noise and silliness."

Lord Petersham smiled at her and said, "I never knew a lady interested in snuff before, Mrs. Barbary. I declare I must send you a jar to try. Oh, very genteelly, in the seclusion of your bedroom!"

Her self-restraint had been remarkable; but later that night, as she was on her way to bed, she could not resist asking Clarissa:

"Is Lord Rohan away?"

Clarissa looked slightly uncomfortable.

"Yes," she said, "he's down at Rohan." And she hoped, with all her heart, that the Ghost had not been encouraging Hesther if he meant to do nothing more about it.

She took Hesther's hand and said:

"You were a *succès fou* tonight. The gentlemen couldn't take their eyes off you. I am as pleased as though I were your proud mama!"

And she *was* pleased, although Hesther did not believe her, for she was as generous as she had ever been, and she wished to give Hesther some of the happiness her friend had never known.

But Hesther had noticed that first, evasive look, and was once more convinced that the Rohans had quarrelled.

The next day she rose early, captured Lucinda from her nurse, and installing herself, began to teach the little girl her letters. She was determined, at least, to make the child fond of her, and she was just congratulating herself upon her success when a door banged below and at once Lucinda sprang from her chair.

"Mama! It's Mama!"

She darted out of the room, and Hesther could hear her calling to her mother down the staircase. Lucinda was laughing; she cried that she was blowing kisses all the way down into the hall.

Hesther sat alone at the table.

Once again she thought:

"I cannot bear it. She has everything, and takes it all for granted. Even her kindness to me. How can I help hating her?"

XXVI

ANOTHER WEEK PASSED without a sign from the master of the house. Hesther did not even know whether or not he had returned to London. Her pride stopped her from mentioning his name to Clarissa, and she was too reserved to gossip with the servants.

One day, talking to Lucinda, she went so far as to refer casually to Lucinda's papa, but the little girl was more interested in the story of Robin Hood; she hadn't seen Papa lately— he often went away to the country.

Meanwhile Mrs. Barbary attended a dinner and a tea party; her good looks, her elegance, and her somewhat serious manner intrigued a number of people, and her origin and her mysterious appearance at Grosvenor Square were both the subject of frequent and vivacious discussion. Some thought Clarissa had chosen her as a foil, a contrast to her own roses-and-cream good looks; others, again, hinted at a more sinister explanation—she was, they suggested, some apparition from the Ghost's past, and it suited Clarissa to be *complaisante*.

There were those (Lady Melbourne was one) who declared the newcomer to be a "dark horse," even an adventuress, and had Clarissa not been known for a virtuous woman, she would have been supposed to be somehow in Mrs. Barbary's power. But, in any case, Hesther was thought intriguing, and not a few gentlemen appeared willing to become on more intimate terms with her, but she treated their advances with cool contempt. To her they were negligible, since they were not Rohan.

And always her jealousy of Clarissa was like something bit-ing at her heart. The sight of her benefactress, moving with what Hesther began to think of as an arrogant grace among the gay drawing rooms of their day, was merely an added re-minder of her own insignificance. The fact that Clarissa always seemed to be enjoying herself was another source of bitterness, for was it not a reminder that, unlike herself, Clarissa had never suffered?

So she thought until one day, approaching her hostess's sitting room, she heard Clarissa say loudly, almost with panic in her voice:

"No, no, I can't! I'd rather die than tell him!"

Hesther glanced swiftly along the passage, and was grateful for the absence of a gilded footman; she stepped closer and put her ear to the door.

The maid, Molly, said something she could not catch, and then Clarissa answered with weariness:

"I shall try again tonight. It's my only chance."

"But, my lady, if it turns out badly once more——"

"I have no choice."

So she has been gambling again, Hesther thought, and has lost more money than she dares confess. What a fool!

"Where is Mrs. Barbary?" Clarissa asked, as though dismiss-ing the subject.

Hesther knocked on the door.

Clarissa smiled at her and said:

"I was hoping you would come in, for I have to ask your forgiveness."

"Whatever for?" Hesther asked, with real surprise. She thought Clarissa looked as pale as her own loose robe of white lace, and she noted Molly's sharp glance over her mistress's shoulder. She did not like Molly.

"Because," Clarissa was saying, "we must abandon the play tonight. I have to go out after dinner. There is someone I must see. Will you forgive me?"

"But of course," Hesther answered, laughing; "the play can wait until another night. I hope your engagement is not a tedious one?"

"Why, no. Molly, I want the carriage in an hour!"

When Molly had gone out of the room Hesther hazarded in a solicitous voice:

"You look tired, Clarissa. That's so unlike you; I noticed it at once when I came in."

Clarissa frowned.

"I am not tired. Hesther, have you read the new Edinburgh *Review?*"

"Not yet. But I would like to if you've finished with it."

And she reflected that she was evidently not to become a confidante. That rôle was reserved for the maid. She shrugged her shoulders. Perhaps one day Lady Rohan would be eager enough to confide in her.

That same evening after dinner Clarissa, who still seemed abstracted, went out directly they had finished their meal. She kissed her companion affectionately, but her appointment continued to remain a mystery.

Upstairs in the drawing room Hesther wandered over to the window. They had dined early, and night had not yet fallen. There were daffodils in Grosvenor Square, and by staring out into the dusk she found that she could still distinguish their paleness beneath the darkly arching trees. A watchman passed, calling the hour. The French clock struck on the mantelpiece, and she turned away from the windows as a footman came in to draw the curtains. Below in the street she heard the rattle of a fast cabriolet stopping somewhere in the square.

She sat down by the fire and picked up the Edinburgh *Review*, but she was in no hurry to read. As was usual when she was alone, the luxury of her surroundings began to exercise an extraordinary fascination on her mind, so that she forgot for a moment her jealousy of Clarissa, and stretched herself like a cat before the fire.

The vivid flames of the cedar logs in the grate; the heavy sweetness of so many flowers; the richness of the satins and brocades decorating the room; the mossy softness of the carpet beneath her feet, all these for a moment swam before her eyes like some Arabian Night's dream, and then her eyes shut, and she slept for a few moments.

When she opened her eyes again Lord Rohan stood beside her on the Persian rug, looking down at her with a strange expression on his face. For once, confused, she sprang to her feet.

"Don't disturb yourself," he said. "Were you so tired?"

"Not at all! I suppose the warmth of the room——"

"Will you please sit down? Or do you wish to keep me standing?"

She obeyed, smiling, and said:

"I cannot have slept for many minutes! It was your carriage I heard in the street just now, I suppose?"

"It was," he said. "Is my wife out?"

"She went out about half an hour ago."

"Do you know where?"

Hesther frankly said that she had no idea, and thought that he frowned. But he changed the subject. Sitting down opposite to her he said:

"I'm not an easy man to deceive, Mrs. Barbary."

"I would never have thought you were, Lord Rohan."

He took a pinch of snuff.

"Why, then, try to deceive me?"

For a moment she shivered, although the fire blazed. She swallowed, and her mouth was dry.

"I—I don't know what you mean."

"I think you do. You represented yourself, or rather my wife represented you, as a widow who has lived quietly in Oxford since her husband's death. In fact, you were some years on the stage, were you not? Nor, I believe, have you ever lived in Oxford."

XXVII

SHE STARED AT HIM but said nothing. Her wits had not quite deserted her, and she knew well enough that silence, in some predicaments, is more prudent than speech. She looked at him almost with defiance, that he should not guess the despair in her heart. So this was where her plotting and scheming had brought her! She would be dismissed within an hour; she would never conquer him now; she would be sent out of his splendid house like any erring servant girl, and Clarissa, her champion, was not even there to defend her. She forgot her dislike of Clarissa now that she needed her; had she known how to pray, she would have prayed then for the intervention of that warmhearted and impetuous presence.

But Clarissa was not likely to come back, and the Man in Grey returned her gaze coolly.

"You don't reply," he remarked at length.

"What can I say?"

"May I ask you something?" Rohan enquired, and continued,

without waiting for permission, "Was this deception your idea, or my wife's?"

"It was Lady Rohan's idea," Hesther answered in a voice so low it was scarcely more than a whisper.

"It would be," Lord Rohan commented grimly; and then, to Hesther's astonishment, he threw back his head and burst out laughing.

"I beg your pardon," he said, "but Clarissa has ever been a bad judge of character. As judge of mine, her ignorance is unparalleled."

She looked at him with so much bewilderment that he smiled once more as he explained:

"She is, as doubtless you have noticed, unconventional. Because once or twice since our marriage I have felt obliged to restrain her, she conceals from me, like a child, matters of which she supposes I would disapprove. Your own career, I imagine, was one of them. She was wrong, as she usually is. It would not at all divert me to talk to a sheltered young female from Oxford, whereas you, Mrs. Barbary, divert me exceedingly. Now do you understand?"

The sweetness of her relief was pricked by an ugly thought; if he knew so much about her, did he know more than he had said? Perhaps he had heard, not only of Swinton Rokeby, but of other men, and of how, in an apathy of misery, it had been her custom at one time to drink herself insensible. Once again she trembled.

"How did you find out?" she asked.

"I have friends in Oxford," he returned. "But you must not be afraid. I shall keep your secret."

Was there a meaning note in his voice, she puzzled, as though he would warn her that he knew not one, but all her pitiful secrets, and was indifferent?

"Even from Clarissa," he continued. "We will not tell her what I know or do not know. It is not her business."

"You are very kind," she murmured.

"On the contrary. I am very seldom kind, as you will find out for yourself if you continue to live in my house. So Clarissa left you alone this evening? I am pleased I came back tonight instead of tomorrow."

"You've been at Rohan, haven't you?" she asked, her heart beating.

His face softened.

"Yes," he said. "The woods are thick with primroses. You will see it soon—we shall go there in a few weeks' time."

He was sure, then, watching her mouth, that he wanted to show her Rohan.

"You know this house tolerably well, I suppose?" he asked suddenly.

"I think I do. Why?"

"Come with me," he said, getting up, "and I will show you some rooms you have never seen."

"Why, you're very abrupt!" she protested, but she got up, too, and he handed her her scarf.

"They're my own rooms," he explained, opening the door, "and I live there undisturbed. I have some fine pictures and a separate library."

As he opened the door she noticed, for the first time, his signet ring, and started at this grinning death's-head in miniature.

He noticed her glance.

"They call me the Ghost," he said, "so for many years now I have worn a skull on my finger. I would be lost without it."

"It's beautifully made," she said uncertainly.

"Try it on."

And it was with Rohan's ring warmly circling her third

finger that she walked for the first time into his own apartments.

Here, in the first room, a small octagonal library lined with richly bound books, an enormous fire burned. There were daffodils on the writing desk, and a slim crystal decanter of wine stood on a little table near an armchair.

"Sit down," he said, "and try a glass of this Spanish wine. It's reported to be excellent, but since it arrived only yesterday, I've had no opportunity to try it."

"Thank you."

"Well," he said, helping himself and standing before the fire glass in hand, "how long have you been here now?"

"About two and a half months." She sipped the wine, and found it cold and fragrant, but for a moment she wished it was gin.

"Tell me, then," he said, "what do you think of it? What do you think of us all?"

Hesther smiled.

"Surely that question would take many hours to answer. How can I say in a minute what has taken me weeks to know?"

"Condense it!"

She closed her eyes, her lips still smiling, and tried to obey.

"I never knew such—such unobtrusive comfort could exist. I never knew flowers could bloom so sweet in winter, or fires burn all day so recklessly, for people who sometimes never come in at all. I never knew the magic of a French cook, or the luxury of reading books fresh from the printer's. When I ride abroad I still expect to be jolted, being used to coaches. I never knew carriages could glide so softly—as I imagine gondolas to move. But I have never been in Venice; I have only read Goldoni."

"You talk," said he, amused, "as though you had found Olympus."

"Sometimes I think I have."

He asked, with melancholy,

"Are we such gods?"

She shook her head then, but her eyes mocked him.

"Certainly not! You are like other men and women, save that life has been good to you. You are more learned, more frivolous, too, I think. You have always had time to study and time for pleasure, but you've had the good fortune also to have had time to separate the two."

"In fact, had you lived in France not long ago you'd have seen us go to the guillotine not only with indifference, but with approval."

"Oh no," she answered with emphasis, "indeed I would not. Yours is the way to live. You would be fools not to have taken the opportunities you were given. And none of you are fools. Lord Rohan, your ring is too big and too heavy; I shall return it."

She dropped the tiny jewelled skull into his hand, where he looked at it for a moment before slipping it back on his little finger. Then again he glanced at her, and her heart beat so violently that she was convinced he could detect her agitation. Apparently he could, for he came close to her and put his hand on hers.

"Hesther, how beautiful you are!"

Many others had said these words to her, only at first to be treated with derision, but her bones melted for this man and his touch set fire to something within her that even Rokeby had never aroused. She, who had all her life been what she thought of as clever; she, who had been as much calculating as she had been ardent, could not withstand Rohan or play cat and mouse with him, for at last her senses had taken full control of her and her ice-cold brain no longer functioned.

And Rohan himself, stirred as he had not been stirred since his boyhood, forgot for a moment his detachment, his cynicism, and his melancholy. He found her mouth and then the warm ivory of her arms. She was no longer Clarissa's protégée, the genteel young widow he had at first supposed her, nor was she the adventuress he had afterwards discovered her to be.

She was the only woman with whom, in his maturity, he had fallen in love, and the passion with which she returned his kiss, the urgency of her mouth, the sweetness of her breasts, the eagerness of her surrender, all made that boyish love of his seem like a dream, or like dead rose leaves faintly scenting some long-forgotten bowl of potpourri. This was real. This was the only thing that mattered, had ever mattered, or ever would, for he thought her spirit the same as his, and sleeping, loving, eating, drinking, talking, they would, he felt, always be bound together, so that neither one would be alone again.

Even after having made love to her he was convinced of this, but he said little, as was his custom, and so she was unsure of him, and felt, as the most beloved woman sometimes feels at such a moment, an appalling, a poignant sense of loneliness. She watched him quietly, and for a long time they said nothing, although they seemed to be at peace, and indeed he was.

It was later, when she was going, that he reminded her how soon they would be in the country, at Rohan.

"And then," he said, "we will be really happy. You shall see."

She crossed the hall and went upstairs in the shadows knowing, for the first time in all her life, what happiness was.

Much later, it seemed to her, she heard the front door close softly and then someone else came stealing upstairs.

It was Clarissa.

She had forgotten all about Clarissa.

XXVIII

Hesther barbary would, for the rest of her life, always remember that month of May they spent at Rohan. It seemed to her then that everything about her surroundings, from the great grey house itself to the acres of green velvet lawns, the banks of vivid tulips, the sombre yew walks, the foaming blossom of the cherry orchard, the bluebells clustering in the beech woods, all these seemed to her as though they had been especially designed to form a tapestry of loveliness and enchantment, an exquisite background to her own happiness.

She worshipped Rohan, loving him with a passion that sometimes almost frightened her, for she thought that if ever he cast her off she would kill herself. Not that he himself was anything but perfectly content with his lot. He had found a woman who never bored him; her mind pleased him as much as her body; he found her tonic good sense as refreshing as was her ivory slimness. She never, he joyfully discovered, made scenes, nor did she chatter, like Clarissa; she was capable of silences he enjoyed, finding them companionable.

But even Rohan did not in the least appreciate with what iron control Hesther refrained not, precisely, from making scenes, but from showing her possessiveness where he was concerned. The fact that he loved her and not Clarissa in no way softened her dislike of Clarissa; on the contrary, there were times when even to see Clarissa sitting at the head of his table shook her with a storm of furious hatred.

She could not endure to think that Clarissa bore his name and shared the dignity of his position, but more intolerable still was the knowledge that she had given him two children. Clarissa, despite her giddy ways, would always be the wife; Hesther could never be anything more than the mistress.

"Unless," she thought, "one day . . . If something happened to her . . ." and then stopped abruptly, horrified by her own dark thoughts.

As for Clarissa herself, she was most certainly not enjoying that spring at Rohan. She hated it.

It had not taken her very long to discover what was happening, and in her first disillusionment she was determined that she would send Hesther packing the moment they returned to London, for it was Hesther's treachery that sickened her, the slyness of her intrigues, and the ingratitude with which she had returned hospitality. It was only after a wakeful night that Clarissa decided to reflect before she acted, and, even so, her manner the next day put Hesther on her guard. Clarissa was too candid, too impetuous, ever successfully to conceal her feelings. But it did not take her long to decide that she would say nothing.

Rohan meant little to her, and if he were in love with Hesther, surely she could not grudge him some happiness after a marriage so wretched as theirs?

The fact that Hesther had behaved monstrously to her, personally, should not, she felt, influence her to behave badly to Hesther; a scene would be vulgar and tedious; she would appear as a dog in the manger, and Rohan's temper, if she sent Hesther away, would be impossible. Nor would this stop the affair, as she well knew; he would merely install Mrs. Barbary in some establishment of her own. And she was too proud to let Hesther know how much her slyness hurt.

And so she pretended, desperately, that she knew nothing,

but she was unable to look Hesther in the face, and she knew that her voice often rang false. It would take Clarissa a long time to grow accustomed to deceit, and she was always a bad actress.

Nor was her own loneliness any easier to endure since there are few ordeals more depressing than that undergone by an unwanted third person in the company of two lovers. Neither Rohan nor Hesther gave away their secret, but sometimes it seemed to Clarissa that their happiness sang, and she would have loved to shut her ears. Her husband was greatly changed, she thought; he was less sardonic and more cheerful; more patient with her and less cutting; she supposed, not without irony, that she should be grateful to Mrs. Barbary. But once again, during that smiling spring at Rohan, her own unhappy thoughts returned to torment her.

She was twenty-five, in all the prime of her brilliant beauty, and she had no one to love or to love her. She might, she thought, have been a withered old maid, like Miss Nuckett, the dame of the village school. Listlessly she reviewed the list of her beaux, and decided she would not care if she never saw any of them again. Then sometimes she would unlock her jewel case and reread Swinton Rokeby's letter, and curse herself for a fool.

She had never seen the young man's face, and never would now. She had never even been alone with him. She had only the memory of his mouth pressed on hers in the darkness, of his vibrant voice, his ribald laughter, and his reckless sense of humour. He was a ghost; she might have dreamed him, in her loneliness, for he could scarcely have been more intangible.

To make matters worse, the very fairness of that lovely May seemed to mock at her solitude; Rohan and Hesther might stroll together in the park before dusk, but when she went out by herself in the grounds the sweetness of the lilac only made her heart more desolate.

"I shall be glad," she thought, "when we return to London."

Hesther said restlessly to Rohan:

"Clarissa knows about us."

"Oh, nonsense!" he retorted, not caring very much whether or not she did.

"It isn't nonsense. I am sure of it."

"What makes you suppose she knows?"

"My instinct."

Rohan burst out laughing. He thought, as he laughed, of Clarissa's beaux; it was seldom, indeed, that she was without a flock of young men all of whom fancied themselves in love with her. He said as much to Hesther.

But Hesther shook her head.

"*She* has never been in love with any of them. That's the difference."

But Rohan did not want to discuss Clarissa, whom he considered to be in any case temperamentally incapable of falling in love, and so he changed the conversation, beginning to talk once more of a colt he had running the next month at Epsom.

Clarissa discovered during that lonely month how devoted she was to her two children. Lucinda, she thought, might grow up pretty; her pale, elfish face was uncommon, and she had her mother's glorious hair. The little boy, Roderick, was an engaging Cupid with a dimple in his cheek and a mischievous grin; both of them adored her, being attracted, as children usually are, by beauty. Clarissa was a vivid contrast to the homeliness of Nanny.

Hesther professed to be captivated by both and took great pains to make them like her, but to Clarissa's secret delight they used her shamelessly; she was good enough to play with until "Mama" appeared, whereupon she was at once forsaken.

This love lavished upon her by the children consoled her for her mother-in-law's approval of Mrs. Barbary, whom she pronounced quiet—rather as though Hesther were a pony—genteel, and well-mannered.

Clarissa's temper rose, and it was with difficulty that she choked back an angry retort. Afterwards she was glad that she had controlled herself. "Old" Lady Rohan lived all the year in the country; she heard little gossip, and existed almost entirely for her flowers. She knew nothing of what was going on. Perhaps she no longer even cared.

When they returned to London, Clarissa discovered that she no longer disliked Hesther so much as she had supposed. If Hesther was treacherous and untrustworthy, well, Clarissa thought, remembering the elopement with Ensign Barbary, that in itself was nothing new, and it was something to see the Ghost so affable. He had not grumbled at her for weeks. He had not even mentioned the subject of her gambling. Nor, she observed, did the pair behave together in any but the most circumspect manner.

Their secret, of course, was soon common property—Lady Melbourne saw to that—and the pretence that Hesther lived at Grosvenor Square as Clarissa's companion or Lucinda's governess had never been discussed outside the family. Now Mrs. Barbary was accepted as the dear friend not only of Lady Rohan, but of his lordship too.

Sometimes Hesther could scarcely believe in her own good fortune, and it was then that, alone with Clarissa, she felt occasional moments of apprehension which she never discussed with Rohan. It was the knowledge, perhaps, that Clarissa could cast her out of the Garden of Eden whenever she pleased. For she was now convinced that Clarissa knew all about the liaison. Watching every direct, candid glance, every movement of Clarissa's proud head, she realised once again that Lady Rohan still had the power to make her feel small, and accordingly hated her the more.

XXIX

But they were all in high spirits as they set out for Epsom on Lord Rohan's coach. They started early on Derby Day, for the Ghost had a horse running in the two o'clock race. The glossy claret-coloured coach was drawn by four perfectly matched iron-greys, driven by Rohan in a many-caped driving coat and a tall grey beaver hat. Hesther wore white, with a cashmere shawl and an apple-green bonnet, and Clarissa had a gauzy dress of blue with azure plumes floating from her fashionable chip hat. They were accompanied by the George Lambs and Lord Petersham, while Toby sat excitedly within the coach with Wright, whose mind was concerned solely with the bets he was about to make.

They were all gay and animated and good-looking, and the day was golden with sunlight; a little crowd collected to see them leave Grosvenor Square.

They had not driven far before they became wedged in the crowd of curiously assorted vehicles all progressing, at a snail's pace, towards Epsom. There were other coaches, as splendid, as gilded as their own; swift curricles nipping ahead past cumbersome farmers' wagons; hired chaises, brimming with cockney families; awkward horsemen bestriding hirelings; gypsy vans; a very fat man in a donkey cart, costers with painted carts, and

some bearded vagabonds with a performing bear. Everyone was
hoarse and cheerful and oblivious of the clouds of dust kicked
up by so much traffic, for this was London's great festival, as
much of a jaunt for the buck as it was for the crossing sweeper,
and the spirit of the crowd was boisterous.

Later that day there would be dancing on the Downs, and
knuckle fights, and spangled acrobats who would continue to
dislocate themselves even as the mad thunder of hooves
drummed the turf amid a tense, breathless silence, and the mute
crowds watched the greatest race of all being run again. Surely,
Clarissa thought, there are few phenomena more eerie than
that brief, deathly silence succeeding so much noise, so soon
to be succeeded by the mightiest roar of all.

Meanwhile the Rohan coach was set in an august position on
the rails, and they were soon, as was the custom of the time,
eating a picnic lunch of patties and sandwiches and champagne.
There were friends to be greeted on the coaches near by, with
the ladies, in their gay dresses, looking like clusters of silken
butterflies, and the gentlemen splendid in their bright coats and
gold-tasselled shining boots.

To add to Hesther's pleasure, the Prince was there, and
most cordial to the Rohan party.

Clarissa, who was in high spirits, soon went to the paddock
with her husband and Sir Harry Mildmay. Hesther, asked to
accompany them, preferred to remain where she was. She knew
nothing of horses or of racing; she disliked crowds, and much
preferred to stay on the coach to watch the fashionable dresses.
Across the emerald strip of the racecourse she could see the
carousing of those common people of whom she was so disdainful; it would appear they had stalls selling gingerbread
and lollipops; she could hear jangling music, the shouting of
showmen, and the pop of guns.

The Ghost's colt was second, and he seemed pleased. It was then that Clarissa suggested they should walk across to the heath and see the fun, for, as she said, they had nearly an hour before the big race. Hesther could think of few things she would dislike more, but to her surprise she was in a minority of one, and even Rohan seemed eager enough to go.

The brown and trampled grass was thick with swarming, shabby figures. There was the sweep, with his black-a-viced apprentices; there was the old apple woman; the Irish mendicant; the Methodist preacher; the blind fiddler; the crossing sweeper; the tumbler; the pickpocket, and the gypsy. Each type was multiplied at least one hundred times, so that the heath was crammed with a live and vital shouting crowd. There were booths and tents from which showmen hoarsely roared the attractions of fat ladies, dwarfs, giants, and other freaks. The pushing, jovial mob was mainly cockney; which is to say that they were perky and alert and ribald and merry. The jests bandied to and fro across the muddied ground were coarse but witty. Everyone laughed, and drank porter, and blew squeaky whistles, and danced jigs.

Hesther perceived, not without distaste, that the Ghost held Clarissa's arm and that they laughed together as they breasted the crowds. She furthermore perceived how much Clarissa was enjoying herself. Clarissa, she realised for the first time, had that gaiety, that zest for living, which finds expression amongst the joy and din of crowds. She walked as though she would have liked to dance, and she had some swift, disarming answer for all the rapscallions who accosted her on pretence of congratulating Rohan upon his colt. She laughed, jesting with them, and Rohan laughed, too, obviously proud of her popularity, and Hesther, watching them, could have murdered her.

It was then, as she followed, her heart bitter with envy, her hand on Sir Harry Mildmay's arm, that she saw Swinton Rokeby.

He was standing, conspicuous because of his great height, staring at Clarissa. He stood among a crowd of thimbleriggers and boxers and acrobats, and the sun flamed upon his copper hair. He wore an old-fashioned dark-green riding coat with tarnished silver on the cuffs.

Hesther, not for the first time, made a swift decision.

She murmured to Sir Harry:

"Forgive me . . . an old friend . . ." and darted across towards Rokeby.

When he saw her he started back in a manner scarcely flattering, but Hesther was past caring.

"Meet me tomorrow . . . Hatchard's Library, noon. Do you hear? It's important."

He said nothing; he glanced at her only for a moment. Then his eye was once more piercing the crowd for Clarissa, and she no longer existed.

She returned to her escort.

"I'm sorry," she said; "a friend with whom I have lost touch . . ."

But Sir Harry was not interested.

"Why, look," he said, "what is this Lady Rohan has found?"

Hesther looked, remembered, and wished herself back on the coach.

For a woman had broken through the crowd towards Clarissa, and Hesther was sure that she remembered that woman.

Clarissa remembered her too.

The gypsy resembled a grizzled she-bear in her gaudy rags. Her hair bristled like the quills of a porcupine, her eagle's face was tanned with the sun and the wind, and her black eyes glittered. She was clutching a goblin child to her scarecrow bosom.

"Your ladyship! Your ladyship!"

Clarissa stopped, delighted.

"I remember you! My lady of Egypt!"

Rohan smiled, pleased, as he seldom was, with Clarissa. He observed for the first time that his beautiful wife was popular with the people, and for a moment he even forgot Mrs. Barbary.

He said:

"You've met before?"

"Gentleman," the gypsy gabbled hoarsely, "ask her, ask her ladyship! I told her she'd marry a man in grey! Long ago, in Bath, I told her that, God bless her pretty face! I told her I'd meet her here at Epsom!"

"That's quite true," Clarissa agreed, and pushed some silver into the gypsy's hand.

"How old is your baby?" she asked, with real interest.

"A year old, my lovely ladyship. But he's my tenth!"

Rohan was searching in his pocketbook. He was happy. His colt had been second, Hesther was in love with him, and Clarissa did him credit on the downs. He had never appreciated Clarissa more.

The gypsy suddenly asked in a husky whisper:

"Where's the dark young lady? The one whose future I could not tell?"

It was as though a shadow fell across the golden day, blotting out the sunshine, and for a moment Lady Rohan was once again a little girl at school in Bath.

"Why . . . she's here, somewhere . . ."

She looked round, but Hesther had vanished.

My lady of Egypt pressed closer, and once again Clarissa was conscious of the smell of wild animals as the gypsy whispered in her ear:

"Let her alone, my pretty love, she'll harm you . . . What did I say so long ago? Would you like to know why I never told her future?"

"I——" Clarissa began uncertainly, and then Rohan produced his guinea piece.

"Good luck to you," he said, a twinkle in his grey eye.

"Good luck to your lordship! And take care of her! They're easy lost!"

"You think I don't?" Rohan grinned.

The gypsy regarded him for a moment with the dead-black eye of a snake.

"Not enough!" she retorted, and turned, then, hugging her brat, and was at once swallowed by the crowd. There was no longer a smell of wild animals, and Clarissa sighed.

"That woman is uncanny!"

"Where's Mrs. Barbary?"

"I expect she's gone back to the coach. Must you still call her Mrs. Barbary to me? Are we not uncommonly formal?"

He said nothing, but offered her his arm.

"Don't scowl at me, Ghost! Don't spoil the pleasure we've had here on the heath!"

"I must admit," he said to this, "I'm proud of you. They like you, Clarissa, and you have damned pretty manners when you please!"

They were crossing the racecourse.

"When I please! You're wrong, as you usually are; the Derby's not yet been run, and I may enjoy it, but so far I've liked the heath more than anything else today."

They strolled back to the coach, ostensibly a loving couple, and Swinton Rokeby, stalking them, went to the rails and stared his fill. Clarissa had not seen him. She would not, of course, have recognised him if she had.

The race would start soon, and he had no right to stray across that strip of green where he did not belong. But he swore to himself as he went back to the booth where his boxers waited, although he was their manager, and there would be a dozen bloody fights before dusk, or so he hoped.

The roar of the crowd died swiftly, and there was a ghostly silence as the horses galloped down past Tattenham Corner. Then as Rokeby pushed aside the canvas of his tent there came the mighty tumult of the crowd. He waited, impassive. Soon, he knew, there would be plenty of business.

Driving home that night in the warm bloom of dusk, Hesther asked Lord Rohan, murmuring casually,

"You haven't yet found a librarian, have you?"

"Unfortunately not."

Then Hesther, pensive,

"I think I know of someone who might suit you."

"You do? Capital! Who is he?"

"He has been a tutor. Quite a scholar, I believe. Shall I try to find him?"

"By all means! Who is this paragon?"

"A young man of the name of Rokeby."

"Why," the Ghost said, lightly flicking his off-leader, "you must send him to me."

"I will," Mrs. Barbary promised.

The London road was choked with vehicles of every kind. There were the public and the private coaches; there were donkey carts and curricles, and battered old chaises and hay wagons, and cabriolets, and vans, and phaetons. A blue and cloudy twilight was falling fast, but the crowds were not too tired to sing.

They sang old songs that their people had first known in the days of Charles II.

The cockneys' festival was over and done with for another year, but, refusing to recognise the end, they still sang.

"I'm sorry it's over," Clarissa yawned, but she was glad to think that there was a cold supper waiting at Grosvenor Square.

Her head drooped, and she slept.

XXX

Swinton Rokeby sat at Hatchard's in Piccadilly and thought himself a fool to wait.

He was naturally impatient, for Hesther was already ten minutes late, and he was by no means sure that he wanted to see her. He knew that he would never have kept the appointment had Hesther not appeared to have been connected at Epsom with a party which included the lovely Lady Rohan. Rokeby, having seen her ladyship near to for the first time, was even more fascinated than he had been at Oxford. He had kissed her in the darkness, he had peeped at her through the theatre curtain, and had marvelled, then, at her beauty. But now that he had seen her close she had become tangible, a woman of flesh and blood, whereas before she had captured his imagination as a spirit, a wraith too remote from his own hard life to exist save as a fairylike legend.

But at Epsom he had stared his fill.

Restlessly he wondered by what unscrupulous means Hesther had contrived to insinuate herself into Lady Rohan's life, and he was still cursing Hesther, watch in hand, when she came coolly enough into the library. She was, he observed, fashionably dressed in a sprigged gown and coquettish bonnet.

"I'm sorry," she said, "to have kept you waiting. But the carriage——"

He bowed, not without sarcasm.

"The carriage, Mrs. Barbary, ma'am?"

"The carriage was wanted for a message."

"The same I held up on the Oxford road one night?"

Hesther frowned.

"I should advise you to forget that adventure!"

He looked at her, his eyes twinkling.

"May I congratulate you, madam, on your dressmaker? Your milliner, too, would not seem to be unskilful. In fact, Hesther, you do me credit!"

She sat down, ignoring his mockery.

"Swinton, what are you doing?"

"I have just waited more than ten minutes for the pleasure of your company. Now I'm savouring it. Any more questions?"

"You know very well I did not mean that. I want to know how you're living."

He frowned, jingling some coins in his pocket.

"I'm still a 'snapper up of unconsidered trifles.' Perhaps I always shall be. Since we last met I've tutored a squire's son in Devon. Yesterday I was in charge of a boxing booth on the downs. Soon, perhaps, I shall go to sea again, and incidentally I have written one or two passable sonnets. And now, my very dear Mrs. Barbary, it's my turn to ask *you* a question—why this touching and surprising interest in my affairs? To put it briefly: What do you want?"

How like Rokeby, Hesther thought, immediately to suspect her of some ulterior motive! She looked at him crossly and wondered why she had ever found him so attractive. Despite his book learning and his long words, he was an impudent rascal, always had been. But of course in those days she had never known a gentleman . . .

She said almost sullenly and quite without the graciousness she had rehearsed:

"I came to offer you an excellent situation."

"Indeed?"

"On condition, of course, that you give up your vulgar friends and low associations."

His eyes wary, he asked:

"May I ask what the situation is?"

"Lord Rohan is looking for a librarian. I have put forward your name."

He was silent, for enlightenment dawned on him swiftly. Mr. Rokeby was not a fool. He knew, as surely as though she had told him, that she was Rohan's mistress, and that, at her command, he himself was to be invited to play some calculated rôle or other in the drama she had created. What it was, he could not for the moment imagine, for whenever he pictured Clarissa's life he visualised her as surrounded by lovers.

Was she jealous of Hesther? Or were they, Hesther and Rohan, proposing to use him against her as a spy of some kind? At the thought of this his face hardened. But he answered smoothly:

"You are kind to remember your old friends. What makes you think I would be a good librarian?"

"You know so much about books, and are intelligent enough, if you would give up your wild ways." She added, a shade too carelessly, "I should have thought you would have been grateful for the post. You admired Lady Rohan so much that night at Oxford; you would perhaps have a chance, if her husband employed you, to be presented to her."

He was silent for a moment, and then he enquired:

"Is it by Lady Rohan's suggestion that I am offered the post?"

Hesther laughed.

"Lud, no! What has her ladyship to do with engaging librarians?"

"Does she know I am the person who held up her carriage last winter?"

Hesther laughed again.

"I expect she has long ago forgotten the whole disgraceful escapade!"

"Suppose she has not? Remember, I kissed her!"

"I think," Hesther said, "she has also preferred to forget *that* breach of taste!"

"I see."

But for a moment he was nonplussed, although he did not let her become aware of it. He was an adventurer, and had never pretended to be anything better. The post of librarian to the Marquis of Rohan offered its own excitements, and had it not been for the two women concerned, he would have accepted it without hesitation. But the more he thought of it, the more revolting he found the idea of an alliance between Hesther and Lady Rohan. He had few illusions about Hesther, and Clarissa, to this cynical romantic, was, as has been said, a legend. He did not think he could resist meeting that legend.

"Hesther," he said slowly, watching her beneath his eyelids, "I do not know if Lady Rohan is your friend or whether you depend on the protection of his lordship—— Wait just a moment, and don't interrupt me! You see, my dear, I know you well enough to swear that you never had one sweet, unselfish thought in all your scheming life, and I want to know just where I stand in this intrigue you're fashioning."

She said, white-lipped:

"I'm not offering you a post to be insulted! Oh no, Swinton, you've sunk too low——"

"Wait," he said; "I hadn't finished! Be patient for a moment more. I must tell you Lady Rohan means more to me than just a stolen kiss in a dark coach. Perhaps if I met her she would be another disillusionment. Perhaps, on the other hand, she would not. At the moment she represents to me all the grace and charm of this epoch. She's the London I've read about —the London that began with Charles James Fox and that will possibly end with Mr. William Lamb. She is something I admire for being exquisite, and incidentally intellectual at the same time. There's a lot of Marie Antoinette in her, and I am sure she would die, if die she had to, just as bravely. But she is obviously a much more intelligent woman than that poor foolish little Austrian Princess . . . Lady Rohan loves politics, but she encourages art, and science too. That I know, having read much about her. She has the looks of Circe and a sense of humour. She'll live, one day, in a world of the future, because she has always lived with so much zest in this world of the present. I suppose there are women like her in every generation, and their contemporaries will always think them frivolous. It's only afterwards that people will know how wisely they used their influence! How cunningly they pulled the wires!"

Hesther suddenly shivered.

"You talk of her," she said, "as though she were dead!"

To her surprise he shivered too.

"I suppose so. I was looking ahead, that's all. Why, she'll live for her beauty, if for nothing else! So you see, my dear, if I'm offered this splendid post on condition I must work against Lady Rohan, I'd politely tell you to go to the devil!"

Hesther put on her shawl.

She said:

"You should know me better! You are asked, simply and solely, to be librarian. The appointment depends entirely on Lord Rohan, who desires to see you tonight at six."

He got up too.

"Hesther," he said, and his voice was not without menace, "I don't know what game you're playing, and I care less! But if I remember rightly, Lady Rohan picked you out of the gutter last year in Oxford! Do you still want me to visit his lordship tonight at six?"

How like Rokeby, Hesther again thought resentfully, immediately to put his finger on anything that was—well—unpleasant. She stared at him malevolently, and once again wondered how she could ever have been in love with him.

"Love," he said jeeringly, as though he could read her thoughts, "is often an ephemeral emotion, isn't it?"

"And don't call me Hesther," she said sharply, "if you decide to apply for the post!"

She wished that she could speak to him frankly, and tell him how much she desired him to intrigue with Clarissa; she wished, for one fleeting moment, that she could explain to him how much Clarissa, without doing anything at all, was contriving to make her feel guilty. But she knew him well enough to be sure that they would never understand one another; Rokeby was peculiar for a man of such low tastes; she could never make him comprehend, for instance, that Clarissa had become more an enemy than a friend.

He was speaking as they walked out of the library into Piccadilly.

"Remember," he said affably, "you're saddling yourself with a hostile critic. Promise you'll never come to me with tears in your eyes, swearing that Lady Rohan doesn't understand you!"

Wright, sitting erect on the box, heard that deep voice, and started violently.

"Do you remember me?" Rokeby asked, helping Hesther into the carriage. "I was pressed once, and held you up outside Oxford. I'm glad to see you, to apologise!"

"Yes," Wright answered sepulchrally, "I remember you . . . sir . . ."

"Six o'clock," Hesther said before he shut the door.

"So be it!"

He cursed himself for a fool as the chaise rolled away, but he knew that he could not keep away from Lady Rohan.

And there was something else. Mr. Rokeby didn't know what it was as he walked thoughtfully away towards the Strand; it was something he himself could not explain. All he knew was that he did not like the idea of Mrs. Barbary being Clarissa's friend. And the more he thought of it, the more hateful this friendship seemed.

XXXI

THAT EVENING Hesther came in to see Clarissa, who was writing letters.

"I'll not be a moment," Clarissa said in a listless tone of voice.

Hesther sat down on the sofa. A small fire was burning, for the evening had turned chilly, and the logs were scented cedar wood. Clumps of overblown roses from Rohan stood in every available corner of the sitting room. The white poodle scratched himself in his basket, and outside, in the square garden, some children were playing with hoops. Clarissa's pen flew for a few moments, and then she rang the bell for Toby.

"Please, Toby, will you take this note at once to Cavendish Square?"

She got up then and came over towards the fire. She wore a peach-coloured wrap and her hair was already dressed for the evening. Her head was turned towards the fire, but Hesther, studying the fruitlike curve of one cheek, was sure that something was wrong. Her voice was nervous, her eyes evasive. When she moved, her long limbs seemed restless, as though she were confined in her own sitting room. Hesther was sure that she had been losing more money.

"You wanted to see me, Hesther?"

"Yes. I know you are dining out, and there is something I must tell you. I have a confession to make."

"A confession?" Clarissa repeated, with distaste. She could not believe that Hesther was about to create a scene, but she was suspicious. Hesther retained her composure.

"Yes. Do you remember a young man who once held up your carriage on the road to Oxford? A Mr. Rokeby?"

Clarissa turned then, and the watcher saw that her April face was suddenly sparkling with excitement and vitality. Nor was her voice any longer listless, but warm with eagerness.

"Your friend the highwayman? Othello? What of him?"

Hesther answered, carefully choosing her words:

"I saw him not long ago here in London. I think he is seeking employment, and you know that Lord Rohan is looking for a librarian. Well, if you are prepared to forget the monstrous manner in which he behaved to you, and if you care to be charitably inclined, I believe he might make an excellent librarian. What do you say? Have I your permission to speak for him?"

In a flash Clarissa remembered how swiftly, after a grey winter, the spring could bloom in all its sweetness. She had been sad and goaded before Hesther's visit, but now she was a girl again, and her heart was light, so that she forgot her cares. Yet she had become more prudent in the last few weeks. Not long ago she would have kissed Hesther, openly delighting in her suggestion, but it was no longer possible, even for Clarissa, entirely to trust Mrs. Barbary, whose influence was becoming every day more marked in her own house.

So she burst out laughing, and exclaimed, very naturally:

"Come, come, Hesther! Do you really suppose I have never been kissed before or since! Of course speak for the young man, and we will see that the Ghost gives him the situation!"

"Very well done, my dear," Hesther thought, "but not quite well enough done to deceive someone who has been on the stage."

Aloud she said:

"I'll mention it to Lord Rohan when I have an opportunity."

It was unlikely, she knew, that Clarissa and the Ghost would meet that night. Clarissa need never know Rokeby had already been in the house.

Clarissa laughed again.

"You will have the opportunity very soon, I believe. Rohan dines in tonight. Now forgive me—I'm late already!"

She was gone before Hesther had had time to decide whether or not there had been a hint of malice in that laughter, the echoes of which still seemed to float in the lovely room.

"What did you think of Rokeby?" Hesther asked at dinner, peeling a peach.

Rohan frowned before he recollected the name.

"Oh! the librarian! An intelligent young rascal! I engaged him. He can work here for a week, and then he must spend the summer at Rohan."

She sighed, well satisfied. A delicious sense of content filled her being. There would be no more coldness from Clarissa. Of that she was certain. She remembered Clarissa's radiant face, she recollected Rokeby's impassioned defence of Lady Rohan and all she stood for. No, their future was inevitable. She felt so pleased that she even wished them well.

"You are in good looks, Hesther," the Ghost told her with courtesy, and then abruptly: "Where is Clarissa tonight?"

"She did not tell me."

"Is she gambling again?"

"That I couldn't say."

He frowned, looking into his glass.

"Can nothing stop that folly of hers?"

Hesther returned with spirit:

"Don't forget, sir, you set her a bad example!"

He did not like this, and retorted:

"I am a good gambler. She is not. Besides, like most women, she never knows when to stop!"

Hesther watched him, worshipping. Never, she thought, would she quite understand this man, and she loved him all the more because he kept her guessing. No one had ever done that before. Even Mr. Rokeby had never troubled to perplex her. He had always been in too much of a hurry.

Rohan pursued, not without weariness,

"Surely you, to whom she is so attached, can prevent her from so wasting her time and my money?"

"I think," Hesther answered, looking straight at him, "she is not so attached to me as she was."

"You're too fanciful," he returned curtly.

Outside the square garden, the tall young man, muffled in his cape, still paced up and down, oblivious of the watchman who regarded his presence with an experienced mistrust.

He had waited, after his interview with Rohan, on the chance of seeing her leave the house, and he was finally rewarded. It was still daylight when two bearers in livery came round to wait with a silver-panelled chair that could only have belonged to Lady Rohan.

He slipped away then into the shade of an overhanging tree growing in the garden, so that he could watch without being seen.

After about ten minutes' time the doors of the Rohan house were thrown open, and by straining his eyes he could even see the porter's hooded chair in the hall. For a moment nothing happened, and then a Negro boy came running down the steps. The boy, Rokeby noticed, was richly dressed and wore a plumed turban. It was the same boy, grown taller, that he had glimpsed in her box at the theatre in Oxford.

While the boy waited, idly swinging an unlit lantern, dusk came flowing, lavender-tinted, to enfold the tranquil square and its shady trees, and then an enormous, gilded footman with huge pink calves came running down the steps of her house, and then she followed.

For a moment a large, lumbering chaise threatened to obscure his view, but it passed before she was hidden from his sight, and for a moment he saw her dimly, standing beside her chair, ghostlike, in the pearly twilight. She wore a dress of shell-pink satin with some scarf of silvery gauze, and he thought that she was smiling as she bade good evening to the bearers. The footman shut her in the chair, the bearers picked up the shafts, and the black boy proudly led the way.

Rokeby came forward and watched the little procession disappear round the corner of Brook Street.

It had already, he thought, the eeriness of something that belonged more to the eighteenth century than to their own days. There were few enough sedan chairs in Regency London, silver-panelled or otherwise, few enough pampered blacka-moors. There was something of Goldoni's time in Clarissa Rohan's exit from her house, and for a moment he could see her clearly enough in a Venice that already belonged to the past.

The twilight deepened as he dreamed, and he thought it was the dusk that had once again made her seem intangible.

"Why," he thought, ignoring the suspicious watchman, "why, beauty like hers belongs to no particular time. Why should it? She belongs to the eighteenth century tonight; really she be-longs to the nineteenth; but perhaps she also belongs to the twentieth century, to an age unborn. Perhaps one day, when she and I are dust, her ghost will cross Grosvenor Square, just as she has done tonight, with a silver sedan chair, and bearers, and a blackamoor to light her home, and then the people of the future, if they see her at all, will see beauty that may never exist for them and think our past world the better for her!"

But Clarissa, as he was to observe, did not, that summer eve-ning, require her Negro to light her home, for the short night was finished before she returned to Grosvenor Square and dawn was breaking, and Swinton Rokeby, tired and hungry, had long ago gone back to the coffeehouse where he lodged.

PART V

Clarissa

XXXII

IT WAS SEVERAL DAYS before they met, and by that time he was absorbed in his work. He was glad to know how much it interested him, for he was sure that she intended to be haughty, and he did not see what he could do about it. By the fifth day, thinking of her, he was plunged in the deepest gloom.

And then, one afternoon, when he was making a catalogue in his neatest copperplate, she came suddenly, impetuously, into the library. She wore, deliberately, her favourite white gauze with a knot of blue ribbons at her waist, and the sun from the window caught the brightness of her hair so that he was dazzled as he sprang to his feet.

It was then that she saw him for the first time.

She had known him to be exceedingly tall, and she remembered that his shoulders were broad. She had not been prepared for the thick, dark copper hair growing so closely

187

over his rather long head; she did not think she had been prepared for the clear, healthy pallor of his skin; but his wide,
impudent mouth was not unexpected, and she supposed she
had always imagined his gay eyes to be more green than hazel.

At first sight he seemed as shy as she was, as indeed he felt,
despite his bravado.

"I thought," she said coldly, "Lord Rohan was here."

He answered, to all appearances calmly, "I have not seen his
lordship today."

There was a pause.

Then she said, fidgeting with her ribbons,

"It would be foolish to pretend we have never met before!"

"It would be criminal!"

"You wrote me a letter——"

"I asked your forgiveness, madam, for a liberty! I said——"

"You are forgiven!"

There was another pause.

"Do you like your situation?" she asked at length, not looking
at him.

"I have known worse," he answered, looking very hard indeed
at her.

"I—— Is there anything you want?"

"Have I permission to address you if there is?"

"In reason——"

"Reason!"

Clarissa laughed.

"So you sneer at reason, sir?"

"I am far from sneering, madam. I never felt less like sneering in all my life!"

And they stared at one another for the first time. It began,
their love, as simply as that, and both understood that a miracle
was happening. It was summer, but spring to them, and the

lilac bloomed magically, and the clock stopped as they looked at one another in the sunset of that long-forgotten library in Grosvenor Square.

She had known until then much that was cold and worldly; he had been all his life an adventurer. But they forgot, looking at one another, their own sophistication. The freshness, the sweetness of youth swept them like a breeze blowing through the windows of the solemn house, as they faced one another like two enchanted children who had grown old before they had learned to be young.

There was no longer a pretence of formality, only an emotion of which they were both afraid, for it was strange to them.

She said, uncertain,

"I must not keep you from your work."

He answered, not listening,

"Last night I saw you set forth in your chair with your black boy. I was waiting across the road under the trees. I don't want to know where you were going—that would spoil everything. But you were like a ghost in the dusk. I waited a long time; you never came back."

She considered this.

"No. I was late. You're a friend of Mrs. Barbary's, aren't you?"

"An acquaintance," he answered firmly.

She smiled, and he hastened to add:

"I can assure you she means nothing to me. Ask her if you don't believe me! She'll most certainly tell you an unflattering tale!"

"She might," Clarissa agreed judicially, and then laughed. "She might indeed!"

They came closer.

She looked at the French clock on the mantelpiece and was astonished to find it ticking.

"I must go—I'm late!"

He went to open the door for her and paused, his hand on the knob.

"Lady Rohan, I hope you don't mind my having found this situation?"

"No," Clarissa said, "I don't mind."

He said:

"Would you not swear there was lilac blooming in this house?"

"It's late for lilac," Clarissa told him.

"All the same, the air is filled with it," he said.

And then he shocked her.

"What am I to do," he asked suddenly, "if Lord Rohan finds out about me?"

"What do you mean?"

He answered, staring at her with his greenish eyes, and she thought his hair more copper-red and his face paler as he spoke.

"Why, I sailed on privateers, you know, and his lordship could ascertain their names! We were called buccaneers—we—we were sometimes high-handed, I suppose, with our prize money, but that's the way of the sea. Still, they were worse to us, the pirates. But now people are overnice, and mix us up together, as jailbirds, and I haven't set sail for three years, but I must confess I could still be prosecuted as a buccaneer. Madam, if they took trouble they could even hang me. There, I never meant to confide in you, but I have!"

Clarissa assured him:

"Your secret's safe with me."

"I do not doubt it," he retorted, "but since Mrs. Barbary doesn't know it, pray will you keep it quiet from her?"

"I will," Clarissa promised, and then, impulsively, "Did many walk the plank?"

"Why, no!"

"Did any?"

"Listen, madam"—and he screwed up his eyes—"there are always those at sea who die more swiftly than they ever reckoned when they were ashore. You see, the ocean's a devil of a mistress! Why, you know how men are pressed and flogged. Some walk the plank, yes, on pirate ships and buccaneers. But when we are taking prizes from the French and Spanish we are condemned the same. Do you think that just, when our men are still being pressed in taverns?"

"You're condemned, I suppose, if you don't hand over your spoils."

"Why, yes!"

"And sometimes you don't?"

"To be frank," he answered, smiling at her, "often we don't! We've sailed away our prize, and careened wherever we could. And that, ma'am, is considered piracy! You see, there's gold buried on the deserted islands where we put in to scrape our ships! Men under whom I've sailed have hidden gold when I was still a child! Men who once commanded solid merchant ships and who are now reviled as pirates! Pirates, you see, is a funny word. I've known men who thought Sir Francis Drake a pirate, and who shall say they're wrong?"

"I never thought of it like that," Clarissa considered.

"Few people have!"

He opened the door.

She hesitated in the hall that seemed to her, too, sweet with lilac.

"You love the sea so much, Mr. Rokeby?"

"Why, yes," he said, "I was born in the West Indies. At Port-of-Spain, in Trinidad. My father was a merchantman, and

I first sailed with him when I was eight. My home, if I have a home, is still there, in Port-of-Spain."

As he spoke he thought of beaches glittering white as salt; of lanky, slanting palms; lagoons of sapphire water, and of the green hell of steaming jungles where parrots screamed and orchids bloomed like weeds.

"There are hummingbirds," he said, half forgetting her, "that are no bigger than butterflies, and they're bright as jewels. They dart about among the blossoms. The flowers are like nothing you have ever seen. There's one they call bougainvillaea that hangs in sheets of purple and crimson everywhere—over everything, even over the cypress trees. Its brightness hurts your eyes."

"Why did you leave *your* bright island for our misty one?"

"I was at sea," he answered, "when I came here first. Oh, and many times before I decided to stay. I stayed because I met an Irish jockey turned horse coper. It's not a romantic explanation, is it, but it's true! I'd always liked horses, and I wanted to know something about them. I lived with him a year and learned many things. One day I took some horses to Barnet Fair, and there wrote a poem to a pretty lady whose husband was pleased with this sonnet of mine. When he discovered that I knew Spanish, he took me home with them to translate a book he had written on philosophy."

"What then?" she asked as he paused.

"Why," he told her, "the lady was too pretty, the husband too suspicious, the book too bad. I was soon sent away. Perhaps also," he added seriously, "I drank too much, for my friend the philosopher drank only water, and I found that tedious."

"And then? Did you never want to go back to your lovely island?"

"I did not," he answered grimly. "My father was killed, in a mutiny off Shark's Bay, and my mother died of pestilence when I was still a babe. Perhaps my island, madam, is not so lovely as I have made you think!"

"Where did you learn to be a scholar?"

He looked at the pure, lovely line of her throat, and looked away again.

"I was educated by the Jesuits. They are good teachers. Not that my scholarship is much these days."

"Will you never go back?"

"Oh yes," he answered slowly to this, "I shall go back one day. Make no mistake! You see, I know where so much gold is buried."

As they waited, talking softly to one another in the hall, the front door opened; in the distance a porter sprang up from the shelter of his hooded chair, and Mrs. Barbary came in from the sunlight outside.

They smiled at her, but Rokeby's eyes were dark. No longer could either one imagine the scent of lilac; when the door shut on Hesther, the rays of the sunset were blotted out, and the great house was sombre once more, and their first enchanted moment was over.

"Good evening, Mr. Rokeby!" Hesther said.

"Good evening, madam," and he ducked his head, unsmiling.

"I must go," Clarissa said, uncertain; "are you coming upstairs with me, Hesther?"

"Of course! Aren't you late already?"

"We are both late. Good night, Mr. Rokeby!"

"Good night!" Rokeby said, and watched them go upstairs together. He observed that Hesther put her arm round Clarissa's waist, and then he muttered something ugly to himself. He went back into the library and shut the door.

Hesther said, laughing, as they walked upstairs:

"You aren't losing your heart to that young adventurer, dearest, are you?"

Clarissa, shaking off her affectionate arm, immediately became Lady Rohan, of whom Hesther was always secretly a little afraid.

"My dear Hesther," Clarissa declared, "my heart is not easily lost. Shall we both try to mind our own business?"

"I was joking." Hesther smiled.

"Then you must keep your jokes for the Ghost; I've observed that he likes them!"

She disappeared with a rustle of skirts—not petticoats, for they were no longer worn—into her own rooms, but Hesther still smiled, for everything she wanted seemed to have come true, and she knew that Clarissa was gambling again.

XXXIII

Clarissa met Rokeby again in August, at Rohan.

They met on a breathless day of heat and thistle-grey clouds that pressed down the thunder until it grumbled somewhere above the treetops and just above their heads.

She had been walking alone by the lake, and it was there that he saw her.

"I didn't know," she said, "that you were here. I was going to pick water lilies, and now the storm's coming . . ."

"I arrived last night. There's a summerhouse on the island, isn't there? Will you trust yourself to me? I'm a seafaring man, as I told you last time we met!"

"I'd be mad," she said, "to go to the island now!"

"Then *be* mad! You need something to wake you! You can't be the Sleeping Beauty all your life!"

"Get the boat, then," Clarissa commanded. "You talk too much!"

"You see," he confided, as they rowed out towards the dusky, tangled island, "you see, madam, our original meeting was really most unfortunate. I was impertinent and you were insincere. We started to act a play then, and I think that both of us hate acting!"

She said, dabbling her hand in the water,

"We're passing all the lilies!"

"I'm indifferent to lilies! I want to talk to you on the island, where there's no one to eavesdrop!"

"Meaning who?"

"Meaning, perhaps, Mrs. Barbary! How you can permit that woman in your house—— But I go too far!"

"You do indeed," Clarissa agreed, "for she is my friend, and I'll hear no harm of her!"

"I beg your pardon!"

Their boat scraped against the bramble-draped shores of the island. He sprang out and gave her his hand.

"Now what?" Clarissa wanted to know.

He picked some cushions out of the boat and answered:

"Now we are going to shelter in this little temple. The rain's beginning."

The island was overgrown with trees and thickets, but there was a clearing in the middle, and there stood the marble "folly," supposedly Grecian, put there by the Ghost's father.

"I've never been here before," she said, looking about her.

"Does anyone come here?"

"Why, I suppose the gardeners do from time to time. But it looks neglected, doesn't it, and ghostly?"

He piled his cushions on the mosaic floor of the temple as rain spattered down on the domed roof.

"Now," he said, "we're marooned together on an island, as I have often wished to be with you; and I only hope," he added, looking down at her with his hands in his pockets, "that the storm will last forever!"

One part of Clarissa silently protested that this was certainly no way for the librarian to speak to Lady Rohan, and the other part experienced a wild tremor of excitement that was strange to her, and her heart began to pound.

"You said you wanted to talk to me," she reminded him, looking down at her dress.

"I do."

He knelt then, so that his face was on a level with hers.

"Will you promise not to be angry with me?"

She shook her head. "How can I promise?"

"Why, then," he sighed, "I suppose you will have to be angry, for say it I will!"

"Mr. Rokeby——"

He took her hand, although at first she tried to draw it away, and insisted:

"I love you so! You knew, didn't you? I loved you the night I kissed you in the dark. That's why I wrote to you when I learned your name!"

"You're a stranger! I don't know you! You're——"

"We have plenty of time! Clarissa, nobody has ever loved you as I do! That you know in your secret heart! Tomorrow you may have me dismissed if you please, but now you *must* listen to what I swore I'd tell you one day!"

She noticed, staring at him, that all the reckless daring had gone from his voice and manner; he was trembling as the words rushed out, and then, as though he saw something written upon her own face, he took her in his arms, and then she was sure that she belonged to him.

"You see?" he said.

She put her face against his shoulder.

"Clarissa . . ."

"Oh no, you must give us time to know. This is just being mad!"

"We *do* know!"

"I'm frightened!"

"You will never be frightened any more with me!"

He put his arm round her then, and she told him something of her life, of the failure of her marriage, and of her loneliness. She found that she could talk to him as she had never been able to talk to anyone. When she had finished he kissed her again, and this time she made no protest.

For a long time they said nothing.

Lying in his arms, surrendering in ecstasy to the embraces of this strange young man, she remembered how once, long ago, she had seen some peasant lovers in the woods and envied them despairingly, thinking such happiness would never come her way. She told him this, and he smiled, saying that when he snatched his first kiss from her in the darkness he had thought that moment all of Paradise that he would ever know.

"And we were both wrong!" she declared gleefully.

"If you were only amusing yourself with me, I should kill you!" Rokeby said.

After a pause she said slowly:

"I felt the same that night in my carriage. I loved you then. I always will love you. And your letter is still locked away in my jewel case."

And she thought, then, that she had been lost from the first moment, when he climbed into the carriage beside her. Looking back, she knew that it had happened, this magic, long before she had ever seen his face; it had been in his voice, in his closeness, his presence; she had loved him even before he kissed her.

She said:

"I waited for you a long time. Now you're like someone who has lit a lamp in a dark room. You must never put out that lamp!"

He told her again:

"No one has ever loved you as I do!" And then he said something that jarred upon her. He asked, "Will you do me a favor?"

"What is it you want?"

"Will you please," he urged, "send Hesther Barbary packing?"

She sat up, then, indignant.

"No, I will not! Don't let's talk of her, since I've already told you she's my friend!"

"I see," he said, and his face was stony.

"You would not be here," Clarissa reminded him, "were it not for Hesther."

"I know that, and I know I should be grateful. But I can't be!"

"What have you got against her?"

"She's bad luck," Rokeby answered shortly.

"Are you so superstitious?"

"Very!"

"It's not only that I like her. My husband likes her too."

"I realise that. I'm not a child."

"Must we talk about Hesther?"

"Do you understand," he said, "she brought me to Lord Rohan's house for one purpose? She *wanted* this to happen! I swear, she's a devil!"

"Swinton," she said, using his name shyly for the first time, "she could never have wanted what has happened to happen, because she could never understand it. Nobody but us could understand. So what does it matter?"

"You need looking after!" he told her.

"*You* are here! Won't you look after me?"

"It's when I'm away——"

"When are you going away?"

"I shall be here for at least a month."

"You'll never leave this situation, will you?"

"Not unless I have to," Rokeby promised, "and that may happen sooner than you think."

"I don't see why."

"Do you see the rain has stopped?"

"I'd forgotten it. Will you meet me here tomorrow?"

"I hope," he said, "I'll meet you here every day! Nobody can see the boat if we hide it beneath the trees, as I've hidden it. This little temple will be ours so long as we're together."

"Don't speak," Clarissa protested, "as though our happiness could ever come to an end! It won't; it never will! How could it?"

"At least," he reminded her moodily, "I've told you the worst about myself."

"A buccaneer! I'd forgotten that!"

So, apparently, had he, for he kissed her again and said:

"Perhaps many years from now, when *we* are both forgotten, your descendants may come out here to this island and sniff about a bit, as people will, and think, on misty days like this, that they see our ghosts!"

"Nobody would be afraid of us," she assured him. "How could they be? Such happy ghosts!"

"Oh, my dear!" he cried, "we haven't come to the end of the story!"

Clarissa shivered.

"I don't want to think of people coming here after us! I don't want to be old and forgotten!"

"Clarissa, how could you be forgotten? You'll always be a legend!"

"Who wants to be a legend? I want you!"

He laughed.

"So do I want you!"

Mist enfolded their enchanted island in ghostly coils, and it was very late before Lady Rohan came down that night to dinner.

XXXIV

SOMETIMES," Hesther said, "I think it would be much better for me to go away."

"Why?" Clarissa asked of her mirror blankly.

"Surely I've outstayed my welcome."

"You keep the Ghost company, and he likes you. What more can anyone want?"

"But you seem—— You're unlike yourself, Clarissa, and sometimes I've really wondered whether you still want me with you."

"I've got a tongue in my head," Clarissa answered drily, "and if your presence were intolerable to me, please believe that I should tell you so!"

"Clarissa——"

"Now, Hesther, I'm late, and in any case I detest intimate talks! Please stop speaking nonsense! Run downstairs and amuse the guests while I finish dressing!"

No, Hesther thought decidedly, this was most certainly not the Clarissa she had known for so many years. This woman

was self-confident where Clarissa had been shy; she was more
ironical than simple, as Clarissa always had been; above all, she
was a little disdainful whereas Clarissa had invariably been
eager to please. And her looks . . . Guardedly Hesther watched
her, and knew that she had never been more beautiful, for her
beauty had the glow that summer that is sometimes to be
found in the deep heart of a rose. With her slimness, her exquisite profile, her mane of red-gold hair, and her radiant skin,
she had always been remarkable to look at, but now there was
grace, a warmth, in every expression and gesture that made her
seem like some glorious painting that had stepped out of its
frame to become alive.

All that, Hesther well knew, closing the door behind her,
was due to Swinton Rokeby, and for a moment she wished she
had never brought him to Grosvenor Square or meddled with
the lives of other people.

"If only," she thought, "it could have been anyone else!"

She did not particularly mind what Rokeby told Clarissa concerning herself, for the Ghost knew all there was to know about
her. But it would be tiresome if Clarissa became jealous of her
own brief love affair with Rokeby. She realised once more that
her own presence in the house depended largely upon Clarissa's
benevolence. If Clarissa really decided that she must go, it
would put Rohan in a difficult position, and he was in some
ways oddly correct.

She thought, not without bitterness, of the many conventional
men with whom Clarissa might have fallen in love had she not,
from the first, set her heart on Rokeby. In the beginning Hesther
had contemptuously dismissed Clarissa as a fool; now, since
the poison of envy was still at work, she decided that if Clarissa
compromised herself foolishly with a scamp like Rokeby she
would be harming the Ghost; she would be more knave than

fool. And then her hatred of Clarissa flamed up once more, and this time, when she wished Lady Rohan were dead, she was not ashamed of her thoughts.

She reflected:

"It would be better for everyone!"

Then, crossing the great hall, she saw that the library door was open, and inside the room she heard Swinton Rokeby whistling.

"Whistle and be damned to you!" Hesther thought viciously; "whistle her away, and yourself too! Away forever!"

As though she had spoken aloud, he strolled to the door and made her a low, mocking bow.

"My compliments, ma'am!"

She pushed past him inside the room.

"I want to speak to you!"

"There was a time," he said lightly, "when you liked being complimented on your appearance!"

A sconce of candles burned brightly on his desk, for the windows were open, and outside the summer night was ice-blue but soft and scented with the fragrance of roses.

Hesther said:

"You owe this post to me!"

"Surely I thanked you at the time."

"You had better be prudent!"

"Fie, fie! But then you always had an ugly temper!"

Listening to his deep, lazy voice, watching his face, white against the deep blue of the night, she knew how much he mocked her and despised her.

Mrs. Barbary liked men to admire her.

She said, speaking scarcely above a whisper,

"Next week there's a great house party here! See to it you're careful! Tell *her* to be careful too! Nobody wants a scandal——"

He interrupted her in a biting, icy voice:

"If you so much as dare to mention Lady Rohan's name I shall turn you, very roughly, outside this room! Incidentally, I shall probably tumble those pretty fal-lals of yours. *Now* do you understand your place?"

He could have said nothing to infuriate her more. White with fury, she spat at him. Rokeby laughed, not a very pleasant laugh.

"Always the lady, Hesther!"

"You lowbred cur!"

"The time has come, my dear, for this interview to end!"

He walked over to the door and held it open.

As she did not move he said, with menace,

"Come, Hesther, I shall count five . . . and then . . . Well, suit yourself!"

She left him in a rush of draperies that were nearly caught as the door slammed, for a night wind had risen. But he had not missed the gleam of hatred in her eyes. He sighed, and went back to his catalogue.

Fifteen minutes later it was Clarissa who opened the door.

He picked up the sconce of candles and went across the room to meet her.

She wore a dress of lilac gauze with diamonds round her throat and on her wrists. Her diamonds glittered.

They whispered, for this meeting was dangerous.

"Have you dined?" she asked him.

"Yes! In the gun room!"

"Was the food eatable?"

"Perfect! You look too beautiful to be real!"

"There's a tedious county dinner party tonight!"

"You'll adorn it!"

"I shall miss you."

"Clarissa, can you come to the lake tomorrow?"

"I think so! Will you be down by the boat at three?"

"I will."

She kissed her hand to him.

"My dear, good night!"

"Good night," he whispered, not daring to come outside the open door.

She went out into the hall, and he returned to his desk. But he could not work. When people fall in love with the violence of these two they are temporarily disorientated, and for a time their passion transforms them into a world where neither one can be accounted entirely sane. Certainly both Clarissa and Rokeby were living at abnormal pressure; there was so much to say that had never been said, because there had not been time; their snatched meetings left them both feverishly dissatisfied; the time between these meetings appeared to them an eternity, so that it seemed to both as though time stood still.

Rokeby sighed again as he shut the door and returned to his desk. He realised that he had behaved with imprudence in making an enemy of Hesther, but he consoled himself with the thought that he had had but little choice in the matter. He was, however, perturbed for other reasons; he had immediately divined the jealous hatred Mrs. Barbary felt for Clarissa, and, knowing both women, he soon came to the gloomy conclusion that his mistress would have been safer, or as safe, living with a rattlesnake in her house.

That was it, he thought moodily, fidgeting with his quill, there was something of the serpent in Mrs. Barbary, and then the recollection of Clarissa's trust in her friend became more distasteful than ever. The whole basis of their friendship, Hesther's ambiguous situation in the house, her eagerness for him to accept his present post, still seemed to him sinister.

"What is she after?" he asked himself aloud. "Has she some

melodramatic plan for ruining Clarissa and taking her place?"

But he did not think Lord Rohan the type of man who would desire, or permit, his wife to be ruined by his mistress.

He could only conceive that Hesther had lost her head, in which case it would soon be made clear to her that she was making a fool of herself, and there was no reason for him to feel that chill of foreboding which for a moment made the great rose-scented room seem cold.

"For even if Hesther tattles," he thought, "and I'm dismissed, that's no reason for us not to meet one another. The island is not the only place in the world."

But he could not for a moment help wishing very much indeed that it was.

XXXV

THEIR MEETINGS on the island continued, and with each meeting it seemed that their love grew. But both were circumspect, so that sometimes one of them would wait in vain, knowing, with resignation, that the other could not come down to the lake without fear of discovery.

There were many guests at Rohan that summer, and Clarissa was busy entertaining them, although she wished a hundred times a day that she could run away from them to find her lover waiting with the boat. But she played her part skilfully, and many of the visitors pitied her, with Mrs. Barbary living in the same house.

Mrs. Barbary, observing this same pity, decided that she would never be likely to forget it. At the same time she cautiously refrained from enlightening Lord Rohan as to his wife's

summer pastimes. That story, Hesther thought, could well wait.
There was no hurry. Later on that autumn, or that winter, she
would make up her mind what to do or say. Not even to herself would she admit the awe she felt of Rohan. But secretly
she was afraid.

And his lordship seemed well disposed towards the young
librarian. He thought him intelligent if erratic.

One morning Hesther, hearing screams of laughter, walked
out onto the lawn beneath the cedar trees, where she saw
Rokeby playing with the children. They were riding on his
back, tumbling his new coat, while a few yards away Rohan
stood, a grin on his face, watching them with indulgence.

Somehow, although she was smiling, Mrs. Barbary's appearance broke up the merriment, and the children soon found an
excuse to run away across the lawn. Rokeby got up, brushing
the grass from his coat.

Hesther said gently:

"Lucinda looks overheated. She is easily excited. Isn't she,
Lord Rohan?"

"I've never noticed it," he answered, "and Rokeby, here, has
been teaching them how to sail a ship. They liked that, didn't
they, Rokeby?"

"Well, sir, they seemed ready enough to learn," the young
man admitted, smiling, and dusted his pantaloons.

He wished he could feel properly guilty whenever he was
addressed by Clarissa's husband, but he found it difficult. From
what she had told him, their ties were casual enough; and,
furthermore, he liked the Ghost. Rokeby was not interested in
politics, but he admired one who had the reputation of being
so good a horseman, a whip, and a boxer, as his employer.
Therefore he smiled at him with the greatest affability, and
declared it to be time he returned to work.

When he had gone Rohan announced:

"I like that young man, Hesther. Not that he'll stay long. He's a rolling stone if ever I saw one and longs to be at sea again he tells me."

"When did he tell you that?"

"Why, last night, when he was talking to me in the library. He's able too; he knows something about books!"

"He's not so young," she answered, scarcely trusting her voice.

"How old?"

"He says he's twenty-eight."

"Well, I wish that *I* were twenty-eight!'"

It was on the island that Clarissa confided how she was haunted by a vice she found herself unable to cure—her passion for play

"I never knew," Rokeby remarked, "you played higher than other ladies."

"I do," she answered in a sombre tone, "as my father did, and I believe my grandfather before him."

"Have you lost much money?"

"Yes," she sighed, feeling a sweet relief in speaking of what she so much dreaded, "I have fearful debts, and one day I shall have to confess to Rohan."

"But how much do you owe? Several hundred pounds?"

"Oh, my dear! If it were only that! I owe"—she hesitated, for even to Rokeby she felt she did not dare admit the truth—"I owe," she finished lamely, "more . . ."

He frowned and said:

"When I go back to that place I know, where the treasure is buried, *I* shall pay your debts!"

She put her hand on his cheek.

"You're never going to leave me. Never! Do you hear?"

"But what will happen to you?" he wanted to know, sincerely troubled.

"I shall have to tell the Ghost in the end. He'll pay them— my debts, I mean. But he will be terribly angry."

Well, he would be, Rokeby supposed, for one must be reasonable. And it scarcely appeared, even to him, that his beloved had shown much sense; and he wished that he could transport himself, on a magic carpet, to a desolate spot named Barracuda Reef, and help himself to the fortune concealed there.

"You see," he said, thinking aloud, "I know the treasure's there, for I helped my father to bury it when I was a lad of fifteen. There were two slaves and my father's bo'sun, a man named Gabriel Tarch. And Tarch is dead."

His voice was grim as he spoke these last words, and she asked, not without apprehension,

"How did he die?"

"On our way back to Port-of-Spain," Rokeby answered, screwing up his eyes as though he saw again the scene he was describing—billowing white sails; the huge sapphire bowl of the sky; a glaring sun; the heaving, glittering desolation of the waves; the gleaming wings of seagulls calling to one another harshly as they trailed their way behind the little sloop. "On our way back to Port-of-Spain this same Tarch, having bribed the slaves, tried to kill my father. He waited until I slept and then, knowing the slaves would turn their backs, he came behind my father with a knife. My father was not armed, but he was a powerful man, and it seems they struggled for some minutes, my father fighting to get the knife. There was no one else aboard, my father having chartered this sloop so that we could hide the stuff quietly. I woke, of course, hearing the noise they made fighting, and ran out from the dark cabin into the brightness of the sun. There I saw my father lift Tarch like a child in his arms and hurl him overboard. I ran to the side and looked while he stood beside me staring. Tarch could not swim—few sailors can—but before he sank, or the sharks got him, he shook his fist and called out something, cursing my father. Then we went on our way."

There was a pause, after which Clarissa asked:

"What about the slaves?"

"They were sold into Haiti," he answered. "And it's thirteen years ago. No one knows about the treasure but me."

"Swinton, you didn't *see* what happened. It was only what your father told you afterwards. It might have been——"

"Why, yes," he agreed serenely, "it might have been the other way about. But I've always given my father the benefit of the doubt."

She considered this, and for a moment they both forgot their own surroundings—the pretty temple nestling among the darkness of arching trees; the tranquil English sky, dappled with clouds; the white carpet of water lilies drifting on the surface of the lake. She shivered, and he put her shawl round her shoulders.

"What was the treasure?" she asked, fascinated despite herself. "Was it—surely I read of—pieces of eight?"

He laughed, shaking his head.

"No. That sounds like some made-up tale of pirates! No! It's a bag of uncut diamonds, big as walnuts, and a great gold bar, part of the prize of a French brig, that was sunk a few months before. If Gabriel Tarch had killed my father, he would have killed me, too, and gone back for it one day."

"Why did they bury it on an island?" Clarissa asked.

"Such plunder is supposed to be handed over to the government. I told you—it's considered piracy to touch it. But many captains do. They get little else, and risk their lives. So they *cache* it."

"And you have never returned for it?" Clarissa pursued, hoping sincerely that the Ghost might forever be spared the revelations of his librarian.

"Never," he answered, shaking his head. "I have always been able to make enough money on my own to live. And there's been no one—no one I have loved enough to wish to realise the fortune. But now I know you I want to return and——"

"You never shall!" she told him in a storm of agitation. "Never! Swinton, promise me that!"

"How can I promise? It might have to be!"

"Oh no!" she protested. "We must always stay together! How could we separate?"

"Listen," he said, taking her in his arms, "one day—who knows—you'll sail back with me to the islands, and we'll go together to find the treasure!"

"That would be different."

Different! It would have meant another life for both, but neither realised it.

XXXVI

THEY stayed on at Rohan until the end of September, and then Clarissa, Rohan, and Hesther returned to Grosvenor Square. Rokeby remained another week to finish his work, and the children were to stay in the country until November.

He was glad of that, for they had become attached to him, called him Swinton, and went to visit him every day. He was lonely, segregated as he was in the great house, and missing Clarissa so desperately.

The library at Grosvenor Square was now in order; he would

have little occasion to visit it, and it would no longer be so easy for him to meet her in London.

When he thought of that, and when he thought of their early-morning meetings in September, he knew that an English September for him would always mean the memory of Clarissa's love.

One morning they had gone out just after dawn to pick mushrooms. He remembered the frosty tang in the air although the sun was glowing through a milky mist; cobwebs were draped like delicate lace upon the hedges, and there were rich clusters of blackberries mixed with the scarlet of rohan and black thorn. Soon their basket was heaped with the pearly buttons of the mushrooms, and then the sun pierced through the mist to warm their bones, and Clarissa took off her shoes and stockings.

Well, he reflected, on his return, that had all been delightful, but it belonged to the past. Now they were in London, and their meetings became more difficult than he had ever imagined.

He had taken lodgings in the city coffeehouse where he usually stayed, and although he saw her twice on the pretext of work undone in the Grosvenor Square library, the second time was dangerous, and both knew that there could not be a third.

She met him for a few minutes in the square garden after dark, and they clung together, feverishly trying to devise ways of meeting. One night, greatly daring, they went to Vauxhall, frequenting only the darkest paths. But that, again, was dangerous. Danger, to both, meant something different: to her it meant the Ghost; to him, Hesther, harmful and malevolent.

He asked despairingly:

"What shall we do? This is unbearable."

"It makes me long for the island!"

"But, Clarissa, what are we going to do?"

"Perhaps soon we could go away together for a few days. I could pretend I was going to try some horses."

"But what will happen after that? What good are a few days when I want you forever?"

There was no answer.

Nor was her life apart from him harmonious. Her gambling debts accumulated and were not paid; apart from this desperate and increasing worry she suddenly discovered that London society had decided to pity her for having Mrs. Barbary to live with her in Grosvenor Square. Clarissa was popular with her friends, and soon that autumn she found her popularity embarrassing. It seemed that Hesther was now too openly Rohan's mistress; her friends—they were many and powerful—resented Hesther.

"My dear," Lady Melbourne said, "don't be a fool! Of course it doesn't matter—Rohan having a mistress—doubtless you're glad he has one! But don't make the mistake of having her to live with you! Turn her out!"

But Clarissa was sulky, and disliked the idea of making a scene about Hesther. The old, girlish loyalty still clung, in remnants, perhaps, but the remnants were there.

"After all," she said to herself, "I'm as bad as she is."

And Rohan was so much happier, so much more genial, since he had fallen in love with Hesther.

"Besides," she thought, during this period of reflection, "if they hadn't got each other, they might find out about my poor young man, and that I couldn't bear."

She could no longer shut her eyes to the fact that on their rare, frustrated meetings Rokeby talked with a furious wildness.

"Come away with me! Come to the islands! We're both young. All our life's before us!"

"How could I leave the children?"

"You could have children by me!"

"Ah, no, Swinton, you musn't talk like that! I can't bear it!"

"And what am *I* supposed to bear? Do you think I can go on sharing you with other people?"

"I don't know what I suppose. But don't *you* make me unhappy!"

"Then come away with me!"

"If I had no children, I would."

"Oh no!" he said, stabbing at her with the bitterness of his own misery, "oh no, you wouldn't! You love being Lady Rohan, don't you?"

She answered with a quiet dignity she had never shown him before:

"Being Lady Rohan has not brought me very much happiness, has it?"

"Why, I don't know," he replied, conscious that he was being detestable, and hating himself, "it's brought you money, and jewels, and splendid houses! Why should you give that up for somebody disreputable like me, somebody who's got nothing to offer you but a pirate's treasure buried on the other side of the world! Oh no! You've got everything! I see your point!"

She thought of the five thousand pounds she owed for gambling.

"I haven't got everything," she said slowly, "and there's a reason why, even if I had no children, I couldn't go away with you."

"Another reason! Well, let's hear it!"

They were at Vauxhall, pacing together down one of those dark and shady paths so much frequented by lovers.

"My debts," she answered candidly. "I could never leave this country owing money to people."

"Clarissa, you still won't believe in my treasure, will you?"

"Yes, I think I believe in it. But my debts are nothing to do with you. I've got to pay them myself."

She did not tell him she had been to a moneylender. What was the use, she thought, of burdening him with the squalor of her life? He did not know squalor existed for her; if he had known, he would only have wanted to sail away and find his treasure, like a little boy, and Clarissa's secret heart did not really believe in the treasure. Somebody, she was sure, had already dug it up; those slaves in Haiti could have bought their liberty by disclosing the secret, and Haiti, in any case, was free now. Not for the first time she wondered what would be the Ghost's reaction if he knew that she was a pirate's mistress.

"Not pirate—buccaneer!" Rokeby protested when she told him this.

"Is there so much difference?"

"All the difference in the world!"

"That was so like men," Clarissa thought, for the difference to her was still obscure.

"I've been odious tonight," Rokeby said abruptly.

"You haven't, because you never could be that. And I know I've been tiresome, what with the children and what with my debts!"

"We can't go on like this!" he insisted.

"Oh, my darling, I know we can't! But later on, next month, we can go away for a few days together. I've told you—I shall pretend to be trying some horses!"

"Clarissa, can't you understand that's no good? A few days! A few snatched, snivelling, miserable days! Hiding in some inn, cowering when the chambermaid comes to light the candles!"

"Well," she said, "there are always the nights!"

"That's not the way it can go on," he answered doggedly.

"Then what? What do you want?"

Behind the dark arbour where they were talking, an orchestra began to play Mozart. Soon, in an hour, there would be fireworks.

He said sternly:

"I can't endure this sort of life. I was never bred for it. I'm not a poodle! If I love someone as I love you, then I must have them completely without sharing! Either you come away with me, or we will finish it! Do you hear? Make up your mind!"

In the darkness her mouth found his.

"I'm sorry," he said again, later, "I've been detestable."

"*I* know we can't go on like this."

"I love you so!"

"So do I love you."

"We *must* go away together! Can *you* bear this?" he asked again with anguish.

"I don't think I can," Clarissa sighed.

"Then, beloved, you *must* come with me to the islands! You must! You've got to! How can we be together if you don't?"

In Grosvenor Square Hesther sat playing backgammon with Lord Rohan. She was a brilliant player, and these games amused him. They amused her, too, for when she lost he never took her money, although he paid her when she won. Hesther would have been a gambler could she always have played backgammon with the Ghost.

"Where's my wife?" he asked suddenly, and—for he was losing—in a disagreeable tone of voice.

"I don't know," Hesther answered truthfully; "she never tells me where she's going."

After a pause, as he moved a man, he said in the tone of distaste with which he always referred to his wife's play:

"I suppose she's gambling again."

Hesther said nothing.

After another move he announced coolly:

"I shall go out and look for her."

"Are you going to leave me alone?"

"I am."

No, she perceived, he was not in a good temper.

She sighed, but she knew it was no good arguing. If he wanted to go, he would, and nothing she could say or do would stop him.

And when they had finished the game he went.

She was left alone in the house with the servants.

XXXVII

It was when she remembered Molly had gone to stay with relations for two nights that she went softly upstairs to Clarissa's apartments.

She let herself into the sitting room, where she lit the candles and looked round her thoughtfully. A bright fire burned in the grate, sparkling cheerfully on the silks and satins with which Lady Rohan loved to surround herself. Hesther went over to the Louis XV writing table. It was not, of course, locked, for Clarissa was neither cautious nor methodical. Stealthily she began her examination.

She found Clarissa's papers somewhat disappointing. If she had gambling bills, they must be concealed in some iron box, possibly at the bank. If she had love letters, they were hidden somewhere else. There were several bills from dressmakers, an invitation to dinner, and a letter from a Mr. Samuel Rogers recommending a new book, of which Hesther had never heard.

There was a half-finished letter from Clarissa herself, praising Lord Holland for a speech she had obviously much admired. That was all.

Hesther picked up a candlestick and went into the bedroom. More firelight here, flickering on painted Venetian furniture of the eighteenth century. A huge bed draped in ivory satin. A faint, delicate scent, to remind her of Clarissa.

"She always had perfume, even as a little girl in Bath," Hesther thought with one part of her mind. The other was busy examining the drawers and cupboards. Quietly, meticulously, she began her search.

She found, after ten minutes, an iron box in the bottom of the wardrobe. That, she thought, must contain some record of the gambling debts. But the box was locked, and there was no key. Mrs. Barbary was annoyed and swore beneath her breath.

It was some time afterwards that she found Rokeby's letters and some diaries in velvet-bound notebooks. These treasures were concealed in a tortoise-shell casket which, perhaps because Molly was not there to remind her, Clarissa had forgotten to lock.

Hesther sat down with the candle and began to read.

Rokeby had written a sonnet to Clarissa, but in this she was not interested, although the sonnet was tolerably good. She picked up a letter which began:

MY SWEET LOVE,
I kiss your heart . . .

There were several more letters, and she read them all.

When she had read the letters she turned to Clarissa's diaries, which were spasmodic but not without interest, since it appeared that she had kept them since her girlhood in Bath.

"I do not like Miss Shaw," Hesther read in one early journal. She turned to the later volumes.

"If I could continue meeting S.R. on the Island I would be content forever. But such sweet Happiness as this can't last. Yet whatever happens I shall have known it, and indeed it is like being enchanted, as though lilac bloomed in a snowstorm, or something as Fantastick. . . . It is too beautiful to last. . . ."

But Hesther was not really interested in Clarissa's love affair, although it was interesting to know that she had been right in her instinct. Nor had she guessed that they used the island as a meeting place. She remembered, not without resentment, that Rokeby had never written her sonnets or love letters during that brief period when they had lived together. He had always seemed in too much of a hurry.

But she turned over the pages hastily, looking for details of Clarissa's gambling debts. But here she was thwarted, for it had not occurred to Clarissa ever to put down in her diary how much money she had made or lost.

Hesther read:

"Gambled tonight . . . was fortunate . . ."

Or, as frequently happened, "Was unfortunate . . ."

How like Clarissa! And how very tiresome, Hesther thought, rapidly conning the pages.

It was then, as a log crashed heavily in the grate and the room grew cold, that she realised she might be caught in Clarissa's apartments. She put everything carefully away and picked up a novel lest she might be questioned on her way out.

She realised her own prudence as she reached the sitting room and saw, in the firelight, as the door slammed, someone coming to meet her. She paused for a moment, startled.

She expected Clarissa, but she saw instead the black boy, Toby, bringing in the poodle from its evening walk. For a moment he stood silent on the threshold of Clarissa's lovely and luxurious rooms.

"Why, Toby!" she said. "I came in here to fetch a book . . ."

"Yes ma'am. Yes, Miss Hesther!"

Even that damned blackamoor, Hesther thought, is on *her* side!

Toby knelt to put logs on the fire. He said no more, nor did he seem to notice her. She walked slowly out of Clarissa's apartments, the novel tucked beneath her arm.

Toby went over to the door and held it open.

"Where's her ladyship, Toby?" she asked casually.

"Ma'am, I don't know."

He remained standing there, black and dumb, as Mrs. Barbary walked down the passage towards her own rooms. It was fortunate, for two people at least, that she had not troubled to read all Clarissa's contemporary diary; she did not even know for certain that Rokeby had sailed as a buccaneer. She knew nothing of the buried treasure, and would, indeed, have dismissed the whole story as a fairy tale.

Clarissa came back dazed from Vauxhall, to meet her husband on the doorstep.

"I don't know where you've been," he said, "but I thought you were gambling. I've been all over London, looking for you!"

"You are most touching! But you see I was not gambling!"

"Thank God for that!"

She was once more overcome by the very thought of her debts. This realisation terrified her so much that she dared not even look at him. Vauxhall, the shaded paths, the music, even Rokeby, seemed non-existent for a moment compared with the burden of these debts.

"If only they could be paid!" she thought wretchedly, and

looking at his stern face she knew that she could never tell him how much she owed.

"Clarissa, you're tired!"

"A little."

"Then good night, my dear!"

"Good night," Clarissa answered miserably, going on her way, a candle in her hand.

She forgot even her debts as she walked upstairs, for once more she was thinking of Rokeby and wondering where on earth they could next arrange to meet.

"Ma'am!" Toby cried, springing up outside her door.

"Why, Toby, what is it?"

"Miss Clarissa, it's Miss Hesther. I found her in your rooms tonight. She tells me she is getting a book, but I think she is reading what she shouldn't!"

"Here! In my rooms?"

"Yes ma'am, yes, Miss Clarissa. She was here a long time!"

"You can go," she said gently.

Left alone, without Molly, and having dismissed her sulky French maid, she came to a momentous conclusion.

She would run away with Swinton Rokeby. She was most certainly not necessary to the Ghost, and her own children were perfectly happy with their grandmother. "Old" Lady Rohan would bring them up better than herself.

And Hesther . . . If the Ghost was fond of Hesther—as fond as she was of Rokeby—then they were better left together. Except for the children. Whenever she thought of the children Clarissa immediately became unhappy.

Miserably, as she tried to sleep, her mind revolved her own immediate problems, so that her tired brain spun like a whirlwind; she was forced to light a candle, and she tried to read, but found no comfort, only a restlessness, an unhappiness she could not conquer, and so she tossed on her pillows, forgetful of the book and of Mr. Samuel Rogers, who had so warmly recommended it to her.

XXXVIII

A FEW DAYS LATER she was able to meet Rokeby in a green glade of Hyde Park. It was a warm, cloudy day and might have been a morning of early spring rather than late autumn.

He was waiting for her beneath the trees, and she thought him pale and anxious. How soon, she reflected, their first joyous love had been transformed into a detestable existence of anxiety and separation! There was no island in London, and there was no excuse to return to Rohan. She looked forward to the future with a sick nervousness; in her home, if she continued to see him, there was Hesther to spy on her, Hesther to use her evil influence on the Ghost. And there were her debts. On the other hand, if she ran away with Rokeby she would lose her children, her home, her friends, everything else that she loved. She would find herself committed to a lawless, roving life. She would live openly, as the mistress of a wild young man, about whom, in fact, she knew nothing except that she craved for him and he for her. But how long, she wondered, would they continue to love one another in the sort of life that she pictured? Would he not find her too helpless, too fine a lady, for an existence she knew would entail many hardships despite his talk of treasure? Where, if she ran away with him, would they run? When she thought, too, that had he been a man of her own world, there would have been no difficulty in meeting him, that old Lady Melbourne herself would have encouraged the affair, she could have burst into angry tears, and it was then that she asked herself, as so many hopeless people have asked,

"Why, *why* did this have to happen to me?"

"Oh, Swinton," she cried, "why could you not have been a soldier, or a lawyer, or a politician, or *anything* in the world but what you are?"

"What am I?" he asked urgently, rather as though he himself desired reassurance.

"A buccaneer!"

"Why, it's not so bad as that! I've been other things, too, more respectable; is not a librarian respectable, pray?"

"I didn't mean that."

"Clarissa, you look pale, and as though you have been crying. Is anything the matter?"

"I *cannot* stand this any longer!" and she began to cry again, stamping her foot.

They walked away together amongst the trees, and he said:

"I can't stand it much longer myself. Not seeing you. Will you put away all your fine ideas and come with me?"

"Yes," said Lady Rohan with simplicity.

For a moment, in his joy, he was speechless. And then, because this love of theirs was teaching him something he had never learned before—a willingness to sacrifice his own happiness to someone he loved better than himself—he said grimly:

"I was mad! I should never have asked you. Do you think in the end I would take you away from your own life, your children, and everything you have? What have *I* to offer you?"

"Ah!" she said, in desolation, "even you don't really love me!"

"I do not?"

And there, in the glades of Hyde Park, where anyone could pass and see them, he seized her in his arms, pulled her close to him, and kissed her half-a-dozen times, not at all as he had kissed her on the island, but rather with despair, as though he knew that he must lose her in the end.

"So I don't love you?"

She said nothing, because she could feel his heart pounding against the iron hardness of his chest, and the ephemeral happiness of this contact made her forget her wretchedness, her worry, and the melancholy doubts that had all night assailed her.

"We could live in Italy," he said suddenly, as though he were talking to himself.

"I don't care where I live! What about your West Indian islands?"

There was an instant's pause. He did not at all want to remind her that he was liable to be arrested for piracy on his own islands. And yet if they were going away together he would have to go back and find the treasure.

"It *belongs* to me!" he told himself obstinately.

Yes, he would have to find it, and sell it—a dangerous transaction. But he would be a rich man then, not merely a vagabond unfit to kiss her shoes. There seemed to him no reason to discuss these matters with her so he asked instead:

"Would Lord Rohan ever divorce you?"

No, she did not think he would. So much depended on his political position; if the Whigs ever came into power . . . of course there were the Hollands, Lady Holland had been divorced; but no, she was sure such an idea would never even occur to him.

"All the same, he might want to marry Mrs. Barbary."

"Marry Hesther!" She was astonished. "Why should he want to do that when they are living in the same house?"

"My beloved," Rokeby reminded her, "they can no longer go on living in the same house once you have left it!"

"Well," she said, thinking of Hesther's spying, "that is nothing to do with me! *Taut pis* for both of them."

She did not tell the tall young man of Toby's report; she knew how impetuous he was; he was capable of dragging Hesther out of the house to shake her, openly, on the pavement.

And then a new thought came to her, curdling her blood.

"Swinton," she cried, "I'd forgotten something—something terrible! My debts, the gambling debts! I can't go away before they're paid!"

"Why," he said, thinking this as good a way of breaking the news as any, "why, there's no question of that! I'm going back to the islands to find my treasure and sell it! Did you think I'd take you away with nothing?"

He listened, unmoved, to her agonised protests. If he went to the islands, she wept, she would never see him again—that she knew, and it was cruel to torture her!

"Then you shall come with me!"

Once again he was becoming reckless; it was a gamble, and they were both gamblers; why gamble only over a faro table? He might never be caught; he could dispose of his treasure in Amsterdam, or in Germany, or in Rome; why should he suppose the steamy heat of the tropics, the vivid sky and sea, the croaking of gulls, meant evil luck to him? He was more superstitious than a woman, and she was the cooler gambler of the two! But after a moment's thought he was suddenly sure that he could not take her with him; women like Clarissa Rohan are not born for their lives to be risked in patched-up sloops beneath a sky of fire; with governors, and magistrates, and iron-barred, stinking prisons lurking just around the corner of all that he had told her of beauty, of hummingbirds, and flying fish, and wild orchids, and passion fruit. . . .

She was speaking, and for a moment it was difficult for him

to wrench himself away from the memory of that hot and violent background that was his but must never be hers. Never! When he came back to her he would be quit of all the sun-drenched bloodshed; it would be a page turned, a chapter done; he reassured himself again, thinking of the treasure,

"It *belongs* to me! It was my father's!"

Clarissa was saying with desperation:

"Swinton, you *must* listen to me! You don't know what my debts are! They're worse than I have ever said! I owe eight thousand pounds for gambling!"

"What?"

For a moment he gaped at her; he thought his ears had played him false.

She continued, with a sad finality,

"I had to tell you. You're the only person I've ever told. Nobody knows. But I couldn't go away without paying them—those debts! It would be too—too——" She struggled for a word, and achieved: "It would be too dishonourable! You see, I pledged my credit. I didn't want to tell you this, but I must if we're going away together. I can't go away—away from London until they're paid. You see that, don't you?"

He gasped:

"You owe eight thousand pounds?"

"Yes! Before we go any further I had to tell you that."

"Well," he said, and whistled, "thank God for the treasure!"

"Swinton, I'll go to the Ghost! I don't care how angry he is! If I'm leaving him, it doesn't matter very much. After all," with bitterness, "he still has Hesther!"

"My beloved," he answered, "I love you, and Rohan doesn't. I'm going to look after you and Rohan isn't. You're coming away with me, not with him. *I* shall pay your debts. You must leave these business arrangements to me! I've *got* to go back to the islands and find my treasure, and sail it home, and sell it where I can!"

"But, Swinton——"

"Listen! you can't come with me, how could you? I'm known in the islands. I'm a West Indian born and bred! But you—— Can't you imagine the stir your beauty would cause if you came out there with me? You're not like other women, dear heart, and never will be! How *could* you come and search for pirate treasure? Be reasonable. You couldn't sail with me without being followed by a hundred ships! Men don't only steal gold in the tropics."

"How long," she asked slowly, "would you have to be away?"

"Less than a year, if all goes well. Perhaps eight months."

"Oh no! I'd rather tell my debts to Rohan!"

"My heart, *I* want to do this for you! I want us to have security in the future. Unless you let me go back, none of it can happen! You see that, don't you? You know I wouldn't take you away from all your luxury only to put you in some Italian gutter. I want to give you a home when we're together—some villa outside Naples where you might be happy! You must see I've to go back!"

"But where will you sell your treasure?"

"Not out there," he said, half-shutting his eyes; "somewhere in Europe."

"But, Swinton, they could arrest you for hiding prize money!"

"They could, but they'll never catch me! I shall be back before you've even known I've gone away!"

"I'd rather go straight to Rohan," Clarissa persisted.

"In any case, I'd still go back. I want to make our future secure! Don't you want me to be a rich man? Just because I've never troubled to think of money before, are you not glad I think of it now I've found you—to make our life for us in the future?"

"Not if it means eight months or more without you!"

"It will pass in a dream," he declared, shutting away his superstitions like something enclosed behind dark curtains in his mind. He had never wished to return before, or find the treasure—the risk was too great. He did not particularly want to be hanged. And he had been happy enough in England acting, horse-coping, writing for newspapers, tutoring, wandering up and down the countryside. More often than not he had forgotten the treasure, and the death of Gabriel Tarch, and the blanched coral reef that was haunted not only by gulls. It was now, when his love for Clarissa obsessed him so that he could no longer claim to be entirely sane—it was only now that he realised how rich he was. It he could but get the treasure and sail back with so much wealth to Europe!

The amount of her debts had for the moment astounded him. He knew that he possessed on Barracuda Reef a fortune many times greater than the sum of money she owed; but he would naturally have to sell his illegal treasure for less than it represented; she did not know this, but he did, he had transacted such matters since he was a lad in his 'teens.

Never before had money meant anything to this wanderer, who had been content with bread and cheese, who had been happy enough to sleep in taverns and in gypsy tents.

Now, loving Clarissa, he would have to find his plunder. To find it and to sell it too.

"I could always pass as a nabob," he said aloud; "you see we could live in Italy, and that's what we'd say if we were questioned."

"Oh, don't go back! Please don't go!"

"It's not your debts I'm thinking of particularly," he told her

with gentleness. "I'm thinking of the future for the first time
. . . *our* future! I'd never let you come away with me unless
I could look after you!"

"But, Swinton, I don't care——"

Once again, oblivious of Hyde Park, he stopped her mouth
with kisses.

"You see," he murmured, when at last he could speak, "it
won't seem like so many months. If I sail this Christmas, I'll
be back in time for the autumn. We'll be at Rohan then, if
we're fortunate, and we'll go to the island every day and pick
mushrooms, and blackberries, and picnic in our summerhouse.
Oh, Clarissa! don't cry! I've *got* to get that prize! Sweet, don't
cry! When we're old we'll laugh about this together! What's
a voyage to the islands! I've made that voyage so many times!
It's like you travelling from London to Oxford!"

"Without you," she said, "to hold my chaise upon the
way. . . ."

XXXIX

Hester was so busy, having her hand modelled for Rohan
by a famous French émigré sculptor that she had no time to
spare for Clarissa's love affair.

She only realised what was happening when one night the
Ghost grumbled:

"The only good librarian I've had for years! And he must
needs be leaving me to sail for the West Indies!"

She was perplexed, and asked sharply:

"For good? The young man must be mad!"

"You should know why he goes," the Ghost answered disagreeably, and once again she recollected how much he had learned of her past life. But he surprised her by saying:

"I imagine he's in love with Clarissa."

She was wary as she laid out the men for backgammon. This was not the moment to tell him what she knew.

"Do you really think so?" she asked casually.

He sighed.

"How tedious you are, Hesther," he remarked, "when you try most to be clever. Throw the dice!"

"I am thinking only of backgammon," Hesther declared.

"Then concentrate! You would play much better if you followed my advice. Double sixes!"

There was a pause, until at last he won the game.

"You're lucky tonight!" Hesther said.

But he was paying no attention. He poured out two glasses of wine and asked her casually:

"You remember Epsom races, don't you?"

"Of course I do."

"You remember the gypsy fortuneteller—the one whom they call my lady of Egypt?"

"Yes," Hesther said, not without bitterness, "I remember her."

"Such women," the Ghost pursued, "are a part of Epsom, and one is glad to give them a guinea. Clarissa, I believe, was told as a child she would marry a man in grey. An odd coincidence."

"Very odd," Mrs. Barbary agreed, replacing the backgammon pieces in their leather case.

"All the same," Rohan continued, "I want no sorceresses in my house."

"Has the gypsy woman been here?"

"No," he said, apparently oblivious to the sharpness of her voice; "no, she has not so far as I know. Nor was I talking of her."

"You're talking riddles, Ghost!"

"Not at all. I was simply musing. Isn't it called musing? Well, while I was musing I came to the conclusion that whatever sort of fool my wife is making of herself I'd prefer no interference! Do you understand? No fortunetellers, nor occult suggestions, nor confidences, nor, above all, tittle-tattling! Another drink?"

"No, thank you! And why should you talk to me like this? Clarissa never tells me anything!"

"I never supposed that she did. I was speaking rather like my lady of Egypt, which is to say, I was talking in riddles. I'm privileged, I suppose, as a husband. You understand, Hesther?"

"It's easy to see you don't love me any more!"

"On the contrary, I do love you and depend on you even more. But that has nothing to do with Clarissa."

"If you found out——"

"Are you going to help me put back these backgammon men, or not? I see; you are. Well, Hesther, there's probably not much for me to find out—or for her, either, don't forget that! We are all pretty much the same in different ways, I suppose. You're very helpful, my dear, and we had a good game; but I was too clever for you tonight."

She thought of Clarissa's gambling debts but could say nothing, since she had no proofs; her hands trembled as she stacked the men in their morocco case.

"I think," he announced, "I shall go to White's for an hour."

"So late?"

"What has that to do with it?"

She sat beside the fire for some time, wondering whether, by some mysterious power or other, Rohan had learned of her ransacking of Clarissa's desk and casket; she did not think so, but she could not help wondering why he had taken such pains to warn her against any discussion of Clarissa's love affair. He

was still, despite their intimacy, incalculable, and she was afraid
of him, but it was clear that she would seriously offend him by
tattling of his wife, and she was glad indeed that she had
resisted the opportunity.

While she sat brooding the door opened and Lady Rohan
came in. She had been, Hesther recollected, to a gay dinner
party, but she did not seem gay. For once her step dragged, and
her pallor was noticeable.

"Why," Hesther said, "you look cold and tired. Shall I make
up the fire?"

"I'm tired," Clarissa said childishly, "of being told I look
tired."

She sat down in Rohan's chair. She did not ask where he was,
but was silent for a moment and closed her eyes as though she
could no longer struggle against her fatigue.

So that was it, Hesther realised, watching her from the corner
of her eye. Clarissa knew that Rokeby was going away, and she
was dying of love for him and of pity for herself. What, she wondered, had made the young man consent to go? She thought
them both fools, and congratulated herself on having managed
her own life more astutely. Then she started, for Clarissa had
opened her eyes and was speaking.

"Why," Clarissa asked, "did you go to my room the other
night and read my letters?"

Hesther controlled herself with an effort.

She smiled, and said tranquilly, "Has that black imp been
romancing again? He should be whipped."

"It doesn't matter," Clarissa answered wearily.

"But I think it does! It matters to me! To be accused of spying——"

In the same flat tone Clarissa interrupted her.

"As you know so much, I'll tell you something else. Rokeby

is going away—back to the West Indies. And I wish I were dead."

"But why send him away?"

"He is not being sent! We've come to a private arrangement, the two of us. Perhaps he will come back—he thinks so. But I'm afraid! I'm so afraid!"

Why she should confide in someone described by Rokeby as her worst enemy, she did not know. She did not really care. It didn't matter very much so long as she was careful not to mention the treasure and their future plans. But she was tired, and worried sick, not only because he was going away, but by the burden of her debts. She felt without hope. Looking at Hesther, the years spun back, and they were girls together in the white-panelled drawing room of a school in Bath. Life had been simple enough then. She had not been married to Rohan, she had never met Swinton, and Hesther had not developed into the devil she undoubtedly was.

"I wish I were young again," thought the twenty-six-year-old Clarissa, "and I wish I were still there. It was dull, but dullness was better. I wish I had known that."

Aloud she said:

"There was one thrush which always sang in the garden. He seemed to sing all the year round."

Hesther began to think her tipsy.

"What in the world are you talking about? Have you said good-bye to Rokeby? Is that the trouble? What do you mean about thrushes?"

"There was one in the garden at Bath," Clarissa answered irrelevantly, and then, looking full at Mrs. Barbary, with her immense blue eyes, "No, I have not said good-bye to him yet. He sails next week from Plymouth, and I shall go down there to see the last of him. If you want to tell Rohan, you may. I shall go, all the same. It won't make any difference."

"It's no business of mine, and you can rest assured I shan't tell him," Hesther retorted, imagining what she might have to deal with if she did.

"People always make promises only to break them," said Clarissa to this.

"Clarissa, won't you go to bed? You look ill!"

"And if I lost my looks there would be nothing left, you mean? Well, perhaps you would be right! And I suppose you think I've had too much wine? You're right about that, too. I have. You're getting very clever, Hesther!"

"Do you want me to ring for Molly?"

"No! And, Hesther, Swinton told me you and he were lovers once, so you can't wound me one day by telling me so yourself, can you?"

Mrs. Barbary was once more torn, as Clarissa had ever had the power to tear her, between pity and hate. For months hate had dominated, like poison, in her mind; now, for a fleeting moment, pity returned, and she put her hand on Clarissa's shoulder, as she had so often done when they were girls at school.

"Clarissa! Please go to bed."

"You're very much in love with Rohan, aren't you?" Clarissa asked with tipsy innocence, and at that question the hatred returned, distorting everything. And Hesther added coldly, "You'd better go before he comes back!"

Clarissa went, like an obedient child.

The next day Rokeby left for Rohan, feeling that he had better be conscientious regarding his lordship's library. She hungered for him, knowing how short a time they had, but he worked all night, and came back to surprise her at Grosvenor Square.

XL

It was a week afterwards that they drove down to Plymouth in a hired chaise. He begged for the peach-lined carriage in which he had first met her, but she was forced to refuse his request, although to refuse him anything nearly broke her heart. But to have taken her carriage would have meant also taking Wright, her crest, her horses, even the Rohan harness. They might, she knew, have been spied on all the way, and they were not yet ready to be spied on.

Afterwards, when he came back and they went away together to live in Italy, it wouldn't matter any more. Nothing would matter then, for they would be together always.

And so she left Molly behind and took only Toby.

She also left behind a purposely ambiguous note for Rohan, telling him that she was going away quietly to the country for a few days because she did not feel well. That, indeed, was true: she did not feel at all well.

So they travelled down to the West Country together in a lumbering chaise that smelled of stale straw, holding hands, but speaking seldom. They were travelling as Mr. and Mrs. Rokeby. Her one pleasure, amid so much pain, lay in calling herself by his name.

She thought dully, looking out of the frosted windows, "It's lasted so short a time . . . not four months. If he never comes back, I can't bear to go on living. I would never have the strength. Oh, why couldn't I have some money of my own! Enough for the future! So that he wouldn't have to do this desperate thing! If something terrible happens, if he dies out there, it will be my fault!"

"You mustn't be sad," he told her harshly at this point, as though he could read her thoughts.

"You can scarcely expect me to feel happy!"

"Clarissa, this voyage to you must seem like travelling to the moon. But it's not, you know; I've made the same journey so often—it's nothing! I swear it's not!"

"There are no Frenchmen on the seas I suppose? No pirates? No people searching for you on the islands for taking prize money?"

"Ah, sweet! You mustn't think of that! I've been back over and over again! Nothing has ever happened!"

"I won't think of it," she answered, pressing his hand. "I don't want you to remember me as someone sad and desolate. I want you to remember how, when we were together at Rohan, we laughed as well as loving one another. We were gay!"

"And you know we'll be gay again! Think, too, of the night I climbed into your carriage! The night I kissed you first!"

She smiled, then, to his joy.

"I thought you a highwayman. Little did I guess you'd turn into a pirate!"

"Not pirate—buccaneer! It's different!"

It was still the same to her, but she smiled again and said nothing. Instead, she looked at him, feasting her eyes upon his pale, rather long face; his wide, humorous mouth; his tilted eyes, and curling copper hair.

"Now, Clarissa, don't look at me as though it were the last time!"

"I wasn't! I just want to remember you for all the months that lie ahead."

They were remarked, at the inns where they stayed, on their way to Devon. She was so beautiful and he so tall; and then, to make them more exotic, there was the silent black page. They were taken for honeymooners, and yet, even in the quiet taverns they purposely chose, people noticed how, despite their passionate affection for one another, they were often sad, and silent for long periods; as though all were not well with them despite their love.

Then it was that landlords and chambermaids furtively questioned Toby, but without success, for they soon observed that the blackamoor was dumb, or as good as dumb. Rokeby was at first inclined to resent the attention they attracted, but he never discussed it with her, for the simple reason that he perceived, not without amusement, she never even noticed it—she was so accustomed to being stared at.

It was when they first approached Plymouth that she felt her heart turn over in her body, and then she clung to him, unashamed.

"You know," she told him, trying very hard to be reasonable, "I don't believe I can bear this. I'm sorry, but I can't—really I can't."

"You must," he said, making his voice sound hard.

A chill grey mist hung over Plymouth so that they clattered, like a ghost coach, down the cobbled streets, and then she sniffed the sea, and her despair grew.

Why, at least, she wondered miserably, couldn't it have been a fine day? It would surely have been easier, then, to bid good-bye to him; the sunshine would have seemed a happy omen. But this damp sea mist defeated her, rising so eerily, making phantoms of them both before they were even separated.

And there were so many things they had never done together, perhaps would never do now

They had never seen the primroses in the woods at Rohan, or been together to the play; they had never even danced together, nor stayed as equals in the same house. They had never been able to be frankly happy, like so many other lovers; always for them had lurked a shadow of deception and of untruthfulness. They were young, and they loved one another, but they had only been able to love in a deserted summerhouse on an overgrown, forgotten island. Always they, who were candid, had been made, by life, to be furtive. They had never been able to be proud of their love before the world. They had had to treat shamefully something which was, to both, the glory of their whole existence.

"You're very quiet, beloved," he said, not without anxiety.

"Only because . . . Swinton, what did you say was the name of your ship?"

"She's called the *Good Intent*. I know her and her captain, too, although I've never sailed on her before."

"He's not a buccaneer?"

"Dear heart, you would wound Captain Richardson to the quick! A more honest merchantman never sailed the Spanish Main!"

It was then that their chaise turned a corner to draw up before their inn, and it was then that she saw the port. Even through the mist she could glimpse so many masts that they seemed to her dazed mind to tower like a forest.

"Why," she told herself, "so many ships sail every day across the world and back again. It's ridiculous to be afraid for him! We're not living in the days of Columbus!"

And she was able to smile very creditably as they went together into the inn.

But their last night together was an agony she would never forget.

They lay awake until dawn in one another's arms while outside, all night, men were loading or unloading cargo, and gulls screamed. They were very close to the traffic of the seas. Whenever they lay quietly together, without moving or speaking, she imagined she could hear the crashing of waves. But, she thought afterwards, perhaps that had been an illusion. Not a dream, because she did not believe she slept at all that night. But it might have been an illusion, a mind picture, of Swinton's voyage, which she so much longed to share.

She remembered, while he slept briefly, his head resting upon her breast, strange stories he had told her of the sea. A phantom barge that sailors saw if their ship was doomed; a great white whale which swam round the seas and back again; it could never rest until all the ships of all the world were sunk. When sailors drowned, they saw for one fleeting moment mermaids with white arms and green hair like seaweed. For a few moments she dozed and dreamed of a salt-white beach where foamy breakers curdled, and behind the beach lay a jungle where birds called, concealed by a tapestry of vivid flowers. And Swinton's treasure was there, hidden somewhere behind all this brilliant blossom. . . . She started awake.

"It's not morning?"

"Yes, it's morning."

They dressed in silence, and then he begged her to come down to the coffee room and meet Captain Richardson.

"You'll feel much happier if you do. He could not fail to inspire confidence, even in you! Please, Clarissa!"

"Of course I will, if you want me to."

They went downstairs together into an oak-panelled room swarming with strange and noisy men. They had brown faces, like mahogany, with gold or turquoise rings stuck in their ears, and some of them wore pigtails. One of them had a bright green parrot perched on his shoulder. They talked loudly, many of them in Devon so broad she could not understand what they were saying, which was perhaps as well, Rokeby told her in an undertone. She felt shy, and drew her hood about her face as she followed him to a table set against the wall. There were several women in the room, crudely painted, dressed in cheap finery, and even at eight in the morning these women were drinking rum.

Rokeby ordered coffee, and in a few moments Captain Richardson came over to join them.

XLI

She liked him at once. She liked his slow, quiet voice, his shining, red-brown face, like an apple that had just been scrubbed, and she liked his steady, clear blue eyes. He did not seem in the least like a pirate. She smiled at him, totally unconscious of the damage she was inflicting upon a susceptible heart.

Rokeby said, with simplicity,

"Captain, this is the lady I hope one day to marry. So, you see, she would like to be reassured as to my safety sailing." And he pressed her hand.

The captain showed very big teeth, like white tombstones, she thought confusedly. He leaned across the table.

"Ma'am, I've known Mr. Rokeby now for a long time around

the islands. I count him one of my friends. I'm glad he sails with me. And if he sails back with me, he'll return safe!"

"You see," said Rokeby, and pressed her hand again.

"I'm sure that's true," Clarissa said, "and I'm very happy to meet you, Captain Richardson. I shall have more peace of mind now."

"Why," Richardson thought, "he's found something out of the ordinary this time! She might be the Queen, only the Queen's not young and isn't splendid to look at like this one is."

"Your servant, ma'am," he said, with old-fashioned courtesy, and to his passenger:

"You'll be aboard by nine, Mr. Rokeby?"

"I will! Clarissa, drink your coffee!"

"In a moment."

She found a pencil and a piece of paper. She scribbled for a moment, and then pushed the folded sheet across the table to Captain Richardson.

"Please take this, sir. If—if anything should turn out badly, you would be very kind to acquaint me . . ."

She drank her coffee then, and he noticed that her hand shook.

He put the address away carefully with his sailing papers and other important documents, but not before he had observed that she was the Marchioness of Rohan, who lived in Grosvenor Square, in London. Then, looking at her pale, beautiful face, at her tragic, dark-rimmed, blue eyes, he quite forgot her grandeur, and leaned over to put his hand for a moment on hers.

"I'll keep an eye on the lad," he said, not without roughness; "you need not fear!"

Rokeby pulled out his watch, the new gold watch that she had given him, with her miniature painted inside.

"Clarissa, I haven't much time. Let's go upstairs to say good-bye."

"Yes."

She got up, and turned to Richardson.

"I shan't forget your kindness, sir. And—good fortune!"

"Your servant, ma'am!" he said again, rising awkwardly to bid good-bye to someone whom he instinctively knew to be sorrowful and alone.

When they got back into the oak-panelled bedroom with its four-poster already stripped she asked:

"How long have we got?"

"About ten minutes. It's better so! Why prolong this misery?"

"Yes, it's better so." She went over to the window, watching the maze of masts, the swarming of cargo. "I like your Captain Richardson," she said without turning round.

He came behind her and caught her in his arms.

"Clarissa . . ."

"Oh, it's too late to say 'Clarissa'! You're going away—you *would* go!"

"So that I can look after you when I come back!"

"When! When! You may never come back!"

His mouth found hers. She noticed, for the first time, that he trembled, and that his face was ravaged. She was so much stronger then that she drew his head upon her breast, and then, miraculously, she became the comforter.

"Swinton, how foolish we are! It won't even be a year!"

"A year! Without you!"

She stroked his head, and put her cheek against his.

"You'll know all the time, my darling, that I'm thinking of you."

He got up. It was he who was weeping; she was still dry-eyed.

"I'll go now," he said, knuckling his eyes, like a child.

"There's nothing left of your baggage. Yes, you'd better go."

They were in each other's arms again, but as though in a

dream, for this was their parting, and nothing else was real.

"Clarissa, I love you."

"So do I love you."

"Our summer's over. But you won't forget?"

"There's next summer. I'll never forget."

"I'm coming back!" he cried, beside himself. "How *could* we forget? I'm coming back! And if you were dead I'd still smash open your coffin to kiss you back to life! That's how I love you! Do you see? I'd scratch open your grave to make you love me!"

He kissed her blindly, so that their tears were mixed, to daub her face, and the door slammed, and then he was gone.

Yes, he was gone; she heard him trampling down the stairs, and then his footsteps died away, and she was alone.

She stood motionless, looking out of the window at a thousand masts piercing the greyness of the mist. Down below at the harbour men shouted and swore, pulling at their oars. Somewhere a clock ticked, and struck nine wheezily. She did not hear it. Nor did she hear a knock at the door until it was repeated at least three times.

"Come in!"

It was Toby, bearing very carefully a cup of coffee.

"No, Toby! I don't want it!"

But for the first time since they had known one another he disobeyed her. He put the cup down and pulled her arm gently.

"Massa Rokeby sent this up before he went. Please, Miss Clarissa! Please drink it!"

She continued to weep.

She sank down on the nearest chair, and sobbed unrestrainedly, like a child. Toby came softly towards her, still bearing the cup of coffee.

"Please, Miss Clarissa!"

"Order the chaise! I want to go! I want to start at once!"

"Yes, ma'am. Yes, Miss Clarissa. When you drink the coffee I order the horses!"

She was his goddess and could do no wrong. He could not understand why "Massa Rokeby" had left her, but, in any case, they were both his special gods, and he could not bear to see her cry.

"Miss Clarissa! Drink! Please!"

She drank, mingling her tears with the coffee.

"Better, missy?" Toby asked, trying to grin.

"Yes . . . thank you . . . please, Toby, order the horses!"

He went out obediently.

He could not tell her what "Massa Rokeby" had said, pressing a guinea piece into his hand before he left. Rokeby had bade him solemnly—he understood Negroes:

"Toby, look after your mistress. Never leave her alone with Mrs. Barbary if you can help it! Do you hear? Always try to be somewhere near!"

"Massa Rokeby," Toby had answered shrilly, "I won't never leave my missy alone with Mrs. Barbary! Mrs. Barbary's no better than deadly nightshade!"

But Clarissa knew nothing of this conversation. She got into the hired chaise feeling more dead than alive, and drove, jolting, for miles, without knowing where she was or what she was doing.

At least she was sensible enough to direct the coachman not to go to the inns where they had stayed, coming down from London. That would have been unbearable.

She stayed alone in more reputable taverns where, not unnaturally, she was taken for a kept woman. She was beautiful, and richly dressed, and had a black page; but she had no carriage, no coachman, and no horses of her own. Yet she seemed so ill and so unhappy that she was not molested, although she was much discussed.

She thought only of Rokeby as she travelled back to London.

She could not then very clearly recollect the island at Rohan, and their meetings in the temple, when they had laughed, and loved one another, and been gay. She could only visualise him at Plymouth, walking out, weeping, into that cold sea mist of early morning. Walking towards a ship where, in spume and gale and storm, he was now sailing half across the world in quest of some bloodstained gold he would not have sought but for her.

She wept then, hiding her face against the straw-bulging cushions of the hired chaise.

It was dusk when she reached Grosvenor Square.

She paid her coachman and tipped him.

She went into her house, ignoring the butler's horror—for it was still light enough for him to see the hired chaise—and walked straight into the library, where a fire burned.

Hesther was alone in the library.

With one glance at her white face, her travel-stained clothes, Hesther came forward, taking her hands, and said:

"Clarissa! He's gone, hasn't he?"

"Yes," Clarissa answered, in a shaky voice, "yes, he's gone . . . I went to say good-bye, but . . ."

Everything seemed dark, and there was a noise like thunder in her ears. She couldn't finish her sentence. With a sigh she fell at Mrs. Barbary's feet. She had fainted for the first time in her life.

XLII

It was a November day of dense, clinging, London fog. The fog hung everywhere in heavy clouds of blackish-yellow. The streets were churned thick with trampled frosty mud, so that carts and carriages smashed against one another in the lowering darkness of a day that was still night, and then the drivers swore, and lashed out, and link boys came running up with flaming torches while the fog pressed ever more heavily down. It was a day straight from Dante's Inferno, and the inky misery grew deeper as the hours passed, so that the only persons continuing cheerful in so much gloom were the crossing-sweepers, and their noses, looming out of the fog, bobbed brighter than cherries as they begged for alms.

Over Grosvenor Square the fog hung in a sooty pall.

Early in the afternoon a little man came shuffling up the darkness of the street. He was short, and of a grubby appearance. He wore a shabby coat, a scarf, untidy breeches, and a motheaten fur cap. He was swarthy, and seemed not to have submitted recently to the formality of shaving.

For some time, lost in the sulphurous gloom of the fog, he paced up and down, trying, in the darkness, to study a document he held. Then, diving from the street towards some great and solemn houses, he walked up to one—to my lady Rohan's house—and knocked imperiously upon the door.

There was a slight shocked pause, and then the door opened. The little man saw a warm glow arising from a fire inside the hall, and the porter, hiding in the shadow of a hooded chair, put away his ale and got up, hesitant.

At the same moment two gilded footmen came swiftly into the hall, and the three of them stared at the little man as though he had committed sacrilege by knocking on the door.

The little man cleared his throat and said:

"The Marchioness of Rohan . . . ?"

"Who are you?" the porter asked.

"I represent Messrs. Barker, Eldridge, and Levy. I have come to serve a writ upon the Marchioness of Rohan in default of a debt occurred by her ladyship on . . ."

"Outside," the porter advised, jerking his thumb towards the door.

"If you turn me out," the little man ventured, "I shall return with a sheriff of the law. This is an ugly matter, and had best be hushed up!"

"Her ladyship is ill," said one of the enormous footmen, like a bear growling.

"Then pray take her this letter! I can wait."

As he said the last words he turned, almost defiantly, towards the huge fire burning in the hall.

For a second the three servants looked at one another.

Then the porter, who was their senior, said abruptly:

"You can't wait! Her ladyship's ill, and you had best not be here when his lordship returns!"

The little man grinned, showing yellow, broken teeth.

"I represent the law! If you put me out, I've told you I'll return with a sheriff's officer! Hadn't you better take this letter to Lady Rohan?"

The porter, being an old servant, decided to show some authority.

"Thomas," he said, "take this person's letter to her ladyship!"

"Very good, Mr. Soames," Thomas said, and at once went upstairs with the paper.

The little man pulled up his coattails, warming his backside before the fire.

"Sad thing," he confided genially; "lovely lady . . . great family . . . gambling debts . . . made a fool of herself, eh?"

"Frederick," said Mr. Soames, the porter, "put down your fist!"

"Yes, Mr. Soames," Frederick muttered, and reluctantly obeyed.

"Now you," said Mr. Soames belligerently, advancing towards the little man; "one more word from you concerning her ladyship, and law or no law I'll throw you into the street! You understand!"

The little man glared at him, rather like an angry ferret, but dared say no more. He had looked forward to this official visit to Grosvenor Square. He had supposed that the servants would have been glad enough to lick their lips with him and curse the woman who employed them. But somehow everything had turned out wrong, for they seemed devoted to her, and he could not understand them at all.

Upstairs, Thomas gave the document to Molly, who gave it to Clarissa and left the room.

She opened it with Hesther sitting by her bed. She turned so ghastly pale that Hesther thought her about to faint.

"What is it?" Hesther asked.

"I suppose," Clarissa said after a pause, "that bad luck goes on and on. For a long time. One can do nothing about it. It's no good trying."

Molly opened the door.

"May Toby come in, my lady? He's got some flowers."

"No!" Hesther said violently.

Clarissa took no notice, and Molly shut the door, not without temper.

Hesther came closer to the bed.

"Clarissa, what's the matter?"

"I can't hide it any longer," Clarissa told her wearily, "it's my gambling debts. I went to a moneylender. He's pressed me for months, and now he'll wait no longer. I'll have to tell Rohan."

"How much do you owe?"

Clarissa looked calmly at Mrs. Barbary. It didn't seem to matter so much any more about the debts. At least Hesther did not know that she was with child. Nobody knew that.

Hesther repeated, as Lady Rohan continued to look as though in a dream:

"How much do you owe?"

"Just on eight thousand pounds."

"Clarissa!"

"You asked me! I can't pretend any longer. This person is waiting downstairs. What's the good of pretending? Even the servants know!"

Not for the first time, looking at her, Mrs. Barbary was conscious of those two violent and conflicting emotions. She hated Clarissa because Clarissa was married to the Ghost, and bore his name, and was indifferent to him. Yet, looking at that white, defeated face, she felt pity. Clarissa was wrecked by her parting with Rokeby. And to be summonsed by a vulgar moneylender . . . Hesther's pity for a moment broke through her hate.

"Clarissa, would you like me to tell Rohan what you owe?"

"Yes, please," said Clarissa like a child, and shut her eyes.

"You know about us, of course, don't you?"

"Yes."

"You don't mind?"

"No. How could I? Am I any better? Will you really tell him?"

"I will indeed," Hesther promised, still feeling pity. "You've been so good to me," she said, astonished to know that she was moved, contemplating Clarissa's goodness.

Clarissa smiled, looking like a pale angel.

"Hesther, we are friends again, aren't we? Like Bath?"

"Of course. I only thought you didn't like——"

"I don't want to talk about it. It has nothing to do with me. I want Toby."

"Toby?"

"Please! He has flowers for me. You see, Swinton ordered flowers for weeks, for months in advance and Toby fetches them. It must have cost Swinton so much money!"

"I'll find him," Hesther said.

Swinton Rokeby had never sent her flowers, she remembered. Jealousy flicked her like a whip, and much of her pity vanished as she went out to call the blackamoor.

Rohan flew into a cold rage when he heard of his wife's debts. He stormed:

"I knew she had debts! But I thought two thousand covered them! Now you tell me eight!"

"She's desperately unhappy."

"You amaze me! Is she really capable of feeling?"

Hesther said slowly:

"She is so much in love with the young man . . ."

"So much in love she takes your leavings?"

"Rohan, you mustn't——"

"My wife's in love with a young cub of a librarian, and owes eight thousand pounds to boot! A pretty story!"

"*You* have been no better!"

"I'll thank you," he said, "not to teach me how to behave!"

In the end, after a wearing scene, he agreed to pay Clarissa's debts only on condition that she sign a paper swearing never to gamble again.

"And," he added, "I refuse to discuss the matter with her either now or any other time!"

Hesther conveyed the message.

"Of course," Clarissa said lifelessly, "I'll sign a paper. . . ."

"Aren't you happy?"

"Very happy indeed."

"Darling, could you not *look* happier, then?"

"I'll try to, Hesther."

"It's all been very difficult!"

Clarissa smiled then.

"I shall not forget what you've done, Hesther!"

She turned over on her pillow, and seemed to sleep.

XLIII

CLARISSA WAS WITH CHILD by Rokeby, who did not know it.

Nobody knew but herself. Soon she would have to tell Rohan.

She lay in bed, thinking of the gambling debts that had been paid, and wondering why all her life should be shadowed with worry. She was the famous Lady Rohan; she was admired, and toasted, and painted. One day, she thought, echoing a morbid mood of Rokeby's, one day, if those pictures live, people will think me beautiful; they won't know Rohan had to pay my debts; they won't know I deceived him with this baby that's not his.

Why, she wondered, in a mood of the darkest introspection,

why should their marriage have wrecked itself from the beginning? Perhaps if they had met later, when both could have
been friends, their lives might have been different. But they had
been too young; they were strangers when they met and married. And they had stayed strangers ever afterwards. Until, she
thought, he met Hesther and I met Rokeby. Then her misery
threatened to choke her, for Rohan still had Hesther. And she
was alone, as she had always been, while Rokeby was sailing
to the other end of the world to find some schoolboy's treasure
in which part of her had never believed.

Hesther came in and said, smiling:

"Clarissa, you can't lie here brooding! You must get up! Why
don't you come to Rohan for a fortnight? Shall we go together?"

"No."

"Clarissa, darling, he'll come back!"

"I wish you wouldn't talk about it," Clarissa said.

"But you must try to get well!"

"So be it. For peace we'll go to Rohan!"

They went, the two of them, a week later.

Hesther could not resist casually asking Clarissa to row her
out to the island.

"I think you forget," Clarissa reminded her, "that once you
read my letters."

"Clarissa, if that little fiend of a Negro——"

"Don't scream at me!" Clarissa interrupted sharply; "my head
aches!"

"Clarissa," Hesther said in her softest, most persuasive tones,
"I've been quite candid with you—I've told you I love Rohan,
and you've been frank with me! I know you love Swinton
Rokeby! And those debts—I don't want to remind you of past
unhappiness, but I was sorry for you—I did what I could . . ."

"Why do you love Rohan?" Clarissa wanted to know.

"Why? How can one answer that?"

"It's true; one can't; it was a foolish question. I don't know why I love Swinton. I suppose we were made for one another. We are somehow incomplete unless we are together. If you feel the same about the Ghost, then heaven help us all!"

There were other matters she would have liked to discuss with Hesther, but the prudence acquired during those last months restrained her. She wondered why, during that brief period of meeting Rokeby in London, she had received, the day of her husband's unexpected return to Grosvenor Square, a sheet of paper on which were printed these words: "THE GHOST WALKS TONIGHT." What was this, she wondered? A cheap joke, or a warning from some illiterate friend? She would never know that black Toby, hearing of his master's arrival and not daring to discuss the matter with her, had given a pedlar a few pence to write these dramatic words, then slipped them himself into the letter box.

She sighed, and Hesther bade her, with briskness, to rouse herself.

That, she thought, would be impossible; with every day that passed Rokeby was sailing further away from her, and in a few months it would be impossible to conceal the fact that she was carrying his child. Once again panic seized her. Was it not bad enough that Rohan, to prevent the shame of his wife being writted, should have had to pay those ghastly debts?

Then the Ghost himself arrived at Rohan, regarding her with the greatest coldness. Impulsively she sat down to thank him once again.

She wrote a letter.

"G, I implore you, put this in the fire, but hear me. I have done wrong, yes, but shall you, in your Heart, judge me? Oh,

G, that would be Heartless and cruel . . . blameless I am not, but . . ."

And another page of apologies, promises, and expressions of humble gratitude, all most distasteful to Rohan, who desired nothing so much as to forget the whole miserable business. He wrote back coldly:

"If you desire to please me, you will adhere to your promise never to play again."

Oh! he was hopeless, Clarissa thought for the hundredth time; he was a dry stick, and she was sure that Hesther could only like him for his estates and titles! Perhaps she would have been a little consoled had she known how icily he had once rebuked Hesther for tattling to him about her play. The Ghost had no love of informers, and wrote to tell his mistress so.

He was in a sullen mood that winter at Rohan, for he had worries of his own quite apart from the annoyance of having to pay his wife's debts. He had become aware, for the first time, how much his liaison was resented in London, and it was Lady Melbourne, naturally, who had seen fit to point this out to him.

Clarissa was popular and beloved in Whig society; it was conveyed to him, uncompromisingly, that, by installing his mistress in his own house, he was subjecting himself to bitter criticism from those of his friends whom he most respected.

He protested:

"She came to the house as Clarissa's friend! On Clarissa's invitation!"

That, Lady Melbourne retorted, had nothing to do with it. It didn't matter how such a business began—it was how it ended!

Rohan left Whitehall in a rage.

He dismissed Lady Melbourne as a snob; she would never have interfered in his affairs had Hesther belonged to her own

world. Nor had it diverted him to hear Clarissa described as a
suffering angel when Hesther had already whispered poison in
his ears, when he knew all about the trip to Plymouth and her
farewell to Rokeby. But he kept silence, hating Lady Melbourne
as he did so.

He supposed that one day Hesther would have to leave his
house, but the idea of parting with her, although she would, of
course, continue to live under his protection, was one which
he viewed with intense dislike. He was used to her; he depended on her company. He liked her where he was, beneath
the same roof. He decided to say nothing until they returned
to London.

One day, however, he learned something which caused him
to change his opinion.

He went out riding one morning with his daughter Lucinda.

The Lady Lucinda Clare looked like a charming little doll
in her long green habit and feathered hat, but she was already
a child with a mind of her own, and just as her father was
about to congratulate her on the manner in which she rode
her New Forest pony she forestalled him, her brow wrinkled
in sincere perplexity.

"Papa, may I ask you something?"

"Of course."

"I don't like to ask Mama."

"Pray, why not?"

"I just would rather not. She might not like it. So I saved it
to ask you."

"What is it, then?"

She enquired earnestly, gazing up at the straight figure tower-
ing above her on the great grey hunter,

"Papa, who is *really* the mistress of the house? Mama or Mrs.
Barbary?"

He kept his voice quiet.

"What makes you ask, Lucinda?"

"I want to know."

"But what put such a question into your head?"

"Oh," she said, "I heard some of the servants talking—they didn't know I was there. They said many things I could not understand, but they said it was Mrs. Barbary who gave the orders. They said *she* was the mistress; not Mama. It isn't true, is it?"

"No," he said, "it is not true."

"Why did they say it?"

"Lucinda, surely you know better than to listen to servants' talk!"

"Yes, but I was afraid for Mama. I don't want Mrs. Barbary to come before her."

"You need not be afraid," he answered drily. "Mama is mistress of the house, and always will be. Do you understand?"

"I'm glad," Lucinda replied. "Papa, will you let me off the leading rein when we get into the park?"

XLIV

So you see," Rohan said, in the library where Swinton Rokeby once had made his catalogue, "you see, we shall have to make other arrangements."

"I only see," Hesther answered, white-lipped, "that you are turning me out of your house!"

"My dear," he said, controlling himself, "there's no need to make a scene! I can assure you that you will not suffer! Can't you rely on me to see you are well looked after!"

She looked at him, her eyes as hard as stones, her full mouth drawn into a thin red line.

"Where should I be without Clarissa's protection? A common kept woman, a baggage no better than Harriette Wilson! You don't mind, do you? You wouldn't care! Well, I'm sorry—I *do* care! Does Clarissa know you intend to turn me out?"

"I don't usually," Rohan remarked, "discuss such matters with my wife!"

"Don't you think in this case you might stretch a point?"

"No," the Ghost retorted, "I do not!"

"Then I'm to go? To be sent out once again into the streets?"

"I've just told you," he said, still patient, "you'll have a charming house wherever you please. Naturally I'll still look after you, and your allowance——"

"But that will mean Clarissa refusing to know me! How *could* she, if you installed me in some house in Maida Vale! I've told you—you want to make a common, kept woman of me!"

"What were you," the Ghost asked wearily, "before you came to Grosvenor Square?"

She demanded, her eyes blazing,

"Is your wife any better?"

"Well, you know," Rohan told her, sighing, "I don't really wish to discuss my wife . . . nor do I permit that you shall. . . ."

"You mean you'll forgive her affair with Rokeby, and still send me——"

"Hesther! Hesther! Will you please to mind your own business?"

"Is that not my business?"

"Why, no," he said, "it's not."

"And I'm to go?"

"I'm afraid so. But not out of my life! Look around, my dear, for any house that pleases you . . . take your time—there's no hurry!"

"I see. There's no hurry?"

"No hurry at all, my dear! All the same, it will scarcely take many months to find something that should please you!"

She knew by this time the suggestion of menace in that last sentence; she turned, left the room blindly, and went upstairs towards her room.

So this was the end of all her social scheming. She was, it was true, to keep him in her life; but for that she thought she would have killed herself. But she, who loved to consider herself grand, who preened herself with joy as she sat in Clarissa's carriage, saluting Clarissa's influential friends, she was to be sent away from Grosvenor Square to live under Rohan's protection as a kept woman.

A gentler nature than her own might have resented so violent a change of fortune, and Hesther's nature had never been gentle. She flung herself upstairs, thinking that soon she would become the mockery and jest of those people whom she had most sought to impress. How they would laugh, to think that Mrs. Barbary was neither more nor less than a courtesan. "And how," she thought savagely, "the ladies will enjoy cutting me!"

Little Roderick, peeping round a corner of the passage, saw her face, and hid, for he was afraid.

But she did not see him; she went into her room and slammed the door behind her. In a few moments he peered out again, like a bright-eyed field mouse, and soon forgot her as he resumed his game.

Outside, it was damp, and iron-grey clouds hung over the world. It would rain before long, but Clarissa did not care. She escaped from Toby and went off alone through the rose garden towards the lake.

She was driven, by some obscure impulse, to seek out the one spot in the world where, months ago—a hundred years ago— she had succeeded in finding the glowing happiness she had known so briefly. She had loved Rokeby for the first time on the island, on a similar day of lowering clouds and driving rain. Now, alone and sick, since she was to bear his child and afraid, knowing he could never return in time to comfort her, she determined to return to the island.

She went down to the shed, took a boat, and started across the lake, which was black and frowning on this dreary day. She set out towards the island.

"Perhaps," she thought, "if I go back to the temple, to our Folly, I shall think it sad, and overgrown with nettles, and wonder how I could ever have lain there, with joy, in the arms of a young man who is still a stranger to me and who's now at the other end of the world!"

Her boat bumped against the tangled bank, and she sprang out, as Rokeby once had done, attaching the boat to the same tree trunk. Yes, everything was the same.

She looked for a moment at the domed marble roof, watching the heavy clouds, the wind-blown trees, naked boughs shivering in a bitter breeze, and thought:

"We never even noticed the weather that day. The sun might have been shining, or there might have been frost, but we always seemed to imagine lilac when we were together."

She tied up the boat and walked through the dark, overgrown path towards the white and gleaming pillars of the temple where she had first learned to love him.

It seemed to her that the nettles had grown higher, the bushes were more darkly arched, and the little temple itself was no longer white, but stained green with moss and with marks of the wind and weather.

She was wearing a thin muslin dress but she forgot the dark clouds as she walked into the summerhouse and the rain began to fall.

She stood for a moment on the mosaic floor, and, hearing the pattering rain, she thought again of that day which seemed to her so long ago. She had been confident then, in all the Zenith of her radiant beauty. She had loved him immediately, with all the ardent response of one whose youth had been touched with frost. Meeting him, she had become alive again; she had responded with all the sunny joyousness of her nature to his passionate love-making.

Now, alone in the grey mist of driving rain, she shut her eyes, and found that she could still see him clearly. It was as though he stood beside her. How easy it was to visualise his great height, his careless dress, his deep, musical voice . . . She shuddered, and opened her eyes again, to find herself standing alone, like a spectre, beneath the domed roof of the little weather-stained temple. The rain continued to beat down.

Then for a moment her love of him, her loneliness, her desperate situation, all combined to make her cry his name aloud, as though by some whiff of magic he might return to her, to kiss her fears away. When she heard a boat scrape against the island shore she turned eagerly, as though in some dream of life, as she longed for life to be, she still expected to greet her lover.

But it was only black Toby stumbling up the path with a shawl over his arm.

To the boy she herself looked like a ghost looming tall and

white against the misty background of the temple. Her face was pale, he noticed, against the vivid brightness of her hair, and he saw that her wet dress clung to her limbs.

"Miss Clarissa! You come home!"

"I know I'm wet. But I wanted to come here. What will you do about the boats?"

"Take Miss Clarissa home. Then come back for the odder boat."

"Very well. Let's go."

"Miss Clarissa, your shawl!"

She said nothing as he rowed her away from the island. But he thought seriously, protruding his negroid underlip. He was supposed to be deficient, but he was not. He had one purpose in life—Clarissa's welfare. He worshipped her, and always had, with a pure and humble love. He did not understand why she had allowed Massa Rokeby to go away, but whatever she did was right. If she had wanted to go with Massa Rokeby to the West Indies, he would have gone, too, back into slavery. It would not have mattered, for he would have been her slave. She was his goddess, who brought brightness with her, the sun, sweetness, and light. When she was not there, he lived in darkness.

"Miss Clarissa, when you get home you go right up to Molly and wash yourself in hot water! Look—you are shaking!"

"I'm only wet!"

But her teeth were chattering.

"You are too wet," Toby replied grimly.

Hesther, coming down from her room, composed, after a desperate hour, met her hostess trailing slowly upstairs.

"Clarissa! You're soaked to the skin! You must change your dress at once!"

"Yes. When I've said good night to the children!"

For the first time since her own troubles Hesther stared full at Lady Rohan. Clarissa's face was deathly pale, her eyes were dark-rimmed, and her slender body dragged, as though she were sick, and tired, and weary of the world.

"Why," Hesther thought, "she must have loved Rokeby so much she's dying of it!"

Aloud she said:

"Clarissa! Are you mad? Change your dress before you go to the children!"

"You've been crying," was all Clarissa said, as she went on her way towards the nurseries.

She seemed indifferent; she did not even wait for Hesther's answer.

XLV

CLARISSA was ill.

It was of course her own fault, but she did not seem to care.

She lay in the great bed that was draped with tapestry, and turned her face most obstinately away from Hesther and from "old" Lady Rohan when they came in to see her.

After two days of fever, coughing, and sickness, the Ghost came in, and sent immediately for a doctor. She protested vehemently; she seemed to have a horror of doctors.

Later, downstairs, Rohan talked to the local surgeon, who was supposed to be clever.

"She has taken a bad chill," the surgeon said, "and her fever is high. There is a fear that it may affect her ladyship's lungs. Were it not for her pregnancy——"

"Her pregnancy?" the Ghost asked.

"Yes. That's the trouble, and the risk—her general condition is by no means satisfactory."

There was a pause.

"You will forgive me," Rohan said, "if I send a carriage for her own doctor in London?"

The London doctor came down, and installed a nurse. Her ladyship's fever continued high, and her heart, he discovered, was not strong.

"Nor can one be too careful," he remarked, "in view of her condition. These early months of pregnancy . . ."

"Quite," Rohan agreed grimly.

When she had been ill for five days and her condition was unchanged Hesther announced to the Ghost:

"I'm going to sit up with her tonight. She is no worse, and the nurse must have some sleep!"

"Can they not get another nurse?"

"I suppose they could, if they thought it necessary."

"Then get one tomorrow! Of course it's necessary!"

"We'll get another nurse tomorrow if you desire it. Meanwhile, you don't object to my sitting up with her tonight?"

"On the contrary! Do you not think I'm grateful?"

He had told her nothing of Clarissa's condition and was determined not to tell her.

She came across to him, twined her arms about his neck, and put her warm lips deliberately on his mouth.

"Ghost, you must not worry!"

Because the closeness of her was something he could not resist, and because he would not make love to her while Clarissa was ill, he got up and said, not without cruelty,

"You haven't forgotten, my dear, what I said to you the other night? You're looking for a new home, I hope?"

"I haven't forgotten," Hesther answered in a low voice.

"You are making enquiries?"

"I shan't come back with you to Grosvenor Square, if that is what you mean."

"That is just what I mean."

She went slowly across the wide hall, where a footman waited to hand her a candlestick, and slowly up the immense, twisting staircase towards Clarissa's rooms.

Outside the door the nurse, a florid woman in a mobcap, came out to whisper with her, as nurses will.

"Mrs. Barbary, I don't like her breathing tonight!"

"You must not worry. I shall sit up with her until tomorrow. Get some sleep!"

"Is she in the habit of taking laudanum?"

"I'm sure she's not. Why?"

"I found some laudanum drops just now in her powder closet."

"Many ladies take laudanum when they cannot sleep. It means nothing. Lady Rohan may have taken the drops once or twice in all her life. I have, too. I tell you, it means nothing!"

"Well"—and the nurse hesitated—"if I go to bed, will you promise, madam, to call me at once if there's any change? And you'll keep up the fire?"

"Yes." Hesther smiled. "I promise."

They said good night, and Mrs. Barbary went into Lady Rohan's bedroom.

Clarissa lay restlessly on the great bed, her face marble-pale, her eyes half-closed. She fidgeted and murmured once or twice, for she was light-headed. Her fingers picked at the sheets.

Hesther watched her for a moment, motionless.

Then, hearing a movement, she turned angrily.

Black Toby sat crouched on the floor in a pool of darkness near the fire.

Hesther spoke to him softly.

"You," she said, "out of here! Do you understand?"

"Miss Hesther, please, Miss Clarissa wants——"

"Do you hear what I say? I'm in charge here. Out of this room!"

"Miss Clarissa wants——"

"Do *you* want to be beaten?" Hesther whispered.

No, Toby did not want to be beaten. He was sure of that. He got up, shaking himself dolefully, like a dog, and, like a dog, slunk out of the room.

Hesther followed him to the door.

"You do not know your place, do you? Your place is downstairs! Don't dare to come up here again unless her ladyship sends for you!"

Toby said nothing. He disappeared like a shadow into the darkness of the passage.

With a sigh of relief Hesther sat down beside the bed. Clarissa asked hoarsely:

"What's all that whispering? Is it Hesther?"

"Yes, my love—it's Hesther!"

"Hesther . . . I feel so ill . . . I'm burning all over . . . my head is torture . . . Am I very ill? I shan't die, shall I?"

Hesther laughed.

"Sweet, I'm just going to give you some laudanum . . . you'll sleep all night, and wake up cured tomorrow!"

"Get it quickly," Clarissa urged.

Hesther went out into the powder closet and poured some drops into a glass.

"This cannot be too much," she said, holding the glass close to the candle. "I don't know how much you are accustomed to take so I have purposely given you very little. Come, drink it up, and sleep!"

"Thank you," Clarissa said, and drank it.

For a few moments she was silent. Then she said:

"Hesther, give me your hand."

Hesther put her cool hand on Clarissa's burning one and felt Clarissa's pulse jumping madly.

"Hesther . . ."

"What is it, my dear?"

"I may never see Swinton again. I wish I'd run away with him. Nobody wants me here. The children are happy with their grandmother or with you. I'm not needed, but Swinton needs me."

"Clarissa, don't talk! Try to sleep!"

"He is on some island where the sun's bright, and where parrots live, and where wild orchids grow. But there's blood on his island, Hesther, and I shall never see him again!"

"Clarissa, try to sleep!"

"Nobody needs me, do they?" Clarissa whispered, tears gemming her cheeks.

Hesther looked at her slowly, dispassionately, and drew her hand away.

It was quiet in the huge bedroom, for the fire was dying and the wind had grown quieter, although a storm of rain still scattered itself, like showers of gravel, against the windowpanes. The fire sank, with a crash, into a crimson ruin.

"I'm so hot," Clarissa declared impatiently. "I might be with Swinton on his island . . . You can look down through the ocean as though it were crystal, and see flying fish . . . And there are coral branches on the beach, and hummingbirds . . . and pirate treasure . . . Do you really think there's pirate treasure, Hesther? And how will we live if there isn't?"

Hesther put her hand on Clarissa's forehead. It was like fire; it almost burned her hand.

"Do you remember Bath?" Clarissa murmured.

"I remember Bath, yes. Try to sleep . . ."

"Miss Patchett and her wigs . . . Halloween, with chestnuts . . . my white poodle——" then with sharpness:

"Where's Toby?"

"He insisted on running downstairs to get some supper!"

"Oh . . . poor Toby! Will he come back soon?"

"Of course! Now will you try to sleep?"

"Yes . . . Hesther, kiss me good night—I'm so tired!"

"Good night," Hesther said, and kissed her on both cheeks.

XLVI

CLARISSA FELL ASLEEP like a tired child.

Hesther got up then and stood beside the bed, looking down at the incomparable beauty of that pale and sculptured face. The loveliness, she observed dispassionately, was flawless and undimmed despite the fever, the sickness, and the pregnancy at which she guessed.

With a sigh she got up to do those things she had to do.

First, she went over to the windows, drawing back the curtains and flinging them open wide, so that rain was blown in with an icy wind.

The fire was dying—crumbling into a heap of ashes. There was nothing to do there.

She went slowly over to the bed and pulled away Clarissa's bedclothes, so that Clarissa lay there, drugged, in the peach-coloured gauze of her nightgown.

But that was not enough. Mrs. Barbary was taking no chances. She dragged at the nightgown, pulling it over Clarissa's head, so that the pale loveliness of her body lay glimmering, exposed to all the bitterness of the wind and to the rain blowing in from the open windows.

Then, for Mrs. Barbary's legs were shaking, she sank down again on the chair beside the bed, but not before she had gone to the wardrobe and found a warm shawl to put about her own trembling shoulders.

The coldness in the bedroom was unbearable.

Clarissa stirred once, drugged as she was, and muttered something incoherent about being frozen.

Hesther said nothing.

She sat quite still, and tears rained down her cheeks.

It had been the same since they were young girls at school together: she had never known whether most to love or to hate Clarissa Richmond.

The white-panelled drawing room at Bath, Clarissa with her sweetmeats and her blue, fur-trimmed hood. . . . Oxford, with Clarissa so gaily picking her out of the gutter. . . . Grosvenor Square and the Ghost, and all she had ever known of happiness. . . . The Ghost dismissing her, to live as his kept mistress. . . .

And now she was murdering Clarissa.

She sat watching Clarissa die and was blinded by her own tears.

Once she murmured:

"Clarissa! I love you! And I'm killing you! God help me, I'm killing you!"

Clarissa, with blue lips, whispered something, but Hesther could not hear. She thought she distinguished the one word "cold." Yes, Clarissa was cold—more than cold—she was frozen.

Hesther sat, wrapped in the warmth of her borrowed shawl, for an eternity, as the night faded and she waited for the dawn.

At six o'clock in the morning she got up from her chair to put an arm on Clarissa's naked shoulder.

It was cold as marble, but Clarissa still breathed hoarsely, lying on her face, her guinea-gold hair tumbled on the lace-trimmed pillows.

Once she murmured:

> "*Cupid and our Campaspe played*
> *At cards for kisses . . . Cupid paid . . .*"

It sounded senseless, and Hesther paid no attention. She wiped away her tears, and made up the fire into a bright blaze. Then she shut the windows, drew the curtains, and went over to the bed, where she dragged down Clarissa's nightgown and arranged the bedclothes so that Lady Rohan was warmly covered.

She waited then until the room was warm again.

It was still dark.

She went out to the dressing room along the passage and knocked at the door.

"Nurse! Lady Rohan seems worse. Will you come to look at her?"

The nurse came hurrying out, her nightcap askew.

She turned Clarissa over upon her face, and Hesther looked away.

"Madame! When did she begin to fail like this?"

"A few minutes ago. I came to you at once."

"Can you go downstairs and send a groom at once for the doctor? And his lordship—— Will you ask him to come up?"

"Yes," said Hesther, and left the room.

Clarissa, Marchioness of Rohan, died two days later of a disease in later days called pneumonia.

She was conscious before she died, but she was delirious; she raved of bright islands, of wild orchids, and of hummingbirds; of pirate treasure, and of Swinton Rokeby.

She called him her poor young man.

"What will happen," she asked once, "to my poor young man if I die before he comes for me?"

She died in the zenith of her legendary beauty.

She is still a legend today.

She will always be a legend. She had not only beauty, but charm and sweetness, and her nature was as candid as her face. She had her faults—she was spoiled and wilful; she would always have her own way; her enemies could do no good, her friends no ill. Nor was she always wise in her choice of friends. But her blind, burning loyalty to those she loved was something that seems to have passed with her death. She had a passion for life, although life was sometimes unkind to her; she was vivid and intelligent, and she passionately espoused a political cause; in fact she loved life, and fought death; she was faithful to her one lover, and called to him, at the end, with her last gasping breath.

Her servants, who loved her, wept when they heard of her death. One of them, a black page, known as Toby, ran away that same night, and nothing more was heard of him for a long time, although Lord Rohan sent people chasing to find him, since he had been her favourite servant.

She died, but she will live forever.

The pictures that were painted of her still glow, or will glow again, in many different galleries. London is dark now, but one day the lights will shine again, the museums will throw open their doors, and Lady Rohan's incomparable face will gleam once more for the people who flocked, for so many years after her death, to warm their hearts with her beauty, to smile at the twinkle in her eye, and to puzzle over the wistfulness of her mouth. They grew to love her, knowing nothing of her, perhaps not even her name.

It didn't matter.

There were always people to cluster about her pictures. They might never have heard of her, but there they stood, gaping, for she was always to remain a honeypot.

Clarissa, Marchioness of Rohan!

Remember those pictures! Remember that long-limbed, graceful figure draped in silvery gauze! Remember the promise of that vivid mouth, the tilt of those deep blue eyes, the brightness of that flowing hair!

Clarissa, Marchioness of Rohan!

She represented, as her lover truly said, all the charm of a gracious epoch. She was deft in politics and warmhearted in friendship. When the two clashed, she chose friendship, and when she loved, she chose to love a wild young man from nowhere. The word "snob" had not been coined in her day, and perhaps could never have been, in her impetuous lifetime.

She gambled wildly, and was repentant too late. She spoiled her children and plagued her mother-in-law. Her servants adored her, and so did the beggars of Grosvenor Square.

She loved to laugh, she loved to be gay. Her husband frightened her, and she bored him, so that they were never friends. That was a pity; they were politically drawn together but otherwise remote.

Yet when she was dead, he missed the gaiety of her presence. Nor was he alone. On summer nights, walking by Grosvenor Square, it seems impossible that so much vitality as Clarissa's no longer exists.

So Rohan thought. Who shall say he was wrong?

It is so easy, then, to shut your eyes and wait, as Rokeby once waited; to sniff the scent of lilac, and to watch, in the dusk, for a silver-panelled chair with bearers in peach livery, and a blackamoor, to hold the link light, to imagine that time stands still, and she is on her way to dine in Whitehall or to gamble in St. James's Street. . . .

But the candles burn low.

They were burning then about her bed, where she lay marble-still, not looking at all as though she had been murdered by Mrs. Barbary.

Rohan, ringing his bell for Toby, was told then that the blackamoor had run away.

Two days later, the day before the funeral, Hesther came in to see him.

He was shocked by her appearance.

She looked as though she had never stopped crying since Clarissa's death. They had nothing to say to each other.

The next day Lady Rohan was buried in the family mausoleum that she had always dreaded because it was encircled by so many dark and gloomy fir trees.

Clarissa had always hated darkness.

Mrs. Barbary was indisposed, and did not attend the funeral.

XLVII

EIGHT MONTHS AFTERWARDS Rohan married Hesther, and they went back to live together in Grosvenor Square.

She had been discreet since Clarissa's death, and had gone, immediately after the funeral, to live in a modest hotel.

Rohan was accustomed to his mistress, and could not get on without her; he married her as soon as he decently could, and watched, not without sarcasm, the hostility with which Clarissa's friends regarded his second marriage.

Hesther, he observed dispassionately, was not received by them.

He was inclined to chuckle about this.

"Wait for a few months," he said to his bride; "they'll soon come leaving cards!"

Hesther smiled at him, but said nothing. He seemed to find their situation funny. She hated it.

She lived with him in his own apartments. She had never, since Clarissa's death, been near her rooms. She seldom went upstairs, except to see the children, and that, as she reflected bitterly, was a waste of time, for they seemed to dislike her since Clarissa's death.

One day, after she had taken them some expensive toys, the little wild Lucinda announced, staring at her,

"You really are mistress now, aren't you?"

Hesther smiled.

"Lucinda, that's not a nice way to talk!"

"The porter says you're our mama since Mama went away! Well, I wish she'd come back!"

"Lucinda," Hesther asked mechanically, very much the schoolmistress, "do you want to be whipped?"

"No, and you shan't whip me! Papa wouldn't let you!"

That, she knew, retreating, was true enough: the Ghost spoiled his children. She went, while the children watched her defiantly.

They had been married two months, and still none of the people she most respected had called on her. She realised that she was an outlaw, that she had made Rohan an outlaw too.

He went frequently to men's dinners, and she dared not object. He saw his friends then, but she never saw his friends' wives. One night, when he was dining with Lord Holland, she went down into the hall and found a crumpled letter addressed to the Marchioness of Rohan.

She opened it, innocently for once, and read:

HONOURED MADAM,

I dislike telling you bad tidings, but you trusted me to inform you.

Mr. Rokeby died very brave and gallant. We had a storm they call a Hurricane in these parts, and needed every man aboard. Mr. Rokeby, although a Passenger, volunteer'd. He climbed to the Crow's Nest, but the ropes were wet, and he slipp'd returning. He fell, his Back broke, and he died in a few hours. He gestured when he was dying. He tried to get up, so as to die on his feet, but fail'd. He said, "Tell Clarissa I tried to die on my feet."

Madam, he was a gallant man, and I fail'd in my Trust. When I come home I would like to wait on you and tell you how bravely, and how gaily, he Died.

I loved him, all the Voyage, as though he were my son.

Madam, Your humble and Obedient Servant,

JOHN RICHARDSON.

"So that," Hesther thought, "is the end of the chapter."

Once again she felt pity for Clarissa, and for her wild young lover who had fought to die on his feet.

"*My* lover once," she thought, "but without any memories—it just happened. But it never meant anything to either one. And Clarissa loved him."

"Perhaps," she thought, trying to convince herself, "perhaps Clarissa would not have wanted to go on living, with Rokeby dead. Perhaps the world would no longer have had any meaning for her."

Despite the horror of that night ten months ago she had never once regretted killing Clarissa. She was utterly ruthless, and Clarissa, innocently enough, had stood in her way. And so Clarissa had to go. If it had not been the way it was, she would, sooner or later, have found another way. Rohan's decision to send his mistress from his house had signed Clarissa's death warrant.

She had hated killing Clarissa and had wept, watching Clarissa die, but she had been determined from that day to kill her. Now she was the Marchioness of Rohan; the Ghost was her husband; she had houses, and jewels, and all the luxury she pleased; she would never want again. She had no regrets. If she had had to live that hideous night over again she would have done exactly the same: she would have committed her crime all over again.

Yet it was strange how much she missed Clarissa. Grosvenor Square was quiet since Rohan's second marriage. It seemed odd never to hear Clarissa's light step, or her gay voice; never to hear the bustle and laughter of her friends; the clatter of carriages driving up to the door; the tinkle of a spinet; the hum of conversation. It was strange never to see the blaze of glittering wax lights in the drawing rooms; to know that Clarissa Rohan would never again give a party.

Hesther sighed, and sprang up from the sofa where she had been reading Captain Richardson's letter. She crumpled it in her hand and threw it carelessly in the fireplace.

As she had said to herself, it was the end of a chapter. More—the end of an epoch.

Rokeby was dead, Clarissa was dead, and in their death they were divided. Mrs. Barbary, perhaps fortunately for herself, had no belief whatsoever in an afterlife.

She stood for a moment looking down at the flames shrivel-ling some sheets of paper that would have changed all Clarissa's existence.

No, she reflected, she would never understand why, hating Clarissa, she had loved her. Weakness, she supposed dispassion-ately, and of course Clarissa had extraordinary charm.

"Too much charm for her own good," Hesther thought, yawning, as the clock struck twelve.

Rohan, she knew, had spent some time sorting Clarissa's papers after her death. He must obviously have read the diaries and known that she was deeply in love. But he had never mentioned these documents to her, and she did not know what he had done with them. Burned them, perhaps, as she had just burned the letter she had opened by mistake.

Then she heard her husband's step, and smiled to herself. She had not seen him all day. She hoped that he would want to make love to her.

Rohan came quickly into the small octagonal room.

"I thought," she said in her soft, lazy voice, "I thought you had quite deserted me."

He made no answer but went over to the fire, as though he were cold. She could not see his face.

"What is that?" he asked suddenly in a harsh voice.

"What?"

"That piece of paper in the grate. *Who* died gaily?"

"Oh, I have been burning a letter I opened, thinking it was for me."

"What letter?"

"Why, Ghost, must you bark at me? A letter for Clarissa from a ship's captain, telling her Swinton Rokeby died at sea."

Very carefully he picked up the two or three charred frag-ments lying beneath the grate and folded them in a sheet of paper which he put in his pocket. Then he turned to face her, and when she saw his drawn and ravaged face she started, knowing that something fearful had happened.

He came directly to the point.

"Hesther, how did Clarissa die?"

The shock of his question made her hesitate. Her mouth felt dry and she could hear her heart pounding against her ribs.

"You know she failed suddenly. I told you! Why must we speak of it again?"

"Do you remember Toby, Clarissa's black boy?"

"Yes. Why?"

Her voice was sullen. For a moment she had been terrified. Now she looked at him defiantly. What could she fear from Toby?

"You sent him out of Clarissa's room the night she became worse?"

"I did! It was no place for him! What do you mean? Why are you talking to me like this?"

"Hesther," and he came close to her, staring at her with those light eyes that were colder than steel. "Toby came back today. He is in the kitchen now. He was starving—he has been a sweep's boy. God knows how he has eaten these months!"

She laughed.

"What is he to do with me?"

"Do you know why he ran away?"

"Oh, he worshipped Clarissa. He's imbecile. I repeat, what has all this to do with me?"

Rohan ignored her.

"He ran away because he thinks you the devil. *Now* do you begin to understand?"

"On the contrary! You have been drinking!"

But once again she was afraid; there was no reason for his

manner, as she knew; but he seemed so strange, so haggard, and his eyes frightened her.

"Hesther," he said, "I want to ask you another question."

"Ask it!"

And she smiled, leaning back in her chair. She was the Marchioness of Rohan, and she was not afraid.

XLVIII

Hesther, do you know where Toby went when you dismissed him from her room?"

"To his supper, I presume," she answered, with a lightness she was still far from feeling.

"No, you are wrong. Toby did not go to his supper that night. It appears that Rokeby, who must have known you even better than I, made him promise never, could he avoid it, to leave you alone with Clarissa. When you dismissed him, he went down to the garden. He's agile, and can climb like a chimney sweep's boy. Did I tell you? For that's what he's been since he left my service. To resume: he climbed the wistaria tree outside Clarissa's window and waited there all night. He dodged you in the darkness when you threw open the windows to let in the wind and the rain."

There was a pause.

Looking at her, he knew exactly how she would appear as an old woman. Her skin flaked to an ugly grey, her cheeks seemed to sink, and she put her hand quickly to her mouth.

He resumed:

"Toby saw you give some medicine to Clarissa. That was before you drew the curtains. But the window was a little open, and he peered through a slit of light. He did not, of course, know what the medicine was, but I have a strong suspicion that you gave her the laudanum found in her powder closet."

She interrupted in a voice so hoarse he would never have known it as her own:

"I swear to God I never poisoned her! That's what you're trying to say, isn't it? That I poisoned her! I never did!"

"Oh no, Hesther," Rohan answered wearily, "you never poisoned her! You were too clever for that, or thought you were. You gave her enough laudanum to make her sleep. Then you dragged the bedclothes off her—you took off even her nightgown—and let in the cold. You watched her die slowly, by inches, and then, when you knew she could not live, you covered her up, and then you went to fetch the nurse."

Hesther made a tremendous effort to control herself.

"And you believe that lying Negro? Will you take his word before mine?"

"Toby is not lying," Rohan said, and took snuff. His hand trembled.

"Then why, if he saw what he thought, did he not tell you then? Why did he run away? He's always hated me! He's——"

"A primitive creature," Rohan interrupted curtly, "who happens to believe in witchcraft. Voodoo, he calls it. I never heard the word before. In any case, he supposed Clarissa dead there and then. Incidentally, as I have told you, he thought you the devil, and so he ran away. He would never have returned had he not been starving."

"Let me see him! Oh, I'll make him——"

He interrupted her again.

"By this time he is over at the stables. He will not sleep beneath this roof because *you* sleep here!"

"And you believe that slave's brat before you believe me?"

He was silent, staring at her. Then he said:

"I *know* you murdered Clarissa! I suppose I always guessed, and shut my mind to the horror. But that's finished now. Now I *know* the truth. I know you killed her! Do you suppose Toby has the wit to invent his story?"

"I may have dozed—I may have let the fire go out——"

"Hesther, here's a mirror! Look at your face!"

"How can you think I could have hurt Clarissa! She was my friend! You know she was my friend!"

"Yes! She was your friend. She loved you, and you killed her!"

He went over to the writing table and set out some papers. She sprang to her feet again.

"What are you doing?"

"You are about to write a confession of what you've done. To me. Come here!"

"I refuse to come near you until you are sane again!"

"Come here!" he repeated. He went across to her and dragged at her arm.

"Let go! You're hurting my wrist!"

"I don't care if I break it! Sit here when I tell you! Now pick up that pen!"

"You're my husband! And you think I killed her?"

"I *know* you killed her! God damn you! Sit down! Do you attend?"

"The servants will hear," she muttered, but she sank into the chair.

She was trembling violently.

"Who will mind if they do? You or me?"

"You'll fetch the Bow Street Runners——"

"Hesther," he said, and his voice was icy, "you don't seem to understand my family customs. I have lived honourably, so far as I know, and my ancestors, for many hundred years, have lived honourably. I'm not talking of duelling, or card debts such as Clarissa had, I'm talking of something spiritual, something you would never understand—you're not bred that way!"

"Let me go! Let me go away from here! I'll never trouble you——"

"I'll let you go when I have finished with you—not before! Listen, Hesther—I never knew murder until I married you! But I do not intend to call in Bow Street Runners! A fine heritage for my son if I did! You fool! Take up that pen and write!"

"Write what? Who for?"

"For those," Rohan said, "who will come after us."

She was broken at last. She loved him. She collapsed, weeping, across the writing table.

"Make haste," he said. "I've no wish to prolong this scene."

She sobbed:

"Will you forgive me if I write what you want?"

"Never! Make no mistake! But you'll still write—at my dictation!"

"You never loved Clarissa!"

He turned away with distaste, avoiding her livid face, her swollen eyes. (For those, he thought again, who will come after us. . . .)

"The sooner this is done, the better!"

"*Why* do you believe I killed her?"

"If we sit here all night," he said coolly, "you will still confess! Until you have, you won't leave this room!"

She repeated, weeping,

"You never loved her!"

"Possibly not," he said grimly, "but she happened to be my wife, and the mother of my son. *You*'re my wife now, you murdering whore! Take up your pen! Do you hear? You may find *yourself* murdered, if you don't!"

Her hand shaking, she picked up the quill.

He dictated, dispassionately.

"Confession . . ."

He continued to dictate for thirty minutes. Before he finished he said:

"You will end up by asking for mercy. As you need that particular quality more than most people, you will repeat the plea three times!"

"I could not bear to leave you——"

"Write that!"

"The devil——"

"Write that too! He must have been searching a mate when he came near to you!"

"Ghost——"

"Write!"

When she was finished the fire had sunk into a heap of pale ashes. He thought again, "For those who will come after us. . . ."

"So Rokeby's dead," he said thoughtfully, as though to himself, collecting the pages she had written at his dictation. And he added after a pause:

"Poor Clarissa!"

"What are you going to do with those papers?"

"Hide them somewhere—with other papers—so that my descendants may one day know who was to blame for this!"

"And me? What's going to happen to me?"

"You?" He got up. "I'd forgotten you! I'd forgotten I married a murderess!"

"Rohan——"

"I'd forgotten how I've depraved myself! Well, Hesther, I warn you now, that although for my son's sake and my family's sake, there will be no scandal—I warn you, I shall never, in private, speak to you again!"

"What are you saying?"

"You understand me," he replied, folding the papers on the desk; "I think you understand me very well! You shan't sleep here tonight or any other night. Go up to *her* rooms if you dare! But go—get out of here! Go upstairs, or go to Rohan! In any case, never come near me again, never speak to me, except in front of others! You see, we've come to the end!"

She stood for a moment facing him.

"But I love you!"

He went over to open the door.

"All that," he said, "is finished! Can't you understand?"

"Can I talk to you about this tomorrow?"

"No," he said, "not tomorrow, or ever! We shall never speak again! Have you got that into your head? You have? Excellent! Now will you go?"

She went then.

She knew that it was finished.

As she crept up the sombre stairs she cried out, although she did not know it, for Clarissa, who had always been there to save her. She knew that she was forsaken without Clarissa.

But the house was strange and dark without her friend.

She suddenly knew that she would give ten years of her life to hear Clarissa calling from upstairs. To hear her voice and her laughter; to sniff her perfume; to see the glittering candles in her room, to know that life was sane and safe again.

But Clarissa's rooms were in darkness, and there was no safety anywhere, for Clarissa was dead.

She called once, feebly, on the stairs,

"Clarissa . . ."

But there was no answer. How could there be? Clarissa was dead. She had killed Clarissa, and now the Ghost had cast her off.

She was alone in the darkness.

She stumbled upstairs to a room in which she had not slept for many months.

She lay on the bed in darkness, and was lost, for was not Clarissa dead?

Downstairs in the hall the porter, dozing in his hooded chair, woke for a moment to see a ghost, so he thought. He smelled a sweet perfume, found his eyes dazed by a shimmer of candles, and imagined, for one ephemeral moment, that he saw the bright, brilliant figure of Clarissa, Marchioness of Rohan, pass through the hall on her way to find her silver chair.

He picked up his candlestick in a shaking hand.

"My lady! My lady!"

But there was no answer here, either; and there were no candles. Yet he was not convinced, even by the dusk.

He crossed towards the door and opened it, his candle flame trembling although he shaded it with his hand.

But outside there was nothing. Only darkness. There was no chair, no blackamoor, no link boys. Just nothing. The square was deserted.

He returned to the hall, where he stood for a moment, warming his hands at the dying fire.

He had been dreaming; and there was another Lady Rohan now. But it seemed to him that the scent of lilac was everywhere —he could not escape the sweetness of this ghostly blossom.

He poured himself another glass of porter, and the door, which he had left open, slammed for the wind was strong.

He grunted. There was no longer a scent of lilac in the hall. So much for dreams.

The beautiful lady was dead, and no ghost had passed his way.

He returned gratefully to the comfort of his hooded chair.

PART VI

Narrative of Mary Rohan

XLIX

April 1940.

I woke up early this morning.

It was still dark.

For a moment I was confused, and at a loss to know why I felt lighthearted, as though a load were taken off my mind.

Then I remembered.

The slavery of the last six weeks is over and done with. I have finished writing the story of Clarissa Rohan. Downstairs, in the library, a great pile of paper lies, neatly tied, upon the long desk near the window, that same desk where, long ago, Swinton Rokeby sat to make his catalogue.

I stretched myself luxuriously, and was not surprised to

realise how tired I felt. I had been too busy, before, to know that I was working myself into a state of exhaustion.

Now, at last, after so much toil, I could sleep. But sometimes one is too tired to sleep. Too tired, too unhappy, and too apprehensive.

I lay still for a long time, maddeningly wide awake, longing for David, longing to tell him the secret that I had discovered about his family. It was all so long ago that I didn't suppose he would mind very much. So much is forgiven the dead.

The birds began to sing, bursting into a sleepy chorus, and at about the same time I thought I heard someone moving beside my bed. I supposed it to be the maid, bringing my coffee, and sat up. But I saw nobody, and, listening to the birds outside, I knew that of course nobody would be likely to call me so early. It was scarcely dawn.

But the swift movement, the sound of a footstep close beside my bed, was unmistakable.

I switched on my light.

There was of course nobody in the room.

So I put out the light again, and lay down, scarcely daring to breathe, as the dawn came filtering through my curtains to fall in streaks upon the floor.

Ever since I wrote Clarissa Rohan's story, ever since I received my own terrible news, I have prayed to be haunted by her spirit. That is why, despite my mother's protests, I have continued to live here alone. I don't want people—real people, I mean. They would only try to cheer me up and make me feel worse. But I *do* want to make friends with Clarissa's spirit. I love Clarissa as though I knew her. I want to know her; *she* was parted from her lover, too; she knows what it is to feel as I am feeling.

She has come to represent to me in this dark and dreadful

world the symbol of a graciousness which is no longer anywhere to be found. It seems strange to say of someone so beautiful that she was *comfortable,* but that, I am sure, is what she
was. All I know is that I need her, to keep my mind off other
things. I want to tell her that things came right, afterwards, for
the family, despite Mrs. Barbary's baleful influence.

I want her to know that her son, Roderick, grew up, and
married, suitably, to father that bearded Victorian statesman
who is David's ancestor and her descendant. I want her to know
that her pretty, wild daughter, Lucinda, married a Russian
prince, and went to live in Petersburg, where she became exceedingly popular, although I am not at all sure that she always
behaved herself! Lucinda, too, left children, so that perhaps
some of her mother's good looks were inherited by these unknown Russian descendants who never appear to have left their
land for ours.

Clarissa's descendants! It seems funny to think of her as a
grandmother, or a great-grandmother. Later, in our times, she is
far enough away to be an ancestress, which is different, somehow, because it sounds ageless.

I would like her so much to know that the Ghost kept his
word, breaking finally with Hesther, Lady Rohan, after learning
how Clarissa met her death; that they never talked again together, save in public; that he sent his children far away from
her, to be educated; that he and his second wife lived, in the
history of the period, as a sinister and lonely pair. It was known
everywhere that they never spoke to one another. He recorded
some of this contemporary gossip later, in a characteristically dry
and sardonic journal.

Meanwhile the black boy, Toby, lived on at the stables, supposedly to help with the horses. No one, any longer, dressed him
in silks and satins, and he grew tall and sturdy, but I learn that

his wits always remained those of a child. Perhaps he had suffered too many privations as a sweep's boy, or perhaps he never recovered from the shock of his mistress's death, but he seemed quite vacant, as he sang and chattered to himself in the sunshine. By Rohan's orders, everyone treated him kindly, but if he caught so much as a glimpse of the second Lady Rohan he would run away and hide himself for hours in the woods, building little stone Voodoo altars, to arm him against her evil spells.

It seems unlikely that the black boy's magic could have harmed anyone, so perhaps it was Hesther's unnatural life that caused her, a few years later, to commit suicide.

She drowned herself in the lake, but all that was hushed up, and I know nothing about it, not even where she is buried.

I went out to the island one day, in a leaking punt. I had to bale all the way across.

When I got there I found it overgrown, and thick with brambles. There was no trace of the little temple where once, long ago, Clarissa and Rokeby had loved one another. The temple had vanished as though by enchantment. I remembered how once she had told him that if ever their ghosts returned they would be "happy ghosts," and I called her name aloud. But nobody, nothing answered. The place seemed sad enough to me —a tangle of trees and bushes and briars. There were nettles, too, growing waist-high. It was a desolate spot—I was glad to leave it. It has been forgotten for too many years.

She had talked of happy ghosts! Why, I thought, even their ghosts are forgotten, just as the temple has crumbled into ruins, while Clarissa lies in the sombre mausoleum I won't even visit, and Rokeby's bones have been coral on the sea bed for so many years; surely, I thought, standing on the neglected island, it all seems a thousand years ago since these lovers were parted.

But I couldn't bear to think of Clarissa's spirit being forever alone.

Of course I see now—I see particularly today—how selfish I have been.

But with David, my beloved husband, missing somewhere in France, I seem to crave Clarissa's sympathy more than that of anyone living. I love David as she must have loved Rokeby. They were together so short a time, and so were we. She lost her lover, and mine, for the moment, is lost too.

Afternoon.

Chaddesley has been wandering around looking like a funeral. How dare he assume that David is dead? He's just like my mother—*why* can't she understand that I don't want her here? I don't want any of them, except David. If he's not coming back, if there's to be no future for us, and if the present is really finished, then I prefer to live in the past.

But I need Clarissa. I want her sympathy—I'm determined to find her!

Surely here, where she was murdered, she must sometimes walk at night, a sad and lovely ghost? What harm could she do, and who would not be glad to welcome her? Why can't people understand that I wish to be alone? I want to find Clarissa. . . .

Later.

I caught Chaddesley telephoning this evening. He looked self-conscious.

I said to him:

"Why did you ring off? Who were you talking to?"

Then I saw his eyes were red, and I was sorry I'd spoken so sharply.

"My lady," he said, "it's not right you should be alone just now!"

"Chaddesley, please don't ring up my mother any more! I don't *want* her here! Can't you understand? I *must* be alone for a little while longer!"

He answered, frankly wiping his eyes:

"Very well, my lady, but you see—his lordship'll turn up one of these days—mark my words if he doesn't!"

Then I was so sorry that I could have kissed him. Of course he's right; of course David will come back soon. "Missing" doesn't mean anything.

That Night.

Something is happening, and I don't like it, for it is not what I have been wanting.

Tonight I nearly caught her.

It began after dinner, when I went into the library.

I had been arranging daffodils all over the house, undisturbed all day long by the soft movements I thought to hear this morning in my bedroom. These movements ceased when I drew back my curtains, and I was almost prepared to admit that I had been dreaming, in the queer half-light before the dawn.

I have been busy all day with the daffodils, forgetting my misery about David, and my longing for Clarissa's ghost. It is not so easy to be sad, on a fair spring day when the daffodils are growing knee-high. It is at night, when the shadows lengthen, and the time has come for curtains to be drawn, that all the old fears and anxieties come back to fret at one's nerves.

I had dinner in the gun room, as usual, and afterwards I sat by the fire, with the spaniels beside me, and read an uncomfortable, worried letter from my mother, which I decided to ignore. Then I turned to my manuscript of Clarissa, and remembered how, six weeks ago, I had stood for the first time before the Ghost's picture in the library. How much has happened, since then—David was not missing on the day I found the secret panel; nobody knew then how Clarissa Rohan died, and no one guessed the curse that Mrs. Barbary brought with her to Rohan.

I thought I would go back and look once more at the portrait of the Man in Grey. So I went out across the hall, switching on the lights, and the dogs came pattering after me.

I went into the library, and, when the spaniels would not come into the room with me, but stayed lurking in the doorway, and soon afterwards ran back across the hall, I suppose I should have known that something was wrong. But I merely thought that they were hungry, and had gone, as was their custom, to scratch at the green-baize door for their supper in the pantry. Now, of course, I know that they were afraid.

They are not the only ones.

I put on the lights, and went over to the picture hanging in front of the secret panel.

He stared down at me with his usual cool expression, his lips curved and scornful, the silver braid of his collar reflected in that frosted hair which gleamed beneath the lights.

For the first time since I had learned his story I realised that marriage with the devilish Hesther had robbed him, not only of his honour, but of something else he greatly prized: of his political career. He seems, from what I can gather, to have abandoned all ambition, when at last he knew what kind of woman he had married; he appears to have lived, even after Hesther's death, as an eccentric and forbidding recluse.

I stood there looking back at him, and mused aloud.

"You were better off with Clarissa!"

Even then I did not begin to understand my own peril. I looked round me, half in fun, half seriously, almost expecting to hear Clarissa's footfall, or to glimpse her ghostly shape moving, where once, long ago, when the room was sweet with roses, she had come to whisper with her lover.

But there was nothing, and so I turned to go.

"Good night!" I said to the Man in Grey, and put out the light by his portrait.

Then I became conscious of a curious illusion. His expression seemed to change in the half-light of the long room; he no longer stared before him with that pride and hauteur I had noticed from the first. I could have sworn that his features became for a moment twisted as though by a grief, a horror, he could not control, and, as he gazed directly at me, I thought I heard a voice cry: "Go away! Go away from here!"

It was, of course, a trick of lighting, for when I moved towards the door the picture looked exactly the same as usual, and the Man in Grey stared superciliously across the long and gloomy room just as he had stared upon his descendants for more than a hundred years.

I turned out the lights and went back thoughtfully to the gun room, where I smoked a cigarette.

That, I supposed (only a short time ago!), was how ghost stories first started. An illusion, a trick of lighting, perhaps only the slam of an unlatched door, ivy scraping at a windowpane, or mice running in the wainscot. Enough, anyhow, to unloose a flock of wild superstitions to terrify foolish servant girls.

I threw my cigarette into the fire and resigned myself to the fact that Clarissa's spirit existed only in my imagination. Then, for I was tired, I decided to go to bed, only to find that I had left my bag in the library.

I went back for it, of course. I hadn't begun to be afraid.

I crossed the hall, and when I saw a thread of light under the door it seemed the most natural thing in the world to me. I thought how careless I had been to leave the library without first having seen that all the lights were out. A second later, as I approached the door, I remembered that I had been particularly careful to leave everything in darkness.

My hand was on the door handle when I heard the thin, tinkling sound of a spinet somewhere inside the room. I think, then, I was more astonished than frightened, for of course there hasn't been a spinet in there for many years.

I called out, "Who's there?" and no one answered, so I pushed open the door.

I had seen a light, but the room was in darkness. For a moment, as I listened, there was silence, and then I heard, somewhere near the secret panel, some scuffling and fidgeting. There was something moving over there in the darkness.

In my ignorance, I called Clarissa's name aloud, as I pressed the switch of the electric light.

But nothing happened—the lighting system is primitive at Rohan, and there are often fuses. I was still not frightened.

I called her name again, almost with eagerness, and then something horrid happened.

I am sure, I will swear, that there was something moving just now in the library, but as I called, for the second time, I felt, like a blow in the face, an emanation, a cloud of evil, that seemed to rise up and choke me, and I knew that, whatever was in the room, it wasn't Clarissa. She could never have been evil.

It was Hesther.

Somehow I had never thought of that. I had always longed for Clarissa's ghost. But I hadn't bargained for Hesther, and Hesther was somewhere there in the darkness. Of that I am certain.

I made a grave mistake then. I was afraid—so terrified that my tongue clove to the roof of my mouth, and I could hear my own heart pounding like a big drum. I had only one wish—to escape the horror that perhaps is still lurking somewhere there in the darkness.

Instead of trying to hide my fears, I fled, slamming the door behind me, and raced across the hall to the sanctuary of the gun room. I thought I heard footsteps chasing me, but I cannot be sure. I ran past the staircase, past Clarissa's sedan chair, and into the gun room, as though all the fiends of hell were biting at my heels.

I was panting, dishevelled, and shaking.

I slammed the door, locked it, and put on all the lights. If they hadn't worked, I should have gone raving mad. As I stood there I heard a strange, gasping noise. It took me several moments to realise that it was the sound of my own breathing.

I found my way mechanically to my chair by the fire and, after sinking down in it, my legs still trembling, I tried to realise what, in my ignorant folly, I had done.

Some obscure wish for Clarissa Rohan's sympathy had sent me searching for her all over the house and the gardens that once had been her home. My own private anxieties had made me, I suppose, more than usually sensitive and fanciful, so that the veil between the past and present had become thin for me, since the discovery of the secret panel, and I have seen nothing impossible, nothing even strange, in making friends with the spirit of a woman who has been in her grave for more than a hundred and thirty years.

Now, in the midst of my own fears, I realise my selfishness in thus trying to call her back from the dead. Her life was short and stormy, and perhaps in death she found peace. How monstrous, then, to beckon back her spirit! And perhaps that is why she has never stirred—for the simple reason that she lies eternally at peace.

Requiescat in Pace.

I never thought of that.

Later That Night.

A few moments ago, writing those words here in the gun room, with its glowing fire, and all its air of cheerful cosiness, the full horror of tonight has returned once more to haunt me.

It has been my fault.

I have tried to meddle with the powers of darkness, to tear aside those veils that must forever be left drawn. Fascinated by the spell of the past, I have trodden wilfully in forbidden places. From my first discovery of that secret panel behind the Ghost's picture, I deliberately shut my eyes to the present. I read and sorted the various papers; then, in disgust and hatred of my own time, and of the war that has torn my husband from me, I became saturated in the past.

There is no other word to describe my obsession.

For weeks I lived by day in and dreamed at night of the great Whig drawing rooms of the Regent's time. I told myself that there were no machines in that gracious age, no bombing aeroplanes, or shattered homes, or tramping, homeless refugees. There was, incidentally, no hygiene, but all the same, I made my choice.

As I wrote until my wrist ached, I thought I heard clattering hoofs, and curricles dashed recklessly through this make-believe world that I had fashioned. Coaches thundered over cobbled streets, lavender-sellers cried their wares outside houses, night watchmen called the hour, and, with dusk, a thousand wax lights sprang to life, to twinkle in these myriad windows of the past. Every evening, at twilight, a silver sedan chair waited in Grosvenor Square, and pirates still sailed the blue waters of the Spanish Main.

This is how Clarissa's world became mine.

When I finished her life story, and came back reluctantly to the hateful life of my own times, I was like some dreamer who has been for an eternity bewitched in fairyland, and who has long ago forgotten the country from whence he came. I still craved the past. It was like an opiate; I knew I had to have it.

That was how, I suppose, I began, in my ignorant folly, to meddle with evil things.

I went searching for Clarissa Rohan's spirit, but of course I could never find it, for she lies somewhere in peace. I searched upon the island, where there was nothing left to remind me of her, not even the little temple she had once so much loved. I looked for her in the park, beneath spreading oak trees, and near the lake, where the daffodils grow thickest. Once, beneath the dark arches of the Yew Walk, I thought I caught the glimmer of a white scarf, but there was nobody, nothing, when I came near.

If I had stopped to think, then, I suppose I should have realized that good and gentle people don't roam the earth so many years after they are dead. Perhaps, for an ephemeral while they leave an impression behind them, something a little like a visual echo, so that the porter at Grosvenor Square may not have been dreaming when he thought that he saw her for a moment, so soon after her tragic death.

But to suppose anything else is, I know now, wicked nonsense, and she will never come back to haunt us.

Yet, in my ignorance, I called to a spirit, and a spirit answered me. *She* rests in peace, but the evil thing that has stalked me tonight cannot rest. For more than a century, I suppose, it has been prowling, invisible, about the halls and corridors of Rohan. No wonder, then, that on winter nights, when the rain was scattered violently, like gravel, against the windowpanes, and Victorian candles flickered in the draught, and doors banged, and the wind rushed down the staircase and across the hall—no wonder people stopped to whisper fearfully, and looked behind their shoulders, and made haste not to linger long in rooms where the shadows lay deep in crannies and in corners.

For the evil must always have been here. Always, from the day, long ago, when Hesther Barbary, or rather Hesther Rohan, committed suicide in the lake beyond the park.

I spoke, just now, of an emanation. Some ghosts steal the forms in which they once lived; I do not believe that she is one of them. I think, I am sure, that she is here, but I am certain her presence is one that breathes, or rather emanates, the vileness that was hers in life. I do *not* believe—perhaps because I do not want to—that she materializes. In the library tonight there was certainly something moving, but there was, above all, the smell, the very essence of evil.

That is Hesther.

And, now that I have whistled, it has come for me, that which once lived in my make-believe world as Mrs. Barbary.

What does it want?

My soul? Does it intend, vampire-like, by the impression of its foul spirit upon mine, to find its freedom? Is it craving exorcism—the rites of bell, book, and candle? Or has the wickedness of a hundred years past increased in malignancy, so that what destroyed Clarissa intends also to destroy me—I who sit in her place?

Just now, writing these words, I heard it outside the gun room; something scratched at the door, and the latch lifted, impatiently shaken. Once again the horror of all that is sinful seemed to pour into the room, almost choking me with the loathsomeness of what waits outside the door.

But I have come to a decision.

The fire is nearly dead now, and in a few hours the night will be over.

When I have finished writing this page, I shall unlock the door, go out into the hall, and confront whatever is waiting for me there.

Hesther Barbary criminally took the place of Clarissa, Lady Rohan.

But *I* am Lady Rohan now, and I'll see her damned before she takes *my* place!

Before the ink of this page is dry, I shall face her, and send her back to the darkness where her spirit belongs. She shall no longer haunt *my* home! One day, when David comes back, and Hesther's shade is no longer earthbound, perhaps we will laugh together about all this. No. On second thoughts I do not believe that there will ever be anything to laugh about.

Because, in one minute from now I shall meet Hesther's spirit face to face.

Now, as I am writing, I can see the door handle twist and turn, and it would appear that whatever waits outside becomes impatient.

I am to blame, I know, for everything that has happened; I broke open a door to which the key was hidden; I fell in love with the past, and have allowed myself to be possessed; I sought Clarissa's ghost, but instead found her own destroyer. No wonder the Ghost tried to warn me.

Poor Clarissa!

I have finished now; the fire is dead, and I am ready to put away my book. Now I shall unlock the door and walk out across the hall; I shall face that thing which was once Hesther, and I shall fight the evil which for so long has menaced Rohan with bad fortune.

May God help me!

EDITOR'S NOTE BY JOSEPH LANGFORD, ONCE LIBRARIAN AT ROHAN

Mary, Marchioness of Rohan, was found dead the morning after writing these notes. She was discovered huddled at the foot of the staircase, and those who found her tell me that her features were distorted by an expression of terror and bewilderment.

The inquest returned a verdict of death by heart failure. Frankly, from what I have gathered, I would never have supposed her heart to be weak.

Chaddesley, the butler, agrees with me, and so, I understand, does Lady Rohan's mother.

Ten days afterwards we heard the news of Lord Rohan's death. He was killed fighting in France, shortly after the French fall.

He left no heir.

The family is finished now, and the house is up for sale.

It is left for me to wind up these disjointed diaries. I only once met Mary, Lady Rohan, but I remember her as a particularly endearing and most delightful young creature. She had no affectations, and it was obvious that she adored her husband.

How she lived during those last lonely months at Rohan is no concern of mine, but my heart bleeds for her. She was young, solitary and sensitive; she was tormented by anxiety. She was, I suppose, the victim of her own lonely fancies. Writing so much about the past, she came to believe that she lived in that past; insisting, as she did, on being alone at Rohan, I imagine that she soon became the prey of her own nervous imagination, with what result her readers have learned for themselves.

As I have said before, the Rohan family is finished now, and there is no heir.

That is why, in this autumn of 1940, I intend to ask permission to publish these documents collected and annotated by the last Lady Rohan. This collection of manuscripts forms a book—her own book; this haunted biography of her husband's ancestress, Clarissa.

Even to me, Clarissa Rohan lives more vividly than any of them, and I have known the family for more than twenty years. I have studied their pedigrees, deciphered their journals, and judged their first editions. I have worked for many weeks in that library where, once upon a time, Clarissa Rohan met her lover, the Mr. Rokeby of whom you have read.

But the family is now extinct. Somehow I find that difficult to believe.

They were occasionally evil, but they were sometimes noble. There was, it is true, much about them that was wild. Yet, sometimes again, they had greatness.

And the Regency Rohan took pains to conceal, for many years, this stain upon his honour. He hid his secret until one day, long afterwards, escaping from the rain, Mary Rohan blundered upon the panel behind the picture known to the family as "The Man in Grey."

It no longer mattered. The line is extinct now. They are all gone; all dead; all crumbled into dust. I have known them for so long that I cannot but feel a sense of intolerable loss.

J. L.

1940.